Murder, She Wrote: Design for Murder

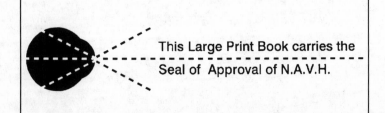

This Large Print Book carries the
Seal of Approval of N.A.V.H.

A MURDER, SHE WROTE MYSTERY

MURDER, SHE WROTE: DESIGN FOR MURDER

JESSICA FLETCHER, DONALD BAIN & RENÉE PALEY-BAIN

Based on the Universal Television series created by Peter S. Fischer, Richard Levinson & William Link

THORNDIKE PRESS
A part of Gale, Cengage Learning

GALE
CENGAGE Learning·

Farmington Hills, Mich • San Francisco • New York • Waterville, Maine
Meriden, Conn • Mason, Ohio • Chicago

GALE
CENGAGE Learning®

LIBRARY OF CONGRESS CATALOGING-IN-PUBLICATION DATA

Names: Fletcher, Jessica, author. | Bain, Donald, 1935– author. | Paley-Bain, Renée,
  author.
Title: Murder, she wrote : design for murder : a murder, she wrote mystery / by
  Jessica Fletcher, Donald Bain & Renée Paley-Bain.
Other titles: Design for murder | Murder, she wrote (Television program)
Description: Large print edition. | Waterville, Maine : Thorndike Press, 2016. |
  Series: Thorndike Press large print mystery
Identifiers: LCCN 2016020851 | ISBN 9781410491695 (hardcover) | ISBN 1410491692
  (hardcover)
Subjects: LCSH: Fletcher, Jessica—Fiction. | Women novelists—Fiction. | Women
  detectives—Fiction. | Large type books. | GSAFD: Mystery fiction.
Classification: LCC PS3552.A376 D46 2016b | DDC 813/.54—dc23
LC record available at https://lccn.loc.gov/2016020851

Published in 2016 by arrangement with New American Library, an
imprint of Penguin Publishing Group, a division of Penguin Random
House LLC

Printed in Mexico
1 2 3 4 5 6 7 20 19 18 17 16

To all the fans of Murder, She Wrote,
both on TV and in print.
Thank you for making this
series such a success.

ACKNOWLEDGMENTS

The Internet provides a wealth of information, but there is nothing like learning the ropes from the folks who walk the walk. Thanks to Jessica Corr, assistant professor of design at Parsons New School for Design, for her expertise on marketing luxury goods. Thanks also to Fran Miano of Creative Cosmetic Labs, Inc., for her tutorial on manufacturing lipstick. Sorry we couldn't use it all. We're eternally grateful to Bruce Bertram, former detective in the Danbury Police Department, for generously answering all questions regarding law enforcement, not just for us but for fellow authors as well.

We consulted numerous fashion sites and clipped every article on the topic from the *New York Times*. It hasn't changed how we dress, but it's certainly given us a new appreciation for the fashion industry.

Thanks as always to our editor, Laura

Fazio, and agent, Bob Diforio, for unfailing encouragement and support.

CHAPTER ONE

Xandr Ebon, in a white T-shirt and jeans, kneeled next to a tall, beautiful woman, a line of straight pins sticking out of his mouth, which made him look like my neighbor's boxer when the poor dog had an unfortunate encounter with a porcupine. "Grrumnph," he said, nodding at me.

"Good morning to you," I replied.

He pulled out one pin at a time and slid them into the side seam of the amethyst-colored gown the model wore, the purple color a beautiful complement to the model's café au lait complexion. "Like that," he said to his dressmaker, who was searching her spools of thread for a match. "It should be a smooth taper. The overskirt will give it the flare."

"If you're going to sew me into the dress, how will I be able to change after the finale?"

"It has to look right for the runway, Dolores," the dressmaker said to the model. "We'll rip it off if we have to." She winked at me.

"You're not ripping anything, Addie. That silk soutache is over six hundred dollars a yard," Xandr said.

"I'll just baste the seam loosely so she can slide out of it," the dressmaker said, grinning. "Don't be so nervous, Mr. Ebon. It'll be fine."

Xandr turned to me with his arms open. "Thank goodness you're here," he said, giving me a quick hug. "Just seeing you buoys my spirits. My assistant sent over the wrong dress, so I have to make last-second adjustments. My patron saint must be Murphy — you know, that law that says that if something can go wrong, it will. Do you know where my mother is?" The words spilled out of his mouth in a rush.

"I left her two minutes ago," I said, trying not to match the speed of his speech. "She's out front talking to an editor from a Long Island fashion magazine."

"Good! We need all the press we can get."

"And Grady is here. So is Donna."

"Your nephew has been an absolute lifesaver, Mrs. Fletcher. He found me the production company that's putting all this together. I don't know how I'd ever have

10

gotten this show off the ground without him. And his wife brought those two huge baskets of flowers that mark the runway entrance."

"They're tickled to have the opportunity to help you," I said. "But now that you're a big-time fashion designer, don't you think it's time you called me Jessica?"

"I don't know about 'big-time,' but I'd be honored to use your first name, Jessica."

"And is it okay if I still call you Sandy?"

"Sure, only not if you're talking to a reporter, okay? To them I'm Xandr."

Xandr Ebon — formerly known as Sandy Black in his Cabot Cove days, when the high school girls swooned over how handsome he was — was readying his collection for his debut as an evening-wear designer during New York's Fashion Week. One of many designers left off the invitation list to participate in the main events at the uptown venue, Sandy and two compatriots had to scramble to find a location to present their work to the public and the press while the city's attention was riveted on fashion design. My nephew, Grady, had arranged for one of his clients — a television commercial company — to create a show setting, complete with a "backstage" curtained off from the runway, rows of white folding

11

chairs for the hoped-for audience, and video and still cameras recording the extravaganza to be uploaded to the Internet the way shows of more famous designers were.

Sandy checked the time on his cell phone, which hung around his neck from a lanyard. He cupped his hands around his mouth and shouted, "Let's go, everyone. We can't run late. We have to be out of here by one o'clock, with everything taken down." He looked at me. "Can you believe it? They're hosting a wedding here tonight. That's the problem with using a catering hall for the show."

He grabbed the arm of a man walking by. "Jack, can you get the music started in ten minutes? We need to hurry things up here."

"Sure thing, Xandr."

"How long does the show take?" I asked.

"Each model has about thirty seconds or less to get down to the end of the runway, turn, and walk back. I have six models, leaving at set intervals. The other designers have about the same time to strut their stuff. Three designers. Twelve minutes, give or take a minute. Then we all come out together. Take our bows. And that's it — we're done."

"So quick?"

"The shows of the big designers rarely last

longer and they have even more models, but that's not counting all the schmoozing that takes place in the audience before and after, assuming they're not making a beeline for the door, hoping to get a good seat at the next designer's event."

"It's an awful lot of work for such a short time," I said.

"And a lot of money, but I can't think about that right now. You're welcome to stay as long as you like and take in the backstage drama, but you'll have to excuse me. I need to make sure everything is ready. I'm a nervous wreck. Can you tell? Please say you can't."

"You'll be wonderful," I said. "Go do what you need to do. I won't stay long, but I'm looking forward to getting a glimpse of what goes on behind the scenes. I'll try to keep out of everyone's way."

As it turned out, that wasn't an easy task. The backstage area was simply one large space with rolling metal racks of clothing used to cordon off each designer's area. Open trunks littered the floor. Chairs were scattered everywhere, but no one sat in them. Instead they were draped with scarves or held piles of clothes, shoes, or handbags. Dressers helped models into gowns, and models checked themselves in mirrors after

13

strapping on shoes with heels so high I marveled that they could stand, let alone walk.

In the center of this chaos was what appeared to me to be pandemonium of its own, the hair and makeup station consisting of two tall director's chairs and a folding table to hold myriad cases of cosmetics. One chair was occupied by a blonde wrapped in a white robe, her foot tapping impatiently while an attractive woman in a pink smock arranged the model's hair into an elaborate updo. In the girl's lap was a box of lipsticks with clear tops that allowed their colors to show. They had been lined up neatly in three rows. The blonde opened each lipstick and tossed it back in the carton, making a jumble of their order. She chose one, slathered it on her lips, and held up a mirror to see the result.

"The gorgeous Mr. Ebon wants dark red for me, Miss Milburn," the blonde said. "I like this one. Do you think *he* will?"

"Don't you worry, Rowena. I have just the one he wants in my smock," Miss Milburn replied. The makeup artist, whom I judged to be in her early forties, patted her pocket.

Another handsome man in a tuxedo lounged nearby.

"Peter, what do you think of my lipstick?"

Rowena asked, pursing her lips at him.

"A very kissable color," he replied, leaning toward her.

"Get out of here, Sanderson," Miss Milburn said. "This one's jailbait, way too young for you."

Rowena pouted. "I am not."

Peter plucked a lipstick from the carton and held it out to her. "I think this would suit you better," he said. "Besides, I'm in love with this lady here." He nuzzled the makeup artist's neck. "You're old enough for me, aren't you, Ann?"

"In your dreams," she said, laughing.

"Baby pink! Ugh!" Rowena said. "Why would I think a male model would know anything about lipstick? The lipstick I make is nicer than this." Her tone reflected her disdain.

"I'm crushed," Peter said, feigning hurt feelings. "Am I not always nice to you? I even brought you a cup of my favorite tea this morning."

"It's not my favorite."

"But you drank it anyway."

"I was thirsty. Here's what I think of your lipstick choice." She held out an arm and dropped the tube on the floor.

"And how old are you?" Ann Milburn asked, picking it up.

Rowena scowled. "My aunt thinks I'm old enough to be here, and that should be good enough for you."

"Your aunt cut a nice deal for you, but it doesn't make you a professional model. You could learn a thing or two from your roommates if you ever stopped admiring yourself long enough to listen."

Rowena set aside the box of lipsticks and slipped off the chair. "I know more than those two losers already, and they'll be begging for my advice when I'm famous. I'll be right back," she called out.

"Oh, for heaven's sake," Ann Milburn snapped. "I'm not waiting for you."

Rowena was not the only teenage model in the room. Most of the young women appeared to be about her age, perhaps a year or two older. I knew that the state of New York had passed a law designating models under the age of eighteen as child performers. The idea behind the legislation was to encourage designers to use older models by burdening them with paperwork and making it more restrictive to hire younger ones. However, there were still holdouts who preferred the less curvy bodies of young teenagers to display their designs. I hoped Sandy was not among them.

I spotted another model teetering on

platform heels, the back of her silvery lace dress hanging open. She was trying unsuccessfully to get someone to zip her up, but everyone else was preoccupied.

"Can I help you?" I asked.

"Oh, would you? I can't reach around to get the darn thing up." She held out her hands, close to tears. "And I have lipstick on my fingers."

"Don't cry or you'll ruin your makeup," I said sternly.

"I was trying to make sure I didn't have lipstick on my teeth. But there's nowhere to wash my hands. And even if there was, if I leave a mark on the fabric, I'll never work again."

"My hands are clean," I said, showing them to her. "Just turn around and we'll get you all zipped up."

She turned her back to me and said over her shoulder, "You have to be very careful. It's a hidden zipper and those things catch the cloth."

"I see that," I said, setting my shoulder bag on the floor. "Just hold still —"

"I'm Babs, by the way. Babs Sipos," she said, looping an arm behind her neck to lift her dark hair out of the way.

"Okay, Babs, here we go." I took the tab of the zipper and slowly raised it, making certain to keep the fabric out of the path of the zipper's teeth. "There! All done."

"Oh, thank you, Mrs. Fletcher." She turned to face me; her blue eyes were outlined in silver to match the dress.

"How do you know my name?"

"I heard you talking with Xandr. Isn't he the most beautiful man you've ever seen? All the models are in love with him."

"He's very good-looking," I said.

"Good-looking and smart. He's been bragging about having a famous writer coming to his show. We're all excited to meet you."

"That's very flattering," I said, "but I write mysteries, nothing to do with fashion design."

She rolled her eyes. "Oh, I know that," she said. "Most people think models don't know anything besides clothes, but we do — some of us anyway. We have normal lives. I love to read mysteries. My parents will be so proud that I've met you. May I shake your hand?"

"We'd better get rid of the lipstick on your fingers before we do that."

"Oh, gee, I almost forgot."

I picked up my bag. "I think I know where we can get you some help."

I walked over to the makeup station, Babs

18

trailing behind, where Ann Milburn was now applying her makeup artistry to a beautiful barefoot redhead who obviously wasn't pleased about something.

"Why would I use some stupid homemade lipstick?" the redhead said.

"She thought it was a perfect complement for your complexion, Isla," Ann said. "It doesn't happen often; I think she was trying to be nice."

"Nice! That's a laugh. It's dreadful," Isla snarled, handing a tube of lipstick back to the makeup artist. "Tell Rowena I don't need her amateur advice."

Ann shoved the lipstick tube into her pocket. "You can tell her yourself, Isla Banning. I'm not your messenger girl."

"Am I finished now?"

"Unfortunately, yes. You're risking a career with those bags under your eyes."

"No one important is going to be here to see them." The sullen-faced model slid off the chair, holding her high heels by the straps. She padded off toward the dressing area.

Since both of the chairs were temporarily empty, I felt comfortable asking the makeup artist if she had any wipes we could use.

"I'm sorry, Miss Milburn," Babs said, holding up her hands and wiggling her stained fingers. "I was just checking my teeth."

"I told you not to chew on your lips," Ann said, grabbing Babs's hand and scrubbing it with a damp towel.

"Hey, Sipos, you're interrupting my makeup session," Rowena snapped as she climbed back into her chair. "Go bother Janine. She's already finished dressing. Oh, and, Miss Milburn," she sang, snapping her fingers at the makeup artist, "I'm back. Let's hurry it up here. I need to get my evening gown on."

"I'll get to you when I'm ready," Ann said, deliberately folding the towel she'd used on Babs and busying herself with her cosmetics.

Babs stuck out her tongue at Rowena.

"Better not do that or you'll smear your lipstick again," Rowena said with a smirk.

Babs's expression was distressed. "Am I okay?" she asked, showing me her teeth.

"You're fine," I said. "You'd better go get ready."

She gave me a soft smile and wandered away.

Ann reached into one of her pockets, withdrew a lipstick, and applied it to Rowena's lips. She stood back, surveyed her work, and nodded. "I think Xandr will like it."

A short gentleman in a navy three-piece suit approached. He was immaculately groomed, from the gel that sparkled in his gray hair down to the clear polish on his fingernails. A heavy gold watch encircled his wrist, and he wore a gold signet ring on his right pinkie. "You have everything you need, Ann?" he asked.

"Yes, Mr. Gould. Caroline brought over all the cosmetics this morning."

He turned to me. "I don't believe we've met. I'm Philip Gould. Are you affiliated with one of the designers?"

"I'm Jessica Fletcher, a friend of Xandr Ebon."

"Mr. Gould's company, New Cosmetics, is sponsoring this show," Rowena put in. "He's a very important man, aren't you, Philly? It's not too late to pick me to be the face of New Cosmetics." She blew a kiss in his direction.

"Behave yourself, Rowena," the makeup artist said. "Look up so I can finish putting on your mascara."

"It's always a little crazy getting ready for a show, and these young girls are a handful," Gould said, chuckling. He picked up the box of lipsticks Rowena had pawed

21

through and replaced each one in its proper slot. "This isn't one of ours," he said, dropping a lipstick into a garbage can.

"Hey," Rowena called out. "Is that one of mine?"

Gould ignored her. "Hopefully, our cosmetics will do the designers proud today."

"I'm sure they will," I said, thinking I'd seen enough of what Sandy had called the backstage drama.

A loud drum solo caught my attention, and rock music filled the room.

"I'd better find a seat out front before they're all gone," I said, raising my voice to be heard over the music.

Philip Gould reached into his jacket pocket and stood on tiptoe to lean closer to my ear. "New Cosmetics is hosting a reception for the designers tonight. I hope you can make it," he shouted, and handed me an invitation. "If you need any more, I'll be here after the show."

I thanked him and walked around the side of the curtain blocking off the dressing area. A projector was splashing kaleidoscope images on the audience's side of the black fabric, the lights changing in time to the music. I found Sandy's mother sitting in the front row, her coat folded on the chair next to hers. When she caught sight of me, she waved me over.

"I saved a seat for you," Maggie said, gathering up her coat. "Did you see Sandy?"

"I did, and I told him you were talking with a reporter. He was happy to hear it."

"I must have written every magazine editor in and out of the city trying to get them to send someone to the show. We do have a couple of fashion bloggers here, but they look like they're thirteen. Hardly Sandy's target customer, but when you're competing with the A-listers, you have to take who you can get."

"Most of the seats are filled," I said, waving at Grady and Donna sitting in the front row across the runway from us. "There certainly are a lot of young people here."

"Xandr's publicist has been soliciting students at the Actor's Studio and Parsons School of Design, selling the tickets at a steep discount to make sure we have a decent crowd. It has to look good on camera. Then we can send the YouTube link everywhere so the people who couldn't make it still get a chance to see the designs."

Maggie handed me the program notes, a slim brochure with a flat-black cover, the names of the designers in glossy black ink. It was very elegant, but not easy to read. Inside was a black-and-white photograph of each designer and instead of a biography, a paragraph extolling their design philosophies.

"All Sandy's dresses are inspired by gems and jewelry," his mother said. "He thought the jewel tones would show really well on the red carpet. He's hoping he can get an actress to wear one of them to the upcoming Hollywood awards."

"Does he have anyone in mind?"

"Not yet, but Sandy's assistant told me there's supposed to be a famous stylist here today," she said, craning her neck to look around the room. "Not that I'd know who she was, but if she chose one of his dresses, it would be a major step in his career."

The music ended, and what had been a competing buzz in the room quieted as those still standing hurried to find seats before the show began. The lights dimmed and the drum solo started up again. An announcer's voice intoned, "Ladies and gentlemen, the collections of Xandr Ebon, Nicolas Flemming, and Akiko Murakami."

Under the words "New Cosmetics Presents," Sandy's name was projected on one side of the black curtain, the other side of which was drawn up to allow the models to enter the runway.

A harp joined the drums as Rowena

stepped onto the runway. A hundred flashes of light greeted her from cameras and cell phones recording her every move, reflecting off the gold crystals scattered over the bodice of the gown, and revealing a sheen of perspiration on her brow. Rowena's expression was impassive, the deep red color of her lipstick standing out against her pale complexion. One long leg showed through the slit of her gold gown, the sparkling material almost matching the color of her hair. The high collar came up to her chin, but the halter top left her arms and shoulders bare.

"That's Rowena Roth, Polly Roth's niece," Maggie murmured.

"Who's Polly Roth?" I asked.

"Ever hear of Runway Public Relations?"

I shook my head.

"Well, it's one of the biggies. Polly Roth heads it up. She agreed to hype the show if Sandy would let her niece, Rowena, wear one of his gowns." She reached into her bag and produced a glossy card with photographs of the model as well as her measurements, height, weight, clothing and shoe sizes, and contact information. "Here. Polly just had these run off. It's Rowena's model card. They all have one."

"I guess that makes her official," I said,

looking at her card and slipping it into my bag.

Maggie snorted. "It'll take more than that. She's only a kid, and frankly, a pain in the you-know-where." She squinted. "Is there a spot on that dress?"

"I don't see anything," I said.

"Must've been the light."

Rowena had reached the end of the runway and turned back, careful not to trip on the train of her gown as Dolores stepped into the spotlight at the curtain's opening and began her studied strut down the runway. Wearing the deep purple silk soutache gown to which Sandy had been making last-second repairs, Dolores sauntered with more confidence than Rowena had shown, hips swaying despite the narrowness of the sheath, which was accented by a tulle overskirt embellished with what looked like amethysts. After the two women passed each other, I saw Rowena stumble a bit as she prepared to make her exit, but Babs was there to catch her arm before stepping into the spotlight herself.

"I hope she didn't take anything to calm her nerves," Maggie said into my ear.

Three more models showed off Sandy's lovely designs for evening gowns in emerald, sapphire, and ruby, before the name on the curtain changed to Nicolas Flemming and the harp and accompanying drums were replaced by steel drums and a marimba. The next designer's Afro-Caribbean creations were elaborate floral patterns, with fabric flower petals flaring out from straight or mermaid shapes. His models wore bright turquoise and shocking pink eye shadow to echo the tropical theme.

The marimba became a flute and the steel drums a Japanese taiko when the name of the last designer, Akiko Murakami, was projected. Her gowns were more severe than those of the other designers, with sharp pleats and geometric cutouts in contrast to her colleagues'. The models wore black lipstick, and what looked like black triangles were sprinkled above their eyes, down their temples, and across their cheekbones.

"Her stuff is supereditorial," Maggie whispered to me.

"I've never heard that phrase," I said. "What do you mean?"

"Those are the kinds of clothes no one will wear but that the fashion press loves. At least that's my definition. Generally if a design makes it into *Vogue,* it's 'supereditorial.' "

For the finale, the three designers accompanied their models onto the runway to

27

the solo drums once again. I was happy to see that Sandy had taken off the lanyard that held his cell phone and had changed from his T-shirt and jeans into a long-sleeved black silk shirt and matching trousers. His blond hair was carefully coiffed so that only a single curl hung down on his forehead.

"My son is even more beautiful than his models, isn't he?" Maggie said, grinning.

The audience rose to applaud as the runway filled with elegant models in gorgeous gowns alongside the beaming creators of the couture evening wear. Babs held Rowena's arm as they paraded to their designated places. Rowena's face was ashen. Was she about to get sick? *That would be embarrassing for her.*

"I guess she found out it's not as easy as it looks," Maggie said to me as she clapped loudly. Sandy waved and bowed and held out a hand to acknowledge his models. He scowled when he caught sight of Rowena, who appeared to be swaying. Then her eyes rolled back and she sank gracefully to the floor.

The audience had already begun filing out and I had to fight my way against the flow to get to her.

"I'm sorry, but I can't kneel down in this

gown," Babs said. "I would help if I could. She must have fainted."

Sandy and I reached Rowena at the same time. He shook her shoulder while I lifted her hand, trying to find a pulse.

"Do you think we should try CPR?" he asked.

I pressed two fingers into the side of Rowena's neck. "Yes," I said, pressing down on her chest, "but I'm afraid we may already be too late."

CHAPTER TWO

Those who hadn't left became aware of the situation and moved closer to get a better look. Among them was a young medical student from Columbia Presbyterian Hospital who had accompanied his girlfriend to the show. He immediately joined me and took over efforts to revive Rowena but failed to get a pulse.

"Get back. Get back," Sandy said in a loud voice to the onlookers. He turned to me. "This is a nightmare, Jessica. It can't be happening."

"I'm afraid it is, Sandy," I said. "You'd better call nine-one-one."

"Is there a defibrillator on the premises?" the medical student called out.

"The caterer says it's broken," someone shouted back.

The medical student conducted his own test of the fallen model. "Skin color, bluish gray. No pulse. Pupils are dilated and fixed," he muttered as if reading from a list. His eyes met mine and he shook his head.

Sandy seemed paralyzed. He held his cell phone in his hand and looked at it rather than touching the keypad, as though it would make the call on its own. I took it from him and dialed those infamous and fateful numbers. A woman answered.

"I'm calling from —" I looked to Sandy. "What's the name of this place?" I asked.

"It's, uh — it's the Starlight Room at Flatiron Catering."

"I'm calling from the Starlight Room at Flatiron Catering. That's right. No, it's not the Waldorf Astoria Hotel."

"Wait!" Sandy grabbed the phone away from me. "Hello? Operator? It's not the Starlight at the Waldorf. We're at the one on West Twenty-sixth Street, eighteenth floor," he yelled into the phone. "What do you mean what kind of emergency? She just dropped dead. Isn't that enough of an emergency?"

Sandy was overwrought; the lead-up to the day's event combined with this unexpected outcome must have tripped his already frayed nerves. He was losing control. "I can't believe it," he groaned, his hand shaking as he held out the phone.

I took it back from him and cocked my

head at his mother. Maggie put her arm around Sandy and led him away from the dead model. "Come sit down, sweetheart."

"Mom, what am I going to do?"

"Operator, are you still there?" I asked. "Oh, thank goodness. Yes, a young woman has died."

"You're sure she's dead?" the woman asked.

"Yes. There's a doctor here and he has confirmed it. She's a runway model, very young. No, I don't know her age. Someone said her name was Rowena Roth. She was in a fashion show of new designs and at first we thought she'd fainted from the excitement. Please send someone right away."

The young physician and I were joined by a tall man in an obvious state of agitation.

"What's going on?" he demanded.

"We have a young woman who's —" I said. "She's — she's dead."

"Oh, no! This is terrible," he said in a husky voice tinged with a Southern accent.

"It certainly is," I said.

"We have to start setting up for the wedding," he said. "I told them. Everyone out and all cleaned up by one. They promised me they would be gone."

"I'm afraid that will have to wait until —"

"I knew it," he said. "I knew it was a

mistake to have this, this stupid fashion show on the same day as a wedding. But Polly, she insisted."

The man, who I guessed was the catering facility's manager, stood wringing his hands and cursing under his breath. I ignored him as I waited for the 911 dispatcher to complete her emergency response protocol, answering her questions as best I could.

"We'll have someone to you directly," she told me. "Do you need me to stay on the line with you until they get there?"

I assured her I didn't need to take up more of her time and that I would remain with the body until the authorities arrived. I thanked her and ended the call.

There was still a clot of curious bystanders lingering by the exit. I didn't see my nephew and his wife. We had made plans to meet in the lobby downstairs after the show.

Sandy, who'd managed to get his emotions in check, recovered enough to take charge once again and began to give out orders. He instructed a security guard assigned to the show to keep everyone away from Rowena Roth's lifeless body, directed the other designers and models who'd been milling about to go backstage and start packing up.

"I'm sorry, Jessica. I think I'll be all right

now," he said, wiping his brow. "I don't know what happened to me. I don't usually get hysterical in an emergency. Such a crazy thing. Who would ever think . . . ?" He trailed off.

"Not your fault, Sandy. This is not what you expected to happen at your show, and especially not to someone so young. But please, see if you can find something to cover her. There are too many prying eyes here. We don't want her picture on the cover of a tabloid tomorrow."

My suggestion was timely. A young man with a camera, a press pass dangling from his neck, approached and prepared to snap a picture of the fallen model. I quickly positioned myself between them to block his view. The photographer changed his vantage point but not before Sandy pulled a portion of the black curtain off the frame separating the runway from backstage and draped it over Rowena. The photographer growled something and contented himself with taking pictures of those of us surrounding the dead girl. The security guard sent him toward the door.

"What happened to her?" another member of the press contingent yelled.

We ignored him. A few seconds later a tall, stately woman wearing a spring green suit appeared from the other side of the large room.

"What's going on?" she asked Sandy.

"I'm so sorry, Polly — it's Rowena," he said, indicating the sheet.

"What do you mean, it's Rowena?"

She was joined by the arrival of two people in navy uniforms with the letters EMT in white on one shoulder and FDNY on the other. They pushed a gurney ahead of them. One carried a leather satchel, the other a portable CPR machine. We stepped away to allow them access to the body. As one pulled the sheet away, the woman who'd just joined us gasped and grabbed Sandy to keep from collapsing.

"I know, I know, Polly," Sandy said to her.

I looked across the room and saw my nephew, Grady, and his wife, Donna, making their way through the crowd.

"What happened, Aunt Jessica?" Grady asked when they reached me.

"A model has died."

"Died?" Donna said. "Just died, like that?"

"I'm afraid so."

One of the emergency medical technicians folded his stethoscope and said to the other, "She's gone."

"No, it can't be," the woman in the green suit wailed.

"Is that Polly Roth?" I asked Grady.

"Yes," he replied. "She heads up the PR agency that's been publicizing the show." He leaned forward to get a better look at the body. "Oh, boy," he said, "that's her niece, Rowena."

"Oh, my goodness," Donna said. "She's just a kid." Donna went to Polly and guided Rowena's aunt to a chair. "I'll get you some water," she said.

The EMTs directed everyone to move back as they replaced the sheet over Rowena and gently lifted her onto the gurney. Philip Gould, the show sponsor, emerged from the side of the black curtain as they were tucking in the gold train of her gown. "Just what we don't need," I heard him mutter to himself. "Okay, gentlemen," he barked at the EMTs, "come on, move. Get her out of here!"

"We're waiting for the police," an EMT said in response.

"Police? Why?"

"Those are our orders," he told us.

Sandy paled. "Do we really need the police?" he asked me. "Can't they just take her to a hospital?"

"It's an unusual death," I said. "Unusual deaths are almost always investigated."

Philip Gould sank down onto a seat next

to Polly and put his arm around her until Donna returned with a glass of water. Then he moved to another chair and typed furiously into his cell phone.

Despite his mother's urging him to sit down, Sandy paced along the runway until the police arrived, shooing away anyone from backstage who poked a head through the curtain to see what was going on out front.

Two uniformed officers and a plainclothes detective arrived.

"Who's in charge here?" the detective asked.

"I suppose I am," Gould said, pocketing his phone. "My firm, New Cosmetics, sponsored this show."

The detective, a barrel-chested spark plug of a man with a steel gray buzz cut, whom I judged to be in his early fifties and who chewed on a toothpick, looked around. "Who else is a witness to what happened?"

"We are," Sandy replied, pointing to himself and to me. "But lots of people saw her fall. All the models backstage." He waved a hand toward the curtain. "My mother over there and —"

The detective gave orders to his officers to take names and statements. They disappeared behind the black curtain. He asked Philip Gould to "hang around," and came to where Sandy and I stood. "Aaron Kopecky, NYPD," he said, showing us his badge. "You are?"

"Xandr Ebon," Sandy answered. "I'm an evening-wear designer. She was one of my models — Rowena, that is, the girl who died. She's wearing one of my gowns. Oh, jeez," he said as he looked at me, his eyes stricken, "how am I going to get the dress back?"

"We'll worry about that later," I said.

Sandy nodded and introduced me. "This is Jessica Fletcher. She's a good friend from back home and —"

Kopecky cocked his head. "Jessica Fletcher? The mystery writer?"

"Yes."

"No kidding? I'm pretty sure I've got some of your books at home. My wife was a big fan."

"That's nice to hear."

"You saw the deceased die?"

"Well, yes, along with everyone else who was here."

"Who is she?"

Sandy answered, "Her name is Rowena Roth. She's seventeen — or was. That's her aunt over there, the woman in the chartreuse suit, Polly Roth. Her PR agency handled press for the show."

"I'll get to her later. How about we find a quiet corner and you tell me exactly what you saw?"

As we started to walk away in search of solitude, the owner of the catering hall intercepted us. "These people have to go," he said, mopping his brow with a handkerchief. "I have a wedding tonight to prepare for."

Detective Kopecky eyed the caterer. "We may be here several hours," he said.

"But my wedding party . . ."

"Looks like the bride and groom will have to elope," Kopecky said.

CHAPTER THREE

Sandy and I told Detective Kopecky what we'd observed, which wasn't much, and he didn't ask many questions. As far as I could tell, he'd been called to the scene of an unusual but not suspicious death of a young person and wasn't viewing it as anything more than that.

"She must have had a congenital heart problem," Sandy offered. "It's always so shocking when someone that young dies like this. I mean, heart attacks are how older people die."

"I've seen a few younger people keel over," Kopecky said. "She never showed any signs of having a cardiac problem?" He angled his head at me.

"I wouldn't know," I replied. "I'd never met her before today." I turned to Sandy. "Had you known her long?" I asked.

He shook his head. "No. Polly — that's her aunt — asked me to use her in the show, which I was happy to do. The only conversations we had concerned the clothes she would wear and what I expected of her on the runway. She was inexperienced — a little cocky — but she learned quickly."

"Well," the detective said, stretching against a pain somewhere in his body and letting out a groan to confirm it, "sorry for your loss. My officers are gathering names of those who are still around in case I'd like to speak with them. Just pro forma. The medical examiner will do an autopsy. That's pro forma, too, in cases like this. What about her family?"

I mentioned Polly Roth again and her relationship to Rowena Roth. "I'm sure that she'll inform other members of the family of this tragedy," I said.

"She's next on my list," Kopecky said. "Thanks for your help. It was a pleasure meeting you, Mrs. Fletcher. If you ever need somebody to fill you in on how murder investigations *really* work, give me a call." He handed me his card. "Nice meeting you, too," he said to Sandy. "Sorry it's under such circumstances."

Grady and Donna had been waiting for my conversation with the detective to end.

"Are you okay?" Grady asked when I joined them.

"I'm fine," I said, "although it's terribly sad to witness the death of a teenager who never had a chance to grow up and enjoy her adult life."

"Do you think it was a heart attack?" Donna asked.

I could only shrug. "That's for the medical examiner to determine," I said. "It's hard to accept that someone that young could die of heart failure, but it does happen."

Donna showed her watch to Grady. "We have to get back to the office," she said, tapping the face.

"I need lunch first. I'm famished," he said. "Aunt Jess, will you join us?"

"I'd be happy to."

Before we left, Sandy, his mother, and Philip Gould approached us. The EMTs had removed the body, and Detective Kopecky was engaged in a conversation with Polly Roth.

Gould shook his head. "Terrible, terrible tragedy," he said. "But I hope this won't keep you from attending tonight's reception." He passed two invitations to Grady and Donna. "We've taken over Capriccio's. Got our reservation in before any of the others even thought about it." He grinned. "They tried to back out when one of the magazines wanted the space, but we had an ironclad contract."

We asked Sandy to extend our condolences to Polly Roth and said good-bye to the others.

It felt good being with Grady and Donna as we left the catering hall and walked to a restaurant they'd suggested for lunch. Although we lived in different parts of the country, my nephew and I had remained close through e-mail and frequent phone calls. He was a terrific young man, married to a wonderful woman. They'd named their only child, Frank, after my late husband, even further endearing them to me. Both Grady and Donna were certified public accountants, but they'd decided that Donna would not seek full-time employment while bringing up their son.

Like many young professionals launching a career, Grady had suffered through some early rough spots, bouncing from one job to another, never finding the right place for himself. I'd thought he'd finally settled down with a firm that handled the payroll for a variety of film and video production companies. But that firm's management had been "creative" when it came to handling the books — "cooking the books" it's often called — and when it went belly-up overnight, the production companies that depended upon it, as well as its employees, found themselves in a bind. Out of a job, Grady and his boss, Carl Zucker, stepped into the breach. They banded together, started their own payroll company, and eventually built it into a respected and lucrative business.

"The firm's name is Zucker and Fletcher," Grady told me at the time. "I held out for Fletcher and Zucker, but we decided to settle it by flipping a coin. Carl won."

With their son, Frank, no longer needing his mother at home full-time, Donna now worked part-time at Zucker and Fletcher.

We walked into a small French bistro near their office but across town from the apartment building to which they'd recently moved. I'd had dinner at their home the previous night after having flown to New York from Boston and was impressed with their new apartment's space compared to the small quarters they'd previously shared.

"What did the detective have to say when you and Sandy talked with him?" Donna asked after we'd all ordered French onion soup and salads.

"He was just following procedure," I said. "Having a very young woman suddenly die of no apparent cause qualifies as an unusual death. Sandy and I told him what we'd observed and that was that. I feel terrible for her aunt and the rest of her family."

Grady sipped his Diet Coke and shook his head. "The fashion world is a strange one," he commented. "I never knew anything about it until I got one of our clients involved in helping stage the show. They're a top producer of TV commercials; they know how to stage a set so it looks like all the other fashion shows, only just different enough to be exciting and dramatic. This was exciting and dramatic all right. I spoke with one of the guys from the production house who was there. He said they were as shocked as everyone."

"Sandy certainly was shaken," I said. "It's an unfortunate way to launch his career."

"You knew him from Cabot Cove, didn't you?" Donna asked me.

"Yes, I did, but not well. I'm sure Grady's told you this, but he was Sandy in those days, not Xandr as he's known now. He was a talented but troubled young man as I remember. I knew his mother back then and recall the problems she had with him. He seemed to think he could charm his way out of difficulties, and many times he got away with it."

"With a face like that, I'm not surprised,"

Donna said. "He looks like he should be a model himself, or a movie star."

"Unfortunately, I think it skewed his expectations," I said. "He always had an artistic bent, though. He won some high school art competitions. Oh, and he also designed costumes for school plays if I'm not mistaken."

"He spent time in Hollywood, didn't he?" Grady said.

"Yes. He —"

The arrival of our lunches interrupted our conversation and we eagerly dug in. When we resumed our chat, the topic turned to my catching up on what was going on in their lives, and the activities of Frank, now almost a teenager.

"He takes after his aunt Jessica," Grady said proudly. "He's a good writer, gets straight A's in his English classes."

"Maybe we'll collaborate on a novel someday."

Grady pressed my hand. "He'd love that, Aunt Jess."

"As long as you wouldn't mind that he'd be writing about murder."

"He's a little young for that," Donna said as she used a piece of crusty French bread to mop up what remained of her soup. "Then again, what kids are exposed to these days can be upsetting for a parent."

I smiled and our conversation turned to other topics, although the vision of Rowena sinking to the floor and my vivid recollection of the fact that the teenager was dead were never far below the surface.

Grady paid the bill and we stepped outside into a crystal-clear day with a cobalt sky above.

"Sure you want to stay in your hotel, Aunt Jess?" Grady asked. "Our pullout couch is really comfortable and —"

"I appreciate the offer, Grady, but the Refinery Hotel is perfectly fine with me. It gives me my own space, and I don't feel that I'm intruding into a busy household. Will you two be at the reception that Mr. Gould is hosting this evening?"

"He gave us tickets," Donna said. "I guess we're expected, but what happened this afternoon takes the joy out of any celebration."

"But the show must go on," Grady said. "We have to put in an appearance."

Donna nodded. "I know."

Grady turned to me. "What will you do for the rest of the afternoon?"

"Don't worry about me. I feel very much at home in New York City. Perhaps I'll take a nice walk, maybe catch a nap at the hotel

47

before the reception this evening."

"We'll see you there, Aunt Jess." He kissed my cheek, as did Donna.

I watched this delightful couple stroll away and my heart filled. Having them in my life was a blessing. My late husband, Frank, and I never had any children. Grady had been like a surrogate son for us and I couldn't love him more than if I'd raised him from infancy. And that went for Donna, too.

I sighed, but my elevated spirits soon came back down to earth. The beautiful young model who'd died intruded into my thoughts everywhere I walked, even while stopping to admire store windows, taking in the variety of people sharing the streets with me, and musing on our lunchtime conversation and Grady's parting words.

"The show must go on," he'd said. The saying originated in the circus world many years ago, its meaning now applicable to almost every aspect of life. I only hoped that what was supposed to be a pleasant week in New York City with my nephew and his lovely wife, and a triumph for Sandy Black, aka Xandr Ebon, didn't turn into a circus.

CHAPTER FOUR

The reception hosted for the designers by Philip Gould, chairman and CEO of New Cosmetics, was held at one of New York's hot spots for people in the fashion industry — or so I was told. Capriccio's was located a block from New Cosmetics' corporate headquarters in downtown Manhattan on a street that had once been down-and-out, but with gentrification had sprung back to life. Small, trendy restaurants lined both sides of it, along with boutiques whose windows displayed the latest in fashion. I was pleased to see an independent bookstore nestled among the eateries but fought the temptation to go in and sign whatever copies of my books they might carry. Maybe another day.

I'd managed to find time to rest at the hotel before getting ready for the reception. I'd worried about what to bring with me from home. Fashion Week in Manhattan is always a festive and high-toned affair, and every newspaper and magazine highlights the cutting edge of fashion being celebrated. But judging from those in attendance at the showing earlier in the day, only the models were dressed to the nines, with some notable exceptions.

Satisfied with the wardrobe I'd chosen — I wore a silk wrap dress that was both practical and pretty — and relaxed from my rest, I took a taxi and walked into Capriccio's feeling refreshed, if a little apprehensive about how Rowena's death would affect others at the party. Sandy Black — I'd not yet gotten used to his new name, Xandr Ebon — had been extremely upset, as we all were. The distress felt by Polly Roth was the most personal, of course. Rowena had been her niece, and she had arranged to have the young woman model in Sandy's show. I could only speculate what dreadful thoughts must be going through her mind at that moment.

The restaurant was surprisingly large based upon its modest exterior. Once inside, I passed a long bar to my left and arrived at a staircase leading to an upper level. A young woman with two large tattoos of birds, one on each side of her neck, stood at a makeshift podium at the base of the staircase. She took my coat after I'd handed her my invitation. She flashed a smile and said, "The party's upstairs. Enjoy!"

I followed the sound of a string quartet up the stairs and arrived at the party venue, a large room with pictures of models in the designers' fashions projected on the walls, and a huge banner that read WHO WILL BE THE NEW FACE OF NEW COSMETICS? From what I could see, the room's perimeter was lined with couches, and small tables with two chairs at each. A bar was set up in the near corner, and a crew of dramatically made-up young women wearing tuxedo suits passed through the crowd offering hot and cold finger food.

The string quartet occupied a raised platform in the opposite corner from the bar, and played classical selections that, while amplified, stayed at a level that thankfully enabled easy conversation. I've never understood why some hosting parties, wedding receptions, and other social events allow the musicians, or DJs, to dominate the scene, making conversation impossible without shouting. It crossed my mind as I entered the space that a sound financial investment would be in companies that manufacture hearing aids. The younger set exposed to such racket on a regular basis will certainly need such devices at some point in middle age. But this musical choice, probably thanks to Philip Gould, who was paying their tab, not only provided an elegant backdrop but kept the volume down.

As I scanned the crowd for Grady and Donna, Peter Sanderson, the male model whom I'd seen behind the scenes at the show, crossed the room to me. "Mrs. Fletcher, I'm so glad that you decided to come."

I was slightly taken aback at the effusive greeting but accepted his outstretched hand.

"Peter Sanderson here. I never had a chance to meet you today," he said, "but someone told me who you were."

"I'm so sorry that the show ended the way it did," I said.

"Really? Oh, you mean what happened to Rowena. Pretty shocking, huh?"

"To say the least."

"I'm really glad that I have this opportunity to get to know you," he said, displaying a grin and a set of very white teeth. "I have the feeling that there's some sort of karma at play."

"Karma?"

"You know what I mean, fate at work. You've had a few of your excellent novels turned into equally excellent motion pictures."

I wanted to move on but didn't want to rudely cut our conversation short.

"Yes," I said, "I've been fortunate in that regard." I didn't add that I wasn't especially pleased with the film version of one of my books.

"I model to pay the bills," he said, striking a pose and then winking at me, "but I'm really an actor."

Ah, I thought. Now I understood what he was getting at. He certainly was good-looking, if not quite as classically handsome as Sandy Black. Peter's hair was brown with blond streaks, and his jaw sported the three-days-without-shaving shadow so many young men affect. And, of course, he had the narrow frame that couturiers like to drape their designs on. This night he wore a tight-fitting navy blue leather jacket with a zipper that went from one hip to the opposite shoulder, and carefully torn blue jeans, a style that continues to mystify me. I don't always notice what men are wearing unless it's out of the ordinary, but I was keenly aware that I was among people for whom the decision of what to wear each morning held great importance.

"Have you appeared in films?" I asked.

"Bit parts, TV walk-ons, but my agent is confident that some juicier parts are on the horizon." He pulled a business card from his jacket and handed it to me, saying, "I've always believed that an actor can do his best work only when he believes in the material, and I believe in your books."

I was tempted to ask whether he'd read any of them but didn't want to put him on the spot. "That's very nice, Peter, but —"

"Let me get you a drink, Jessica. I may call you Jessica, right?"

"Of course," I said, waving excitedly at a woman in the crowd, "but I hope you'll excuse me. There's someone I need to catch up with."

"Promise me we'll have a chance to talk later," he said.

"Let's see how the evening progresses," I said.

I hoped I'd disengaged politely. The woman I'd waved to was giving me an uncertain smile, probably trying desperately to remember where she'd met me when, in fact, we'd never set eyes on each other before. "Your dress is lovely. I've been admiring it from afar," I said as I squeezed by her, having spotted Sandy's mother.

"I didn't see you come in," Maggie said.

"Easy to get lost in this mob," I said.

"I'm relieved that so many people have shown up," she said, "after what happened to Rowena. I was afraid we'd all be talking to ourselves. Have you heard anything new about it?"

"No. I'm sure that nothing will be determined until the autopsy is completed. How is Sandy holding up?"

"Oh, he's fine," his mother said. "He's over there, conferring with his financial backer."

I looked in the direction she indicated and saw him at a table with a middle-aged man.

"It must be expensive launching a new line of clothing," I said.

"Incredibly so," she said. "Raising money for his line has taken up most of Sandy's time. Investing in new fashions carries with it a lot of risk."

"I can imagine. Who is Sandy's financial backer?"

"Jordon Verne. They met when Sandy was in Hollywood." Her face turned sour. "That's a part of Sandy's life I'd just as soon forget, and I would have thought that he would, too."

"I meant to ask you about that —" I started to say when Babs Sipos, the model who'd been next to Rowena when she collapsed and whose dress I'd helped zip up, tapped me on the shoulder.

"Hi, Mrs. Fletcher," she said.

"Hello, Babs. I was hoping you'd be here. I see that you've changed into something more comfortable."

She laughed. "We were supposed to wear our gowns to the party, but I couldn't wait to get out of mine." She looked at Maggie. "Oh, sorry. I didn't mean to insult your son's designs. They're beautiful, but I —"

"That's all right, dear," Maggie said, but her voice was cold. "I know what you meant, but please don't say that in front of anyone else. We have press and other important people here. We don't want them taking away a negative impression. In fact, I see the editor of *Couture Model.* Excuse me, please."

"Oops," Babs said after Maggie had walked away. "I always put my foot in my mouth. I hope that won't keep me from getting another job with Xandr."

"I don't think his mother will tell him not to hire you," I said. "How are you feeling this evening?"

Her lips turned down in a pout. "I still can't get over what happened to Rowena. I never knew anyone my age who died."

"It's a terrible tragedy," I said. "She seemed fine when I saw her at the makeup station. Did she show any signs of being ill?"

"Well, she did run to the ladies' room before we went on. I was afraid she wouldn't make it back in time — it was on another floor — but she did. I thought it was just nerves, you know. I told her that I was sick to my stomach, too, my first time on the catwalk, but she brushed me off, said she wasn't nervous at all."

"Was Rowena a good friend of yours?"

"No one was her friend," Babs said, taking me aback. She saw my expression and rushed on. "I mean, she could be really snarky, had a real California-girl chip on her shoulder, even though she's from the Midwest." She quickly added, "But that doesn't mean she deserved to die, of course."

"No, of course not," I said. "Are you from New York?"

"Nope! I'm a small-town girl, too, the 'all-American' type, or so it says on my model card." She pirouetted in front of me. "Can't you tell?" She pointed to her nose. "See? Freckles."

"Did you come here with your family?"

"Not exactly. Well, I mean, my mother accompanied me when we first came two years ago, but then she went back home after dumping me with her cousin in Queens. But my mother's cousin and I didn't get along, so I moved in with another model."

It's bad form to ask a woman her age, but that rule doesn't apply to a very young woman. I asked.

"I'm eighteen, but I'll be nineteen next month."

I tried not to show my surprise. It's a courageous move to leave your sixteen-year-old daughter with a relative she doesn't know in New York, or any other large city for that matter, but I didn't express that thought.

"Why do you think Rowena had a chip on her shoulder? It would seem to me she was fortunate to have an aunt who could get her a job modeling. I assume that's what she wanted to do."

Babs smirked. "She wanted to be a model, and she thought she knew more about the business than anyone else. She played at being an authority on everything, even mixing up her own makeup and always lecturing everyone about what they should be doing like she was an expert. I mean, it was her aunt who was the expert, not Rowena."

Babs looked to where some of the other models from the show (I recognized their dresses) stood in a knot of partygoers. "See that girl in the amethyst gown? That's my roommate, Dolores Marshall. Rowena was mean to her. I even heard her use a racial epithet once to her face."

Dolores's complexion testified to her mixed parentage — perhaps African-American or Hispanic, and Caucasian.

"Is that the right word, 'epithet'?" Babs asked. "I mean, you're a writer. I figure you'll know."

"If you mean a nasty slur, you've chosen the correct term. That's an interesting vocabulary choice."

She shrugged. "I had good teachers and I read a lot."

"Did Rowena have a roommate?" I asked.

Babs pointed. "Two. Isla and Janine. Isla's the redhead in emerald and Janine's the brunette in the ruby gown. I like her dress the best. I asked Xandr if I could wear it, but he said the platinum one went better with my coloring. Whoever he sells it to better hire someone to help her zip it up."

I thought that at the prices Sandy was likely to be selling his gowns for, that wouldn't be a problem for his buyers.

A waitress reached us and I plucked a mushroom off her platter. Babs waved her away.

"Aren't you having anything?" I said. "Can't," she said. "Have to watch my weight."

I couldn't help laughing. She was a matchstick in her miniskirt, calf-high boots, and a pullover black shirt cut low.

"We're all hoping Mr. Gould picks one of us to be the 'new face' of New Cosmetics," Babs said. "Don't dare risk anything that might make him count us out."

The redheaded model waved to her, and Babs twirled around grinning.

"Go talk with your friends," I said. "It was nice to see you again."

We separated and I headed for the bar, where I ordered a white wine from a young bartender with a goatee. *Another actor, if I don't miss my bet,* I thought. As I turned away in search of someone else to talk to, I felt a finger poke my back. It was another bearded young man, dressed in a tan safari jacket and jeans, who carried a notebook.

"Jessica Fletcher?" he said.

"Yes?"

"Steven Crowell," he said, "the *New York Post.* Got a minute?"

"Yes, I — but not if you want to speak about what happened today at the fashion show."

"That *is* what I wanted to talk to you

about," he said. He didn't look old enough to be a reporter for any newspaper, let alone a large one like the *Post.*

"Why would you want to talk to me?" I asked. "I was just an onlooker like everyone else. Maybe you should speak with Sandy — er, Xandr Ebon. Rowena, the model who died, was working for him."

"I already spoke with him. He promised to get together with me privately once the party is over."

"Then you don't need me," I said.

"He happened to say he's from the same town in Maine that you live in."

"Cabot Cove," I said. "Sandy grew up there and —"

"Sandy or Xandr?" he asked, his pencil making scratching noises on the page of his notebook.

"I'm sure he'd prefer Xandr," I said. "That's the name he's using now professionally."

"What do you think happened?" Crowell asked.

"What happened is that a young and beautiful fashion model just died. It's certainly unexpected and dreadful, but I didn't know her. I can't help you."

Crowell looked around before saying, "I get the impression that she was disliked by just about everybody."

I stiffened. He was wading into the sort of gossip that tabloid newspapers are famous for, and I wasn't about to contribute to the rumor mill.

"I just told you that I didn't know her," I said, but I couldn't help thinking about what Babs Sipos had said about Rowena. I wondered if he'd spoken with her.

"Yeah, but you write murder mysteries, so I thought you might have a particular slant on it. Any thoughts?"

"If I were guessing, I'd say the unfortunate young woman must have had a congenital weakness and succumbed to it. I feel terrible for her family. Now please excuse me."

It occurred to me that I'd already had to extricate myself from two awkward conversations, and hoped that it wasn't a harbinger of what the rest of the evening would be like. As it turned out, subsequent conversations, almost all of them with people I didn't know, were pleasant enough and didn't find me looking for excuses to escape. I enjoyed time spent with Grady and Donna, whose contribution to the fashion show had been enthusiastically acknowledged by Philip Gould, who introduced me to his wife, Linda. She was a head taller than her husband, heavily made up, and very thin.

patted my handbag and smiled.

"You must call me so we can talk about
our next project."

And your acting aspirations, I thought.

I managed to slip away without confirming that I would call, and was halfway to
the staircase when I thought I saw Detective Kopecky standing by the bar, a drink in
his hand. I backtracked to be certain I was
right.

Why would he be at the party? I wondered.

I approached him and said, "It *is* you. I
thought I recognized you. How do you
come to be here tonight?"

"It's a pleasant way to spend an evening,"
I said. "Don't you think?"

"Do you have an interest in fashion?" I
asked.

He chuckled and sipped his drink. "One
look at me and what I wear and you'll know
the answer."

"I think you look just fine," I said.

His bloodred tie contrasted with the pale
blue button-down shirt, gray tweed sport
jacket, and gray slacks that he wore.

"What about your wife? Is she a fashion
fan?"

"My wife always said that I had a terrible
sense of clothes," he said pleasantly. "Eve-

Although close to my age, she was obviously
a devotee to plastic surgery with a forehead
so smooth it limited the facial expressions
she was able to form. I wondered if having
a husband surrounded by beautiful models
motivated her to keep herself looking young.
Philip, as he insisted I call him, took pains
to thank me for coming. He also told me I
looked lovely, but only after revealing that
his company, New Cosmetics, was putting
out a line for "mature women."

"About time you paid some attention to
the women who really support the business," his wife remarked coolly. "Those
baby-face models don't care about quality
as long as there's glitter in the tube."

Philip laughed. "I promise there won't be
any glitter in the new line."

"Just cat's eyes and flaming lips," his wife
said with a small smile.

"We have to follow the trend, Linda."

"No, dear. You have to lead it."

I caught up with Sandy later on and had a
truncated conversation with him. His mother's allusions to her son's Hollywood days
as being unpleasant enough for him not to
want to relive them crossed my mind a few
times during the evening, but I didn't raise
the topic when I saw him. He appeared to
have the weight of the world on his shoul-

ders, and I wondered whether it was Rowena's death or the lengthy meeting he had with his financial backer that was the major contributor to his heavy mood. Or could he possibly be more bothered by the temporary loss of the gold gown Rowena had been wearing when she died? There was a piece of me that bridled when he'd expressed worry over that. A child's death — and that was what she was, a seventeen-year-old child — should take precedence in our thoughts over any inconvenience it occasions. Although I suppose that's naive on my part. Most people see the world only from their own narrow perspectives. And to Sandy, Rowena was a model he'd been pressed into hiring by her aunt, nothing more.

I hadn't expected to see Rowena's aunt, Polly Roth, attending the festivities, and her absence was understandable. I thought with sympathy that she carried a miserable burden having to notify the other members of Rowena's family about their loss.

On my own, I wandered around the room, eavesdropping on snippets of conversation. I heard one elegantly dressed woman tell her companion, "Yes, he's gorgeous, but his evening gowns crease too easily. You don't dare sit down."

"Then how do you get to an e companion asked.

"Either you put it on after you have someone waiting there with I just can't be bothered."

Out of the corner of my eye, I caug of emerald. "I borrowed her coat here tonight."

"You didn't," gasped her brunett

"Why not? She's not using it."

"Hey, Phil, care to give the *Po* regarding your 'new face'?"

"You'll hear the announceme everyone else does, Crowell."

"I heard her husband caught ther grante, as they say."

"I wouldn't mind seeing that fac from me at the breakfast table."

I decided to call it a night after tw and started to make my way tow stairs, but was intercepted by Peter son again.

"Jessica! You can't be leaving. We had a chance to continue our chat."

"Perhaps another time," I said.

"Still have my card?"

since she died — breast cancer last year — I've been trying to dress better."

"Oh, I'm so sorry. I didn't know."

"Of course you didn't," he said, waving away my apology. "As for fashion like these people define it? As long as my clothes don't have gravy stains on them, that's good enough for me." He looked back at the bartender. "Buy you a drink? They're cheap, just a buck in the tip jar."

"Thank you, no," I said. "I'm on my way out, but may I ask you again what brings you here? I'm just curious."

"That man over there, Mr. Gould, gave me a pass to the party. I got talking to him this afternoon. I had nothing else on tap this evening, so I figured a couple of hours with the city's beautiful people might be fun. Since my wife — there I go again — since she passed, I try to fill my off-duty hours."

"I understand," I said. "I hope you enjoy the party."

I had started to walk away when he grabbed my elbow. "I meant it about buying you a drink, but not here. I know a nice little bar around the corner, quiet, and they make good drinks. The food's not bad either."

"Are you proposing to give me a lesson in

how *real* murder investigations are conducted?"

He laughed. "As a matter of fact, I figured that maybe you could teach me a thing or two, like the way you solve crimes in your books. What do you say?"

I thought for a moment before replying. It was my intention to go back to the hotel, pick up reading a good novel where I'd left off, and get a good night's sleep. But I've always been an easy mark given a chance to probe the mind of a law enforcement officer. Besides, I wasn't sleepy yet, and the limited hors d'oeuvres hadn't made up for a lack of dinner.

"That sounds nice," I said. "Yes, I'd enjoy that very much."

We were halfway to the stairs when Grady and Donna caught up with us.

"Come back to the apartment for a nightcap?" Donna asked.

"May I take a rain check?" I said. "Detective Kopecky and I are going out for something to eat."

I read the glance between my nephew and his wife.

"And to talk shop," Kopecky put in. "I got some cold cases I want to run by her."

"See you tomorrow night, Aunt Jess?" Grady asked, a slight grin on his face.

"Of course," I said. "You two enjoy the rest of your evening."

"And you do the same," were Grady's parting words.

CHAPTER FIVE

The restaurant that Kopecky led me to was called Jill's. It was everything that he'd said it was, quiet and sedate, with low lights and with guitar music coming through the speakers. Kopecky was obviously a regular; the bartender greeted him by name, indicated we were to take two stools at the end of the bar away from other patrons, and asked the detective if he wanted "his usual."

"That'd be fine, Jake," Kopecky said.

"A diet soda for me," I said.

I expected that because we'd just recently met, conversation might be difficult, but Aaron, as he asked me to call him, turned out to be a talker. In a half hour I'd learned much about him, his childhood in Brooklyn, his two years at John Jay College of Criminal Justice, a stint in the army where he rose to the rank of sergeant, his decision to join the NYPD, starting out as a patrolman in some of the city's toughest neighborhoods, and his eventual promotion to detective. He started to recall one of his most difficult cases for me, stopped, laughed, and said, "Here I go again, running off at the mouth. My wife always said that my mind's on vacation but my mouth works overtime. That's a song title, you know, by a piano player named Mose Allison. I have his album. I like jazz, but not too loud. You like jazz?"

His enthusiasm brought forth a smile from me. "Yes, I like jazz — but not too loud."

We ordered calamari — "crisp, please" — and two bowls of lobster bisque that Kopecky claimed was the best in New York.

"You married?" he asked between bites and spoonfuls.

"I was. My husband, Frank, died a number of years ago."

"I bet the guys swarm around you like bees to honey," he said.

I shook my head.

"No boyfriend? A pretty lady like you?"

I thought of George Sutherland, my Scotland Yard inspector friend in London. I wouldn't call him "my boyfriend"; we were a little too old for that. Romantic sparks had flown back and forth on occasion, but neither of us had taken our mutual admiration and warm feelings for each other to another level. But I was not about to talk to Aaron Kopecky about George.

"Do you have a girlfriend?" I asked, thinking I should.

"Me? Nah."

His eyes might have misted, but I couldn't be sure in the low light. After a period of silence he asked, "So, what's your take on what happened today at the fashion show?"

"Is this what you meant when you said we'd be 'talking shop'?"

"Yeah, maybe."

I sighed. "My take on Rowena's death? I really don't have one, except that a lovely young woman's life has ended prematurely. Why do you ask?"

"Oh, I don't know. It's just that I have a funny feeling about it."

"Why?"

"Healthy young people like that model just don't drop dead like that."

"But you said this afternoon that you'd seen a few young people 'keel over.' I believe those were your words."

"Yeah, I did, but I've been mulling it over. You were with her before the show. Did she look like she had a heart problem, you know, breathing heavy, funny color, blue fingernails, things like that?"

"No. She seemed perfectly healthy to me,

but one of the models said Rowena got sick to her stomach before the show. She attributed it to nerves. It was Rowena's first time modeling in a show."

"See? That could mean something."

I considered what he'd said before adding, "It could. But you don't know yet that she didn't die of a heart attack — nausea is one of its symptoms — or of some other natural cause. The autopsy will show if she had a heart defect. It's not unheard of, even in young people. Are you suggesting —"

He cut me off with a hand on my arm and a smile. "That's just me. You're right. Probably some medical problem. I'm not suggesting anything. My wife always accused me of seeing bad stuff around every corner. She said that being a cop soured me on the human race; nothing but bad people out there."

I started to reply but he added, "My wife, she was right, always was. She knew me like a book." This trend of thought led to a lengthy description of his deceased wife. I found it charming that he needed to talk about her now that she was gone. His comments, while at times critical of her, were mostly positive. It was clear to me that he missed her very much.

At the same time, I found myself becoming weary.

I stifled a yawn. "I really should be going," I said.

"Right. My wife always said I put people to sleep with all my talk and —"

"No, no," I said. "It's been a long, difficult day, and seeing that young woman simply drop dead in front of me took an emotional toll. I just need a good night's sleep."

He paid the bill and we walked outside.

"Do you see any taxis?" I asked.

"You don't need a taxi," he said. With that he led me around the corner to a battered Subaru with fading paint. "One of the perks of being a detective," he said. "That shield in the window lets me park anywhere. Of course, you don't keep a nice car in the city. Never pays. Someone is always going to come along and dent your fender. So if you don't mind riding in my rust bucket, come on — I'll drop you off."

For the first time since I'd run into him at the party, I was vaguely uncomfortable. I really didn't know him, and the thought of getting into his car gave me pause. But he was, after all, a detective, so I climbed into the passenger seat and he drove straight to my hotel. Before the hotel doorman emerged from the building, Kopecky jumped out, came around the car, and opened the door for me.

"Thank you for dinner," I said, "and for the ride."

"No sweat. My wife always said that a man should open the car door for a woman."

"It's a nice gesture," I said.

"Nobody else does it anymore," he said.

"Well," I said, "I appreciated it very much. Good night."

"My pleasure. Hey, I really enjoyed being with you. Hope I didn't talk your ear off. I didn't give you much of a chance to talk about you. We'll have to do it again soon, huh?"

"That would be fine," I said.

Once in my hotel room I thought about my evening with the detective. It had almost been like going out on a date.

A date?

I smiled as my mind filled with memories of the dates I'd gone on with my late husband, Frank, before we'd married, and of times spent with Scotland Yard inspector George Sutherland.

I got ready for bed and cracked open the novel where I'd left a bookmark, but my mind wandered, reliving the day's activities. It had been exciting to be present at Sandy's fashion show, and I hoped his designs would be successful in the market. But the day that had started out upbeat had turned tragic with the shocking death of Rowena Roth. When she sat in the makeup chair, I hadn't noticed any telltale signs of illness. What could have caused such a sudden reversal in her well-being? That she didn't seem to have any close friends was sad. You expect a young woman of that age to be surrounded by her peers. Babs had said she was "snarky" and had a chip on her shoulder. Perhaps competition for jobs kept models from making intimate connections with one another. I'd have to ask Babs — if I saw her again — if that was often the case.

By the time those thoughts had run their course, fatigue had overtaken any thought of reading, and I climbed into bed.

Yes, it had been quite a day, and I hoped that the following one would be free of intrigue and surprises.

But it was not to be.

CHAPTER SIX

One look out the window the next morning told me that it was good that I'd brought a raincoat, rain hat, and umbrella with me from home. The rain was coming down hard, and a brisk wind splattered it against the panes.

I ordered room service — an English muffin, raspberry preserves, grapefruit juice, and coffee — and turned on the TV. It was unlikely that Rowena Roth's death would be grist for an item on the news. She wasn't a big-name model. Besides, people die every day in New York of natural causes and don't rate news coverage. But at the tail end of a local news segment, the female anchor said, "New York's Fashion Week was marred yesterday by the unexplained death of a model. More after these messages."

The station cut away to a series of commercials and I hit the MUTE button.

I sat back on the couch and thought about

Rowena's collapse, which then led to a recollection of what Detective Kopecky had said at the bar at Jill's, that he had a "funny feeling" about Rowena's death. He'd quickly explained it away by saying that his wife used to blame his vocation, saying that being a policeman had caused him to see — how did he put it? — "bad stuff around every corner." I suppose that's an occupational hazard for all law enforcement officers who spend their days dealing with the less savory segment of the population. But Joseph Heller gave us something to think about in *Catch 22* when he said, "Just because you're paranoid doesn't mean they aren't after you." Even for a jaded cop, there *is* "bad stuff" around many a corner.

I put aside those contemplations when room service arrived. By the time the tray was set down and I'd signed the check and turned up the volume again, the television news program had moved on to the weather, which was forecast to improve later in the morning. I switched off the TV and enjoyed my muffin, paging through *USA Today,* which had been delivered with my breakfast. The national newspaper featured photographs and brief articles on the major designers in New York for the fashion event, but no mention of the less famous names, nor of the demise of a first-time model named Rowena.

Showered and dressed, in shoes I hoped could withstand puddles on the streets of New York, I went down to the lobby, where I picked up a copy of the day's *New York Post* and settled in an easy chair to peruse it. Rowena's death was summed up in a single line in the paper's famed "Page Six" gossip section. I'd expected that the young reporter who'd spoken with me at the reception, Steven Crowell, would have written something more substantive, but he evidently hadn't unearthed enough information to warrant an article.

I had a busy day ahead. Sandy had invited me to visit his studio in Manhattan's Garment District that morning, and I'd made tentative plans to stop in to see Vaughan Buckley, my publisher at Buckley House, later that afternoon. I'd left lunch open in the event Sandy — or his mother, Maggie — wanted to extend our get-together, and had promised to meet with my agent, Matt Miller, at five. My nephew, Grady, and his wife, Donna, had invited me to dinner again, but I'd called to beg off, suggesting that we do it the next night. I needed some time for myself, something I increasingly crave as I get older.

The rain had stopped and the sun was trying to push through the clouds when my taxi driver, a pleasant sort, dropped me in front of Sandy's building on West Thirty-fifth Street, between Eighth and Ninth avenues, a brick industrial structure that had probably been there since the nineteenth century. It was in the heart of the Garment District as evidenced by the flurry of activity that swirled around me — clothing racks lining the sidewalk, trucks double-parked, horns blowing, and attractive young women rushing down the street, probably models on their way to auditions and photo shoots. The energy was contagious, and I picked up my step as I entered the building and checked the long roster of tenants posted in the narrow lobby. Xandr Ebon Fashions was on the top floor.

The elevator might have been as old as the building itself, although I surmised that it had been added later. It creaked and stopped at each floor with a jolt before reaching the top. I stepped from it and was almost bowled over by a man pushing a clothing rack down the narrow hallway. "Sorry," he muttered, and continued on his way. It was loud as I stood in the hall. Myriad voices competed with one another. Some yelled. Some laughed. It was chaotic.

I walked down the hall until reaching a sign in elegant script indicating I'd found the right place. The door to Sandy's studio was open and I was about to step through it, but angry voices from inside stopped me.

"It's not your job to tell me what's wrong with my designs," a man shouted.

"I worked in an *atelier de flou* for thirty years," a woman retorted. "I tell you, it's not draping properly."

"It drapes on her the way it's supposed to," the man replied, louder this time. "Who's the designer here?"

I recognized the man's voice as belonging to Sandy. His was low-pitched but had a discernible nasal quality to it.

Another man said, "Knock it off, Xandr. I don't have time for your temper tantrums!"

"If everybody would just leave me alone," Sandy moaned.

I stepped out of the way as two women stomped out of the showroom. I recognized Addie, the dressmaker, in a white lab coat with a tape measure draped around her neck; she rushed past me down the hall. Right behind her was the model Dolores Marshall from the fashion show, who was also Babs's roommate. Standing nearly six feet tall in a fur-collared parka, black tights, and lace-up boots, she was an imposing figure as she came to a halt upon seeing me.

"Hello," I said. "I don't know if you remember me. I'm Jessica Fletcher. I saw you at the fashion show."

She cocked her head as she tried to place me.

"We got to say hello but only briefly while you were being fitted."

"Yes, right," she said in a well-modulated voice. "You're the mystery writer. Xandr told me about you."

"I'm so sorry about what happened to Rowena." As I said it, I remembered what Babs Sipos had said about Rowena making a racist remark to Dolores.

"Yes, it was a shame," Dolores said, not sounding especially bereft.

"Do you mind if I ask you a question?"

She looked at me quizzically. "Try me."

"Do you know if Rowena was suffering from any medical ailment?"

"Only if being a spoiled brat is a medical ailment. Otherwise I have absolutely no idea. Why would you think I would?"

"I just thought that when models get together they might talk about such things."

"Rowena and I never talked about any-thing — *pleasant,*" she replied.

"Oh," I said, "I'm sorry to hear it."

"You can try one of the other models.

There might be someone who could stand her. Anything else?"

"Actually, I'm here to see Xandr Ebon," I said, "but I did want to tell you that you looked beautiful in the show."

She tilted her head. "Thanks. Sorry if I was rude. As you can see, I'm just leaving. I stopped by to return my dress. He's in there." She indicated where she meant with a flip of her head, sending her thick mane of inky black hair into motion. She stepped past me and headed for the elevator. "He's a little edgy. Must be post-runway blues," she said. "He should be happy. His name's in the *Post* this morning." She disappeared behind a clothing rack.

"Yes, but —" I started to say. It was only because Rowena had died.

I drew a breath and entered Sandy's studio. I didn't know what I was expecting, but it certainly wasn't a bare space with exposed pipes and peeling paint. The tall windows were grimy with soot. Panels of fluorescent bulbs hung from long stems affixed to the ceiling. It wasn't a big room but was made smaller by a large table along one wall flanked by racks of clothing, one of which held gowns I recognized from the show. Several people in white coats milled around. In the center of the studio was a small circular stage set in front of a threefold mirror. An apparatus to make chalk marks on fabric stood to the side. I skirted one of the clothing racks and peered into an office, where I saw Sandy talking with the man who'd been pointed out to me at the reception as his Los Angeles financial backer.

"She promised to come tomorrow," I heard him say before he caught sight of me.

"Hello?" I called, waving, not sure that I should be intruding.

Sandy turned. "Jessica," he said. "What a pleasant surprise."

"You invited me to come this morning. I think I'm on time."

"I did? My mind is a sieve today. Too much going on. Of course I did. Come in, come in. This is Jordan Verne. Did you meet last night?"

Verne shook my hand. "I don't believe I had the pleasure," he said.

"Jordan and I go back to my L.A. days," Sandy said.

"Do you live in Los Angeles now?" I asked Verne.

"Most of the time."

Verne was a wiry man in his fifties who exhibited a nervous energy even when standing perfectly still. In contrast to Sandy, who wore ragged jeans with a pea green

T-shirt with an indecipherable design on the front, Verne was dressed in a black leather blazer over narrow black trousers. His gray shirt had a high collar, against which sparkled a black tie with silver metallic threads.

"I've always enjoyed my trips to Los Angeles," I said.

"It has its benefits," he said. "At least it doesn't snow."

"Jordan is really high on my designs," Sandy said.

"For good reason," I said. "They're lovely."

"Lovely designs don't necessarily translate into sales," Verne said. "Marketing does. And you can't get by on your good looks alone."

Sandy's face reflected his reaction to his financial backer's negativism.

"The fashion world is one that I know very little about," I said.

"What do you do for a living?" Verne asked.

"I write novels."

"What kind of novels?"

"Jessica is a famous mystery writer," Sandy said. "Always on the bestseller list."

"Really? Good for you. I'm afraid I don't read much. Just the financial papers. That's mystery enough for me."

Verne told Sandy that he was leaving for another appointment. "Just remember what I said, Ebon. This isn't a game. Big bucks are at stake. You need to step it up." He nodded at me — "Nice meeting you" — and left.

I took the chair opposite Sandy, in front of a heavy glass bowl filled with pins that was perched on his desk. "So, have you heard anything new about Rowena Roth?" I asked.

"No. Nothing in the *Times,* but there was a small bit in the *Post* this morning."

"Yes, I saw it."

"They mentioned me."

"So I noticed."

"I actually got a couple of calls from manufacturers thanks to that mention," Sandy said.

"I suppose there's always something good to come out of the bad," I said.

"I just hope that Polly gets over this quickly and gets back to work promoting the line. This is such a critical time when the designs are online and people are weighing what to buy."

It was tempting to scold Sandy about his callous remark, but I didn't want to embarrass him. At that moment, a woman interrupted us to show Sandy a selection of sketches. He gave the boards a cursory look and said, "Are those possibilities for the charity ball?"

She nodded.

He flung them on the desk with such force that they slid off the side, nearly toppling the glass bowl, which I reached out to steady before it followed the boards to the floor.

"I'm sorry. I . . . I . . . didn't mean to do that," he said, leaning down to help gather the boards. He handed them back to the woman and said, "Not now."

She hurried out of the room.

Sandy pulled at his hair. "In case you couldn't tell, I'm a little tense today, Jessica. Nothing is going right. We were supposed to lend one of the gowns to a fund-raising event the Council on Fashion Design is holding to benefit a scholarship program. It was an honor to be asked and they specifically requested the gold one, which, as you know, I no longer have." He spread out his hands in a gesture of defeat.

"Won't they accept another gown? I thought the purple one was especially lovely."

"I don't know, and if they don't, I've lost a golden chance to get in front of the most important eyes in the business." He snorted. " 'Golden chance.' Some irony, huh?"

"I bet it will work out," I said to break the tension. "How about showing me around? I came to see the studio of a man your mother swears is a soon-to-be-famous designer. You can't disappoint me."

We walked into the main space I'd seen before and Sandy opened his arms wide. "What's to see, Jessica? This is it." He pointed to one rack of dresses. "Those are the gowns from the show, except, of course, the gold one. I'd like to know when I will get that one back, but no one seems to be able to tell me."

"Did you call the police?"

"I had one of my guys do it." He looked around and shook his head sadly. "You know, you're only as good as your last success, Jessica. I'm sure it's true for writers as well. And I have to make the sales right away or the buyers forget." He wandered over to the rack and ran his fingers over the dress Babs had worn in the show. "I had three orders for this platinum one this morning and I'm sure I could have sold the gold to the same people if it was here — but it's not." He sighed again.

Sandy's self-pity was getting me down, and his staff seemed to be tiptoeing around him, not a pleasant atmosphere in which to work — or to visit. I was now eager to leave but wasn't sure how to finesse it. Sandy saved me when he returned to my side and said, "Sorry. This is a bad morning. Let's take a walk. I need some fresh air."

"Yes, some fresh air would be welcome," I agreed.

We rode the elevator down, crossed the lobby, and emerged on bustling West Thirty-fifth Street.

"Where are we going?" I asked.

"Any place to get away from the studio. I swear, Jessica, I'm ready to explode."

I fell silent as I followed him to the corner of Eighth Avenue, where he crossed against the traffic and continued to the east side of Seventh Avenue. He paused at the corner. "This is it!" he proclaimed.

"What's 'it'?" I asked.

"The hall of fame for fashion designers. Seventh Avenue. Fashion Avenue." He pointed to a sign that confirmed that the avenue bore both names. "Look," he said, pointing to a bronze plaque embedded in the sidewalk. "This is the Fashion Walk of Fame. This is my inspiration."

I looked down to see what he was refer-ring to. When I lived and worked in Manhat-tan, I'd not had much reason to visit the

Garment District, nor was I aware of the plaques, a succession of them with the names and brief bios of leading fashion designers.

"Twenty-eight designers in this Fashion Walk of Fame," Sandy said. A smile lit up his face, and I noticed several women on the street turning to admire him. He seemed unaware of them. "Look, Jessica! Calvin Klein, Halston, Perry Ellis, Beene, Donna Karan, Oscar de la Renta. The greatest. One of these days, Jessica, if everything goes right, I'll be the twenty-ninth to have a plaque here."

I had to smile at his youthful exuberance.

"I don't doubt for a minute that you will," I said.

His upbeat tone turned somber. "But it'll never happen if fate keeps conspiring against me," he said.

"Where's your mother today?" I asked, hoping to distract him.

"I don't know. She said she had something to do and would see me later."

"Let's grab some coffee. My treat. What's your favorite place?"

"Well, there's Culture Espresso. Best coffee and pastries in the city."

"Terrific! Is it nearby?"

"It's not far."

I realized as we walked to the coffee shop that until that morning I hadn't known Sandy Black very well, and I knew his new persona as Xandr Ebon even less. My knowledge of his early years in Cabot Cove was scant; I'd met Maggie through the Friends of the Cabot Cove Library — we'd worked on several projects together — and she was a frequent customer at Loretta's Beauty Shop. I knew Sandy had been a popular if lackadaisical student, who through force of personal magnetism — and generous help from friends — had managed to pursue his goals on the West Coast with great fanfare, only to come back East a few years later. Since his mother's glowing accounts were my only source of information about the designer, his demeanor that morning had taken me aback. I had expected an ambitious professional, but he was more like the spoiled young man he'd been during his teenage years, when every disappointment was caused by someone else and every failure was excused by a mother who praised his talent.

It wasn't that I was unfamiliar with artistic people. I'd gotten to know plenty of them and respected the strain they were under to succeed in their chosen and difficult professions. A number of years ago, I'd been involved in a Broadway play that had been adapted from one of my novels, and seen firsthand the fragile egos and competitive nature of their lives. But Sandy demonstrated a selfish side that made me uncomfortable. I would have preferred to see him strive for success than whine when it didn't come right away. I know I've been accused of being a "glass half-full" sort of person, but I can never see the advantage of wallowing in pessimism when there's always an opportunity to make things better.

At the coffee shop Sandy was greeted by name as two of the young women behind the coffee bar vied to serve him. He turned to me. "Best cookies in the city," he said, smiling. He fished in his pocket for money and waved off my objection. "They're even better than my mother's, but don't tell her I said so."

Buoyed by his sudden return to positive, I seconded his order of cappuccino and we managed to find an empty table along the wall where we drank our coffee and nibbled on delicious chocolate chip cookies.

Given his better mood, I was surprised when he brought up the topic of the dead model again. "You asked me if I'd heard anything new about Rowena. I haven't. Have you?"

I shook my head. "An autopsy is being performed," I said, "and I imagine that the family will be notified of its results. Whether we'll learn them is another question."

He shook his head. "She was all wrong for my designs."

"Was she?"

"She sure was. That's the problem with doing people a favor. It comes back to bite you. I let her model in the show as a favor to Polly Roth and Philip Gould. Never again!"

His mood changed as rapidly and often as the city's traffic lights, and I was tired of his self-centered complaints.

"I really should be going," I said. "I have — I have a lunch appointment." It wasn't true, of course, but was an acceptable white lie.

"Just as well," he said. "I'd better get back and see what I can salvage from the ruins."

We stood to leave but were stopped by a young man who approached Sandy. "Xandr," he said. "Congratulations on your show, man."

"Thanks. I think it went well for the most part."

"Did you hear about Latavia Moore?"

Sandy shook his head.

"The famous model?" I said.

"Yeah," the man said.

Although I knew practically nothing about the world of high fashion, the name Latavia Moore was familiar. She was a favorite of the paparazzi, a supermodel whose face looked out from the cover of dozens of high fashion magazines. A well-publicized society marriage and an equally well-covered divorce landed her a role on a reality television show, and made her gorgeous face and figure familiar to a whole new audience.

"What about her?" Sandy asked.

"She's dead, man. They found her in her apartment."

Sandy's eyebrows flew up. "I hadn't heard that."

"How old was she?" I asked.

"I'm not sure," the man replied. "Twenty-five, twenty-six maybe."

Sandy grabbed his shoulder. "How did she die?"

"All I know is that she's dead. Say, weren't you and her — ?"

"Old news," Sandy said, brushing aside the man's question and striding to the door.

"I'm so sorry. Was Miss Moore a friend of yours?" I asked when we got outside.

"Not really."

"Well, thanks for showing me your studio."

"It'll be bigger and better someday," he

said. "I'll tell my mother you stopped by. Maybe we'll catch up again while you're in town."

"Count on it," I said.

I watched him walk up Thirty-eighth Street and disappear into a crowd of people.

Since I had canceled our plans for the evening, I called Grady and was pleased that he was free for lunch. I settled in the back of a cab and thought about Rowena. The death of a healthy-seeming teenager was puzzling. And now another sudden death, that of supermodel Latavia Moore. My visit to New York was supposed to deliver me from my computer and the murder that drove the plot of my latest novel. I'd welcomed the chance to spend time relaxing with my nephew and his family, to experience New York's famed Fashion Week, and to catch up with old friends like my publisher, Vaughan Buckley, and my agent, Matt Miller.

A pleasant holiday.

Yet two models were dead.

It must be a coincidence.

Then why was I so ill at ease?

CHAPTER SEVEN

My nephew and I met up for lunch in a coffee shop a few doors from the building in which he had his accounting office. Spending time with him has always been a joy. Enthusiastic, hardworking, and kind, Grady has a ready smile and an inquisitive mind, more interested in what you have to say than what he's thinking, a trait too rare in today's society.

"How was your visit to the design studio this morning?" he asked after we'd been seated at a table near the window.

My response was prefaced with a grimace. "The world of fashion is unlike any other, it seems to me, except maybe for filmmaking. The artistic temperament looms large."

He laughed. "I know what you mean," he said. "Our clients in the production business can be difficult at times, egos getting in the way, emotions on the surface, but nothing like the fashion folks. The head of the production company I recommended to Sandy told me about some tense moments with the demanding Xandr Ebon. He's the masculine version of a diva. What would that be called? A divo?"

"That sounds right," I said, laughing. "He is high-strung."

"You knew him back in Cabot Cove?"

"Barely. His mother, Maggie Black, and I were acquainted, but I never had much interaction with Sandy."

"Didn't you tell me he used to design costumes in Hollywood?"

"Yes, but I know nothing about that period in his life, other than it seems not to have worked out the way he'd expected." I thought back to the comment Maggie had made at the reception about wanting to forget about her son's Hollywood years.

"Did he ever work on a blockbuster movie, something I might have seen?" Grady asked between bites of his tuna on rye.

"I have no idea," I said, "but you've got my curiosity up, Grady. I'll go online and see what film credits he has."

"You heard about the other model that was found dead?" he asked.

"I did. She was quite a famous name. How did you find out about her?"

"I saw it on television this morning."

"Oh," I said, thinking that the report I'd missed when the hotel's room service arrived was probably about Latavia Moore rather than Rowena Roth.

"Do you think . . ." Grady started.

"Think what?"

"That there might be a connection between two models dying?"

I laughed. "You're starting to think like a mystery writer. Is my vocation rubbing off on you?"

He looked smug. "Well, I was at least partially responsible for your becoming a famous author, wasn't I?"

"You were, indeed!"

Unbeknownst to me at the time, my nephew, Grady, had given my very first attempt at writing a whodunit to a New York City publishing house, and by some miracle the book was accepted. No one was more surprised than I when *The Corpse Danced at Midnight* became an overnight bestseller. Not only did it take this widowed Maine schoolteacher out of her quiet small-town existence, but it launched me into a whole new career writing murder mysteries — and on occasion helping to solve real ones.

"I figured I'd ask," Grady continued, "because you link up seemingly unrelated murders in some of your books."

"That's just my novelist's mind at work," I said. "Besides, no one is using the term 'murder' with these two cases." I didn't mention Detective Kopecky's "funny feeling" about Rowena's death.

Grady's eyes lit up and he pointed at me. "But you're already referring to them as 'cases.' They wouldn't be cases if there wasn't something funny going on, would they? I remember you saying once that fiction is often based upon real events."

"True, but so far these deaths are unrelated. Besides, we wouldn't even know about the famous model dying if she hadn't been a celebrity." I paused, then said, "I would suggest that you finish your tuna salad sandwich before it gets cold, but the tuna was served cold."

He took his last bite and looked at his watch. "I'd better get back," he said. "Glad you were free for lunch. Donna was disappointed when you canceled dinner tonight, but now she can attend her book club, so it worked out okay. Are we set for dinner tomorrow night at our place? Frank wants to read you his latest story. He got an A on it."

"Looking forward to it," I said as I paid the bill and we stepped outside. As we did my cell phone rang. "Excuse me," I said, and answered it. It was Detective Kopecky. "Go back to work," I said to Grady. "I'll call later."

"Sorry, Detective," I said. "I was just saying good-bye to my nephew."

"I can call another time," he said.

"No, this is fine. I didn't expect to hear from you so soon. How did you get my number?"

"Oh, the NYPD has its ways."

"I see."

"I just figured that since we already talked about that model's death, and now there's this other one, I —"

A truck roared by blowing its air horn.

"Hold on please," I said, ducking into a doorway and holding my free hand against my other ear. "I'm sorry. It's noisy here on the street. You were saying?"

"I wondered whether we could get together, you know, to bat around some ideas. And I figured that I gotta eat and so do you. So are you free for dinner? I really enjoyed last night."

I hadn't expected that he was calling to invite me out again, and took a moment to consider.

"Jessica? Mrs. Fletcher?"

"Yes, I'm here." A fire truck roared by, its siren screeching. "There's so much noise here," I said.

"Not like that town you live in, huh?"

"Nothing like it."

"About dinner. If you'd rather not, it's okay."

"It's just that I'm meeting with my agent at six. I'm not sure what time I'll be free."

"Sure, I understand. Just thought you'd be curious about this new case I've been working, you know, the death of this other model, the famous one, Ms. Moore. I've been on it all day and thought it might interest you."

"I, uh — yes, I'd enjoy dinner tonight. Is seven thirty too late?"

"It's perfect. How about I pick you up at your hotel, then? I'll take you to one of my favorite joints, nothing fancy."

"That'll be fine," I said.

I hung up and shook my head. Initially, in our brief conversation, I'd decided not to accept his invitation. I wasn't eager for another *date.* But then he mentioned the death of Latavia Moore and that he was working that case, and I changed my mind. It was like dangling a worm in front of a fish. I bit.

My curiosity had gotten the better of me, which my dear friend and Cabot Cove's favorite physician, Seth Hazlitt, claims is an affliction of mine like asthma or sinusitis. When I'm offered to discuss murder with a professional like Detective Kopecky, or any seasoned detective for that matter, my inquiring mind almost always takes over.

As I walked uptown in the direction of my next appointment, I thought of having met Scotland Yard inspector George Sutherland in London years ago when he was investigating the murder of my dear friend Marjorie Ainsworth, a world-famous writer of murder mysteries. I'd been at her mansion when the deed occurred, and Inspector Sutherland had spent considerable time with me discussing the case. Our mutual attraction had bloomed. We've remained close, our friendship cemented by our strong feelings for each other that threaten to advance the relationship to another level. But we're both wary of moving too fast in affairs of the heart, and content ourselves with knowing how much we care for each other.

Of course, having dinner with Detective Kopecky had nothing to do with personal issues. I was not at all interested in him romantically, and he, as a relatively recent widower, probably felt the same about me — at least I hoped he did. As he said, he needed to eat and so did I, and we could enjoy a companionable meal and talk about what interested us both. I'd admit to being curious about this latest death of a fashion model. If Rowena Roth's death was the result of natural causes, was it the same with Latavia Moore?

Enough making excuses for having accepted his dinner invitation, I told myself. *If my inquisitiveness draws me to those who investigate murder, so be it.*

It was good to see my publisher, Vaughan Buckley, again. We seldom get together in person, and each time I do I'm reminded of what a splendid gentleman he is. His assistant brought us coffee and we sat in his spacious office with windows affording a lovely view of the city. I caught him up on what I'd been doing, and he consulted with my editor on a printout of the sales of my various books published under the Buckley House banner. I mentioned having been at the fashion show and Rowena's death.

"I read about that in the *Post,*" he commented. "And there's another model who just died, isn't there?"

"I'm having dinner with the detective who's working both cases," I said.

His eyebrows went up. " 'Working both cases'?" he said. "Is foul play suspected?"

"Not that I know of."

He cocked his head, and a knowing smile

crossed his lips. "But Jessica Fletcher's fertile brain is in overdrive," he said, more a statement than a question.

"No, nothing like that," I offered defensively.

"Maybe the basis for your next novel?"

"I hope not," I said. "I know nothing about the fashion world. The amount of research needed would be daunting."

"Well," he said, "if you *do* decide to set your next book in New York City during Fashion Week, I can put you in touch with someone who knows it better than anyone else. Claude de Molissimo wrote the definitive book on the New York fashion scene." He pulled a copy from a bookcase and handed it to me. "Here. Take it with you. It wasn't a big seller," he said, "but I was pleased to publish it. His insight into what makes the fashion world tick is impressive."

We chatted a little longer before he walked me to the elevator. "Olga asked me to send her best to you," he said. "She's visiting a cousin on the east end of Long Island this week. She's disappointed not to be able to catch you while you're in town."

Vaughan's wife is one of my favorite people, and I asked him to return the greeting.

I killed time between seeing Vaughan and

my meeting with Matt Miller by browsing shops, including a luggage store where I treated myself to a stunning leather shoulder bag that had been drastically discounted, which appealed to my New England sense of thrift.

As usual, Matt was on the phone when I arrived. I retreated to his conference room to wait, and perused the book Vaughan had just given me. Its author, Claude de Molissimo, had written for *Women's Wear Daily* and other fashion publications. The photo on the back cover showed a smooth-faced, white-haired, plump octogenarian in a plaid jacket with an ascot peeking from his open-collared shirt. I flipped through the pages that detailed the organization of the textile and apparel industries from the sweatshops in impoverished countries where so many of our clothes are made to the rarefied workshops — *ateliers* to use the French word — of famous designers in Paris, Milan, New York, and London who contribute to the wardrobes of wealthy clientele.

"What have you got there?" Matt asked when he joined me in the conference room fifteen minutes later.

I held up the book so he could see the cover.

"Hey, I know that guy."

105

"You do?"

"Yeah, saw him at a garden party in the Hamptons last summer. Can't miss that shock of white hair. Makes him unique."

"Did you have a chance to talk?"

"Not really, but if you ever need to get in touch with him, I can get his number from the hostess. She knows everyone out there."

I thanked him and we spent a pleasant hour together. Among many things Matt had wanted to discuss with me was an offer for the audio rights to some of my newer books, which impressed me. But he felt he could negotiate for a better advance and royalty and wanted my permission to turn down the offer, which I granted him. He's been my agent for many years and I trust his instincts.

As I waited for the elevator in Matt's building, my mind wandered to my pending dinner with Detective Kopecky, and I began to regret having agreed to see him. I'd turned down dinner with Grady and Donna because I wanted time alone, and here I was making plans for dinner with someone I barely knew. Seth Hazlitt would undoubtedly find it amusing, and I could only imagine the comment he would make about it.

I was waiting in the lobby when Kopecky

arrived. While he'd claimed the "joint" we were going to was "nothing fancy," he was dressed in a nice gray suit, white shirt, and tie, and didn't look as though he'd been through a tough day. He was freshly shaved and sported a pleasant aftershave lotion.

"You look beautiful," he said.

"Thank you." Finding his comment strangely personal, I resisted returning the compliment.

We drove to where he said he'd called ahead for a table at a place called Jeremy's Ale House, on Front Street in the South Street Seaport section of the city. Kopecky parked directly in front of a NO PARKING OR STANDING sign and hopped out of the car to open the door for me.

"Ever been here before?" he asked me.

"No. I don't know it at all."

"It's kind of a hangout for cops, always has been. It's just far enough away from One Police Plaza so the brass can't keep an eye on its customers. It's got the best crab cakes in the city, and chips like you've never tasted before."

"It sounds like fun," I said as we climbed the front stairs and entered the noisy restaurant.

Kopecky leaned close to my ear and said in a low voice, "Most cop hangouts are Irish places, you know, Irish pubs. That's why I like this place. You don't have to be Irish to get in." He laughed to be sure that I hadn't taken him seriously.

As with Jill's, where we'd gone the previous night, a number of customers and staff welcomed Kopecky by name. But the atmosphere at Jeremy's was as different from Jill's as it was possible to be. The interior was dim, most of the lighting, as far as I could tell, coming from suspended television sets and neon beer signs hung on the red-brick wall. We squeezed past the packed bar of drinkers holding foam cups of beer and managed to get a small table as far from the throng as possible, which pleased me. It was a boisterous crowd, with a lot of loud talk and raucous laughter. I looked up and was stunned to see women's bras hanging from the dropped ceiling, the acoustic tiles covered with graffiti made by multiple-colored markers.

Kopecky was definitely overdressed for the occasion, and I was, too. This was the definition of a dive bar, more like a clam shack in Maine than any restaurant in New York I'd ever been to.

"Hope it's okay that we came here," Kopecky said. "I mean, you're probably used to places like '21' and the Waldorf."

"Oh, no," I said, "this is fine."

"They have great seafood. I figured, you being from New England and all, you'd appreciate that. It gets pretty loud sometimes. That's because cops come off a shift and have to unwind."

"I can understand that," I said, although most of the bar patrons looked more like college kids or young Wall-Streeters than off-duty officers.

"You drink beer?" he asked. "They'll make you a drink, but most people order beer."

"A beer would be fine," I said. "I enjoy a beer now and then."

Kopecky went to the bar, ordered our beers, and returned to the table with them. "It's kind of a do-it-yourself place," he said. He raised his foam cup and said, "Here's to seeing you again, Mrs. Fletcher."

I touched my cup to his and said, "Good to see you, too, but please call me Jessica."

"Jessica it is," he said, grinning. "I'm Aaron."

"I remember."

I started to ask a question about his job and crime in the city, but he began telling me about his late wife.

"Mary, she was a saint to put up with me," he said. "She never liked coming to places like this — you know, too noisy. We didn't have many cop friends. Mary was uncomfortable with them." He laughed. "Imagine, being married to a cop and being uncomfortable around other cops."

"Too much shop talk, I imagine," I said.

"Yeah, that's it," he said.

We ordered from a menu of small dishes, including the crab cakes he'd touted, calamari, two shrimp cocktails, and onion rolls and butter. Kopecky told more stories about his wife and their life together, and it was plain to me that he was desperate to share these tales of their long married life together with someone, anyone.

I took advantage of a lull in his virtual monologue to ask what it was that he wanted to "bat around" regarding the deaths of the two models.

"That's right," he said, wiping his mouth with the napkin that he'd tucked into his shirt collar to cover his tie. "I was at the apartment today of that model who was found dead."

"How was she discovered?" I asked.

"She never showed for an appointment with her agent yesterday, and he came to the building this morning and got the super to open the door. There she was, on the couch."

"Was she fully dressed?" I asked.

"Yeah, she was. I know what you're getting at. No sign of sexual assault."

"And no signs of a struggle? Was everything neat and orderly?"

He shook his index finger at me. "You'd make a good detective, Jessica."

"I'm not sure I would, but thanks for the compliment. I take it that you're content with this celebrity model having died of natural causes."

His face screwed up in thought. I waited for his answer.

"Tell you the truth, Jessica, I'm not so sure of that."

"Oh? Why?"

"I had a chance to look at the body while the medical examiner did his work. Not that I'm a doctor or anything, mind you, but I have seen a few corpses in my thirty-three years on the force."

"I imagine you have."

"Something struck me as wrong."

"Which was?"

"Her eyes. When the ME held them open, I got a good look. There were these little red dots I'd seen before with victims who'd been strangled."

"Petechial hemorrhages," I said.

"Yeah, I knew you'd know about those things. I never can remember how to pronounce it."

"Did the medical examiner agree?"

"He's a young guy who doesn't like to be told anything," Kopecky said. "I asked about those red dots, those —"

"Petechial hemorrhages," I put in.

"Right, those. He blew me off, said she probably choked on her dinner."

"Was there any food near the body?"

"There were a couple of plates with some crumbs on them."

"Did you have a chance to see her tongue?"

He shook his head.

"Sometimes when someone is strangled or smothered, they bite their tongue."

"You know a lot, Jessica."

"I've taken a few courses in forensics," I said modestly.

"Yeah, well, I suppose we have to wait until the ME does his thing — the autopsy, that is."

"It's always best to wait for the official findings," I said, which ended the conversation about the model's demise.

Kopecky abruptly asked, "Got a boyfriend?"

I couldn't help laughing. "You asked me that last night."

"Yeah, but you didn't really answer."

"I'm a little old for having a *boyfriend,* but I do have a friend whom I like very much. We don't see much of each other because he lives in London. He's an inspector with Scotland Yard."

"That's impressive. You and he, are you — ?"

"As I said, we like each other a great deal."

"That's good," Kopecky said. "I mean, it's good that there's somebody special in your life."

I couldn't be sure, but I sensed that he was fighting against tearing up.

"Let's call it a night," I said. "It's been a long, busy day for me and I need some sleep. Sounds like it's been a long, busy day for you, too."

"Just another day," he said as he picked up the check.

"You sure I can't take that?" I asked. "You treated last night."

He put his hand over his heart. "My wife, if she was alive, would kill me if I let a lady pay the tab."

He pulled up in front of my hotel.

"I really enjoyed having dinner with you," he said. "I know it's not a fancy place. I kind of forgot about the bras on the ceiling. I hope you weren't offended."

"Not at all. It was an *interesting* bit of decor," I said, choosing my word carefully.

He laughed.

"Anyway, I enjoyed dinner, too. Thank you."

For a moment I sensed that he was poised to lean across the seat and kiss me good night. I opened my door, which sent him through the driver's door and to my side.

"Maybe we can do this again sometime," he said.

"I'm not sure how much longer I'll be in New York," I said.

"That town you're from? Cabot something?"

"Cabot Cove."

"Right. Cabot Cove. In Maine. You know, I've never been to Maine. Well, good night, Jessica."

"Good night, Aaron." I hurried into the hotel, hoping that I wasn't going to get a surprise visitor once I got home. Detective Aaron Kopecky was a very nice man, but he needed something from a woman that I couldn't — no, wouldn't — give him.

CHAPTER EIGHT

I awoke the next morning to a city filled with speculation about the demise of two models, seemingly within hours of each other during Fashion Week. Could a serial killer be on the loose? The morning television shows were interrupted by a news conference in which the city's chief of detectives briefed the press. As the camera briefly panned across the other dignitaries behind him, I was pretty sure I saw Aaron Kopecky standing to the side. The chief of detectives declared there was no evidence to support that the deaths were related in any way. While the toxicological results would take some time to come back, he reported, the city's medical examiner hadn't found anything to indicate foul play in his examination of seventeen-year-old Rowena Roth. Similarly, the postmortem on supermodel Latavia Moore was deemed "nothing of concern so far," notwithstanding Kopecky's suspicions about the little hemorrhages that he'd noticed.

Nevertheless, official statements by the police department didn't tamp down rumors that whizzed around the Internet and fed gossip columns, both off- and online. Twitter was alive with comments linking the two young women, although it was unlikely they'd ever met. Under the headline DEATH STALKS THE CATWALKS, the *Post*'s front page featured a glamorous photograph of Latavia in a dress with a deep décolletage, her long bare legs crossed. Boxed on the lower right was a head shot of Rowena that looked as if it came from her high school yearbook rather than her model card or anything her agent might have provided. Inside, an article bylined by Steven Crowell offered the shocked reactions of friends and associates of Latavia Moore, accompanied by more photographs from her glamorous life. At the close of the piece, the reporter quoted Xandr Ebon, whom he described as an up-and-coming designer whose clothes the other dead model was wearing when she collapsed on the runway. "It was a terrible tragedy. She was a beautiful girl with natural elegance. She would have gone far," he'd said of Rowena.

My schedule for the day included two

panel discussions that were part of the Fashion Week calendar. Maggie Black, Sandy's mother, had secured a pass for me to a series of talks and demonstrations taking place at an event space on Eighteenth Street.

"There's so much to see and do during Fashion Week," she'd told me when she invited me to attend Sandy's show. "I want to make it worth your while to come to New York. He needs our moral support, but I promise it'll be great fun for you, too."

I'd assured her that there was always plenty for me to do in New York City, not the least of which was having an opportunity to visit with business associates and, best of all, family. But Maggie had gone ahead and signed me up for a hair and makeup demonstration; an art show of canvases by fabric designers; a panel discussion on how the fashion world would have to adjust to the graying of America; and an immediately sold-out lecture on the role of luxury goods in the modern world — all taking place in the same building or one nearby. What especially lured me to the panel on the graying of America was that among the panelists was Claude de Molissimo, the author published by Buckley House whom Matt Miller offered to put me in touch with. I'd

Googled him on my laptop at the hotel after my dinner with Kopecky and was impressed with the accolades he'd received for his book, although there were some negative comments, including one about his "bombastic views." This was obviously a man who knew the fashion world inside and out and had ruffled more than a few feathers.

Instead of ordering breakfast at my hotel, I bundled up — New York was experiencing a cold snap — and marched briskly uptown until I finally spotted a luncheonette off Sixth Avenue, where I sat at the counter perusing the newspaper over poached eggs and toast. Comfortably full, I determined to work off my meal and save money by walking downtown instead of taking a cab.

My route south took me to Times Square, where despite the frigid temperatures, a young man wearing white cowboy boots, a matching Stetson, and practically nothing else, strummed his guitar while standing on a concrete median as pedestrian and vehicular traffic streamed by. The "Naked Cowboy" — his title was emblazoned across the back of his white briefs — was a street performer who certainly attracted a lot of attention. Cell phone photographers grouped together across from him while he posed for pictures with a succession of female tourists. I couldn't see if they tipped him for the service, but if they had, I didn't want to know where he put the money.

The triple-X movie theaters are long gone, and pickpocketing is said to be a "lost art" in that part of the city, but when I crossed the street amid a throng of people, I hugged my shoulder bag to my side. It always pays to be vigilant, especially in an unfamiliar environment.

When I had safely crossed, I happened to look up at the news crawl that was making its way around one of the buildings overlooking Broadway.

BREAKING NEWS, FASHION WEEK EXCLUSIVE:
WHILE NEW YORK CITY DETECTIVES DENY LINKS IN DEATHS OF TWO MODELS, TOP DESIGNERS BEEF UP SECURITY AT SHOWS.

The press has a tendency to dramatize events, I thought. Everything these days is "breaking news." But were authorities protesting too much? By strongly denying there was a connection between the two models, were they inadvertently convincing the public of the opposite? My mother used to say "A maid convinced against her will is

119

of the same opinion still." She didn't know the origin of the reference, but she quoted it every time I tried to persuade her to change her mind.

"Hey, lady, you're holding up traffic here," a woman's voice called out to me.

"Oh, sorry," I said, looking around.

A female police officer raised her baton and saluted me. "We gotta keep everything and everybody moving," she said.

"I'm on my way," I called back, hurrying to make the light at the next corner.

I finally reached the address on Eighteenth Street and joined a flow of people inside where a large poster pointed in the direction of the panel discussion I wanted to attend. The seats were filling up rapidly and I scouted them in search of a good vantage point. There was a vacant one two rows removed from the dais where the panelists would sit, and I headed in that direction. It wasn't until I'd reached it that I realized that I'd be sitting next to Steven Crowell, the *New York Post* reporter who had written the piece I'd read that morning, and who'd approached me for a comment at the party the night of Sandy's ill-fated fashion show.

"My lucky day," he said as I sat.

"I'm glad you feel that way," I said, not eager to encourage conversation.

"Mind if I ask you a question?" he said.

I sighed. "No, of course not, but please respect that I know nothing about the death of the model — of *either* model."

"Yeah, sure, but why are you so involved in Fashion Week? You're a mystery writer, not a designer, or press."

"I'm a friend of one of the designer's mothers. We're from the same town."

"Cabot Cove, Maine," he said, uncapping a pen with his teeth and poising it over a reporter's pad resting on his thigh.

"That's right. I also have family here in New York, and I'm meeting with people in publishing. So Fashion Week is not the only reason —"

"Xandr Ebon is your friend's son, right?"

"Yes."

"Did you know him back in Cabot Cove?"

"Not well," I said, pleased with the interruption when the moderator took the microphone while other panelists filed in and found their seats behind placards bearing their names. The hefty Claude de Molissimo was hard to miss with his mane of white hair, glowing, red-cheeked face that could have belonged to a man thirty years younger, and a stylish white bush jacket over a pale blue shirt and vibrant red-and-white ascot. The moderator welcomed everyone and then introduced each member of the panel, saving de Molissimo for last. It struck me that while she had lavished praise on those who were introduced before de Molissimo, her comments about him were surprisingly short and lacking in enthusiasm, confirming my impression that he was not a beloved figure in fashion circles.

The panel's topic addressed the question of how the fashion world would have to adjust to the increasingly aging population of America, not a particularly scintillating subject for the majority of audience members, who appeared to be in their twenties. One of the panelists, a Ph.D. in data science, launched into a lengthy presentation of facts about America's growing number of people falling into the "senior citizen" category. The number of people over sixty-five years of age would more than double between 2009 and 2030, he reported. They would compose nineteen percent of the population by then, and, according to a statistic quoted in 2012, they represented the age group with the most money, their average annual income more than seventy-five thousand.

That led to the next panelist, a young woman whose thesis seemed to be that regardless of how many Americans were sprouting gray hair, fashion still had to focus on youthful designs and open the doors to young designers.

A third member of the panel, billed as a psychologist-cum-designer, debunked the notion that older people wanted designs created for them. "They want to remember when they were young," he intoned, "and would resent designs blatantly conceived to cover up their added weight and wrinkled skin." There seemed to be a murmur of agreement in the young audience, which did not include me. I thought that his remarks were offensive.

De Molissimo evidently agreed with me. He'd listened quietly as the others made their points, a scowl on his broad face. When the psychologist-turned-designer concluded his remarks, de Molissimo pulled a microphone close to him and said in a booming voice, "What we're hearing here today is what's wrong with the fashion world, and always has been." He went on for another ten minutes despite the moderator's attempt to cut him off, his diatribe aimed at the cult of youth in the fashion world, teenage models seeing plastic surgeons, outlandish styles that no self-respecting woman would ever be seen in, and all of it fueled by money. He saved his final salvo for models' agents, whom he termed "bloodsuckers preying on egotistical young women who think there's something glamorous about tottering on a catwalk in obscenely high heels for a few minutes."

Until he spoke, the panelists' comments had been dry and boring, but de Molissimo's attack garnered everyone's attention, including Steven Crowell, who laughed when de Molissimo stopped talking. "That's why he's hated in the industry," he said. "His book rattled a lot of cages."

"He certainly doesn't pull any punches," I said. "I have his book to read." I retrieved it from the oversize bag I carried that day and showed it to Crowell.

Our attention returned to the dais, where de Molissimo suddenly stood, announced he had an appointment to get to, and walked away, leaving a perplexed moderator whose panel had another half hour to go.

"Excuse me," I said to Crowell, getting up, squeezing by others, and following de Molissimo from the room.

He'd stopped at a coffee service in the lobby, where he grabbed a glazed donut from a tray.

"Hello," I said.

He turned and glared at me.

"Sorry to bother you, but I heard your

talk inside and —"

"*You* were in that room?" he said.

I was taken aback. "Shouldn't I have been?" I asked.

"Frankly," he replied, "you're a little old to be in that crowd."

"I am?"

His stern expression softened. "I wasn't sure anyone there had made it out of middle school. You'll have to pardon me," he said. "I'm not in the best of moods."

"No pardon needed," I said. I took his book from my bag. "Vaughan Buckley, my publisher at Buckley House, gave me this copy. Would you autograph it for me?"

His face brightened and he pulled a pen from his breast pocket. "Vaughan, eh? He's a good man."

"No argument from me."

"You're a writer, too?" he asked, signing his name with a flourish.

"Yes, Jessica Fletcher. I write murder mysteries."

He let out a loud "Ha! Sure, Jessica Fletcher. What're *you* doing at Fashion Week? Researching your next book? If you are, I can tell you where all the bodies are buried."

"I was hoping that you would," I said with a smile, despite it not being my motivation in pursuing him.

"Really? You want an inside look into this so-called industry? Come on, let's have breakfast. It's on you. I'm a little short of cash, but I'm rich in knowledge."

We went to a luncheonette across from the building in which the panel had taken place and sat at a booth. De Molissimo ordered steak and eggs, with a side of hash browns. Since I'd finished breakfast barely an hour ago, I stuck with tea and toast. As we sat there, he picked up where he'd left off at the panel, berating anything and everything about the fashion business and Fashion Week in particular. He was especially harsh on plastic surgeons. "They take these gorgeous young girls, some as young as twelve or fourteen, and promise to make them even more beautiful by using injections and or even the scalpel. 'Sculpting,' they call it." He paused to use a piece of toast to soak up the yoke from his fried eggs. "You know Dr. Edmund Sproles?" he asked.

"The name is not familiar."

"You want to see the really dark side of the fashion biz, spend time with him. He's gotten rich catering to models, hundreds of them who flock to his fancy Park Avenue office, his bills paid by parents who think their daughters are God's gift to the modeling world. The modeling business is so viciously competitive that these pretty young kids think that if their thighs were slightly narrower, or their nose was tweaked just a little, or their lips were a tad fuller, they'd have a leg up on the competition. It's pathetic."

"I thought that was starting to change a little," I said.

"Not enough for me. You have some advertisers using what they call 'real-life' models — there was the Dove campaign. But despite New York's efforts to encourage older mannequins, if you peruse the fashion layouts, many of the models are barely past puberty and look like walking sticks."

"It must be hard living that way," I offered.

"Worse than hard. Modeling agents are no better than the doctors. They encourage these kids not to eat so that they stay skinny, and then take big commissions. Half of the models I know are anorexic. Every time I see one with a little meat on her bones, I root for her, but I know that she won't get the lucrative jobs apart from the few designers who specialize in what they call 'full-figured women,' or even the still fewer who design for 'plus-size.' "

I assumed that I was considered one of

those "full-figured women," which suits me just fine. I couldn't help smiling at his passion for what he believed in. The question did cross my mind as to whether he exaggerated the situation and burnished his iconoclastic reputation in order to financially benefit from his views. His curmudgeonly role in the fashion industry seemed to have brought him a lot of notoriety, and he'd successfully used it to write a book and find a wonderful mainstream publisher for it.

"Tell me more about this Dr. Sproles," I said.

De Molissimo's face screwed up in disgust, as though even to have mentioned the name was distasteful. He finally said, "I don't mind plastic surgeons making older people look younger — even if I did, it would be a waste of time — but to screw up the faces and bodies of kids for them to fit some crazy definition of what's beautiful — well, that brings my blood to a boil. All across this country, teenagers are literally starving themselves to death to match some warped vision of how thin a person should be to look good in clothes. It's insanity! And I lay that at the feet of the fashion industry. Ready to leave?"

"Yes." I hesitated to tell him that there

was another program I wanted to stop in on for fear that it would set him off on another tirade.

We parted on the sidewalk and he extended his beefy hand. "Nice meeting you," he said, "and thanks for breakfast. Next time it'll be on me."

"It was my pleasure."

"And say hello to Vaughan Buckley for me."

"I certainly will," I said as he walked away, "waddled" being a more accurate description.

My encounters that morning initially with Steven Crowell and closely followed by Claude de Molissimo made me determined to do a little research at the earliest opportunity. First, I would do what I'd promised Grady, and that was to look up Sandy Black's Hollywood credits as a costume designer. And second, I would see what I could find out about this Dr. Edmund Sproles. Why? I couldn't tell you at that moment. But he obviously had intimate knowledge of many models, and I wondered whether that included Rowena Roth and Latavia Moore. Could Rowena have died from anorexia? Did Latavia? That was a possibility I hadn't considered before. Rowena had been as slim as a willow branch, but she hadn't struck me as emaciated. Some models in fashion magazine layouts look as if the wind would knock them over. Rowena had been sturdier than that. I'd never seen Latavia in life, so I couldn't judge if she'd been starving herself to stay on top.

The truth was that not only was I interested in the idle speculation that there was something suspicious about their deaths, but I'd also begun to toy with the idea of setting my next murder mystery during New York's Fashion Week.

When in Rome . . .

CHAPTER NINE

I had time before the next panel convened and settled on a couch in the building's lobby with what my dear friend and Cabot Cove's favorite physician, Seth Hazlitt, likes to call a "newfangled fruit phone." My skills on the phone are limited — I haven't mastered typing with my thumbs and I'm not sure I ever will — but I was able to figure out how to access the Internet, and managed to locate a database site for movie information.

Because I wasn't sure what name Sandy had used during his years on the West Coast, I started with the professional name he now went under, Xandr Ebon. There was one Xander but no Xandr, and one Ebon and several Ebonies and other variations, but no Xandr Ebon. Going back to basics, I typed in Alexander Black and was disappointed once again when his name did not appear. But I did find three films on which a "Sandy Black" had worked, first as a "costume trainee," then later as a "costume assistant," and finally as a "costume design assistant." Of course it could be another Sandy Black. The same name could belong to a woman rather than a man. But I chose to believe that Sandy had found some success in Hollywood even though his mother had said she'd wanted to forget his time in California.

I didn't recognize the names of the films on which Sandy Black was credited, but that wasn't surprising. Between my writing schedule and my travel schedule, I couldn't remember the last time I had bought a carton of popcorn and sat down in a movie theater to enjoy the show.

I had just typed Sandy's name into Google to see if I'd overlooked anything when the phone rang. It was his mother, Maggie. I pressed the answer button.

"Oh, Jessica, I hope I'm not interrupting anything important."

"Your timing is good, Maggie. I think I may have missed the hair and makeup demonstration this morning, but there's still ten minutes before the next lecture I'm signed up for."

"I wonder if I could prevail upon you to skip the lecture and help me out."

"Is something wrong?"

"Not wrong exactly, but awkward." There was a long pause.

"What is it, Maggie? Can you tell me?"

"It's just this. Polly Roth wants to go to Rowena's apartment to gather up that poor child's things, and she asked me to accompany her. I hate the idea. I'm never good with these maudlin scenes. Just ask Sandy. Or maybe you shouldn't. Anyway, I lied and told her I couldn't because I was meeting you for lunch."

"Well, you're welcome to meet me for a late lunch," I said. "The lecture is over at one."

"Thanks, but she wouldn't take no for an answer. She said to bring you along and she'd buy lunch for the three of us. I didn't know how to get out of it."

"So you need me to accompany you to Rowena's apartment?"

"If you wouldn't mind. I'd be so grateful."

"Are you certain Polly is comfortable sorting through Rowena's belongings with a stranger?"

"I think she simply doesn't want to do it alone. That I understand. I wouldn't have wanted to do it myself either. I still don't want to do it, but I couldn't turn her down."

"Where did Rowena live and what time should I be there?"

I wrote down the address and instructions for finding the building. Maggie said Rowena shared her apartment in Brooklyn with two girls who were working and not going to be home. At the party, Babs had pointed them out as Isla and Janine, two other models who'd been in the show.

Before leaving the Fashion Week venue, I stopped at the table outside the room where the sold-out lecture on the role of luxury goods in the modern world was to be held. I turned in my ticket, explaining to the woman sitting there that I was called away unexpectedly, but that she was welcome to give away my seat if anyone wanted it.

"Too bad you can't make it, but thank you," she said. "That's our hottest ticket. A Parsons professor is speaking. I have a long waiting list for that one. Someone will be delighted."

Back on the street, I consulted a city subway map and concluded that I'd better take a taxi if I didn't want to get lost in the labyrinthine streets of Brooklyn. Getting around Manhattan is fairly easy as long as you stay north of Fourteenth Street, where the even-numbered streets run east, the odd-numbered streets run west, and the avenues alternate north and south. The exception is Broadway, a winding cow path in the days when the Dutch ruled New Amsterdam. It still wanders at an odd angle.

New York's outer reaches are not as well plotted out, and only those who live in those environs can claim enough familiarity to find their way from one place to the next. I don't qualify. When I lived in a West Side high-rise, my days were spent mainly in Manhattan, what New Yorkers from the other four boroughs call "the city."

My cabdriver dropped me off at the door of a four-story brick building in Red Hook, across the street from a dilapidated wharf on the Buttermilk Channel. The neighborhood appeared to be in the process of gentrifying — several buildings sported scaffolding — but hadn't reached that exalted status yet. There wasn't a store in sight, and parked out front was an abandoned jalopy with a sheaf of tickets tucked under the windshield wiper.

I pushed the button next to a piece of masking tape with three names on it, one of them Rowena's, and an answering buzz released the lock on the door.

"Is that you, Jessica?" a voice called down.

"Yes," I replied. "Where do I go?"

"The elevator's on the fritz. I'm afraid

you'll have to walk up."

"I can manage. What floor are you on?"

"The fourth."

Grateful for my regular exercise routine, I climbed the stairs, walked down the cracked white tile of each landing to the next flight, and climbed again until I reached the fourth floor. There had been two apartments on each floor, and I headed for the one with the open door.

"Maggie?" I called as I entered the apartment.

"In the kitchen."

I walked through a narrow room, lined on either side with an assortment of what must have been cast-off furniture from relatives. There were two couches, and across from them three chairs, one of them a desk chair on wheels, and a small table so piled with papers that I doubted it had ever been used for dining, or even as a desk in its current location. A thin-screen television set was mounted on the wall opposite the sofas that, unless I missed my guess, were probably where the roommates took their meals — whatever models actually eat — while they watched their favorite shows. At the back of the room, on the left side, were three doors, one to the bedroom, one to the bathroom, and the last to the kitchen, a small box of a

136

room barely accommodating a sink, hot plate, tiny refrigerator, and my friend Maggie emptying a grocery bag.

"Polly's in the bedroom packing up," she whispered. "I just got our sandwiches. Thank you so much for coming."

"Don't even think about it. What can I do to help?"

"Why don't I introduce you first?" She took off the dish towel that had been slung over her shoulder and draped it across the faucet. "Polly," she called out. "Jessica's here."

Maggie led me to the door of the bedroom, but we didn't go in. From what I could see, the beds and the floor were covered with clothing. More clothes were hung on a rack that likely came from one of the Garment District showrooms. The only light fixture was a bare bulb in a ceiling socket. A narrow window provided some additional dim lighting.

"These girls were — are — absolute slobs," Polly said, wiping her hands on a white coat similar to what Sandy's employees wore at his studio. "I'm sorry this is your introduction to my niece." She thrust out her hand and I shook it. "But I appreciate your giving up your lunch date so Maggie can help me."

"Actually, I met Rowena the day of the show. She was a beautiful girl. May I offer you my sincerest condolences?"

"Thank you. I almost remember seeing you there. I was so frazzled that day, I'm not sure of anything I saw." She ran a shaky hand through her blond hair and sighed. "My sister-in-law in Ohio couldn't face coming East to pack up Rowena's things, and from the looks of this place I'm grateful she made that decision. How could I ever face her again if she saw how I allowed Rowena to live? Of course, you didn't *allow* Rowena to do anything. She just decided what she wanted and did it."

"Why don't you take a break now that Jessica is here? Are you ready to eat?" Maggie asked. "I was about to put out the sandwiches."

"I'm not very hungry."

"Even so, you need to keep up your strength, and so do we."

"Of course. I'm sorry, Maggie. I seem to be thinking only of myself today."

"Go wash up while Jessica and I set the table."

Polly closed the door to the bedroom and went into the bathroom.

"Set the table?" I mouthed to Maggie, and cocked my head toward the masses of paper

138

covering its surface.

"I can take care of that mess," she whispered back. She retrieved the grocery bag from the kitchen and began filling it with the papers from the table.

"Let me do that," I said. "You take care of the sandwiches."

I made a separate pile of magazines and catalogues, and stacked them on the floor between the sofas. I would have attempted to sort the mail by recipient if the envelopes were there, but when Maggie carried in two plates, I just swept off what was left on the table, dumping it in the paper bag, which I dropped on top of the magazines. Two cards had floated to the floor in my hasty cleanup, and as I gathered them up I noticed one was a business card from the medical office of Dr. Edmund Sproles. The other looked as if it had accompanied flowers or a gift. A message in red crayon read "R — Sorry for the disappointment! Hope this cheers you up." It was signed "Love, P." Without thinking, I tucked them both in my jacket pocket, intending to write down the pertinent information about Dr. Sproles when I had a moment.

Polly emerged from the bathroom, her nose pink and her eyes red-rimmed. She stuffed a tissue in her pocket and rolled the desk chair over to the table. "Where did you get these?" she asked Maggie, who was placing a third plate on the table.

"I found a deli, Defontes, up Columbia Street," she replied. "Their sandwiches are huge, so I only got two and cut them in thirds. One is corned beef and Swiss and the other is eggplant. Figured I'd give you the whole New York experience, Jessica."

"They look delicious," I said.

Maggie put out three bottles of water but no glasses. I wondered if the girls who lived there even possessed any. Given how carelessly they kept the apartment, Rowena and her roommates probably did little or no entertaining there. Where did young people in the city spend their leisure hours? Was all their social time passed in clubs and bars?

We sat quietly and ate, each of us caught up in our own private thoughts. I was wondering how a seventeen-year-old had managed to manipulate her parents and her aunt into allowing her to move to New York City to pursue a modeling career. Had she even graduated from high school? From Polly's remarks, I gathered that Rowena was a willful young woman. She was not particularly sensitive to others' feelings, given what Babs had related about Rowena's relationship with Dolores and other models.

I had witnessed her speak disrespectfully to the makeup artist and the executive from New Cosmetics, but was her behavior just an adolescent showing off in front of adults? My train of thought raised many questions and I decided I would never have a better opportunity to find out about Rowena than while I was in the company of her aunt.

"I understand Rowena lived here with two other models who were in the show with her," I said to Polly.

Maggie answered for her. "Isla and Janine. Isla was the one wearing the emerald gown — green is such a good color for redheads — and Janine was the brunette in the ruby dress."

Polly started as if she suddenly realized there were other people at the table. "I convinced them to let her live here," she said. "It was a mistake. I see that now. She would have been better off living alone or with girls in another business."

"Why do you say that?" I asked.

"I think they were jealous of her, of her connection to me, and of how easily she got a job in their field, you know, waltzing into Manhattan and being in a show during Fashion Week your first time out. Not many who can do that. Oh, they were happy to have someone to share the rent, but they weren't nice to Rowena."

"How do you know?" Maggie asked.

Polly wiped her mouth with a napkin and seemed to weigh her response. "She told me. She complained that they helped themselves to her clothes — 'stole' was actually the word she used — without permission. And they ate her food and never repaid her, used up her toothpaste without replacing it. Just little annoyances, but it showed they didn't respect her."

"Three is a difficult number," I said.

"You're right, Jessica. Two against one is always hard," Maggie put in.

"Well, Rowena got some of her own back," Polly said with a wry smile. "She made a play for Janine's boyfriend, not that she was really interested. And she confided in me that Isla Banning, whose model card says she's twenty-one, is actually twenty-five. I don't know how she found that out, but she was quite pleased with herself about it."

If Rowena let Isla know that she'd discovered her secret, it was not bound to endear her to her roommate, I thought.

"It sounds to me like she was able to hold her own," Maggie said.

Polly paused. "I guess. But I was hoping that if Rowena lived with girls in the business who were a little older, they would mentor her and maybe settle her down a bit. I was lobbying to have her chosen as 'the new face of New Cosmetics.' It would have been so good for her self-confidence. She was such a beautiful child — but difficult. I always attributed it to, well, insecurity, and was sure that once she found a little success she would blossom. But she didn't seem to appreciate all that had been done for her. She kept expecting more."

"She was very high-strung; lots of artistic people are," Maggie said diplomatically. I had a feeling that she was thinking of Sandy.

My first impression of Rowena had been that she was a spoiled young woman, and nothing I was learning from her aunt changed that view.

"Did she have other friends here," Maggie asked, "people who would support her when she was feeling down?"

Polly shook her head. "She could come to me, but she rarely did. Babs Sipos was nice to her, but Rowena didn't take to her. As a child, she always had difficulty making friends. I think she rejected them before they could reject her, but perhaps that's just my armchair psychoanalyzing. I never had any children of my own."

"Did she have a boyfriend?" I asked.

Polly hesitated. "Not that I knew of.

Unfortunately, she was always attracting older men. She said boys her own age didn't interest her, but, frankly, I think she frightened them away. There was someone. She was wearing a fur coat last week that I know she didn't bring with her from Ohio. When I asked her about it, she said it was a 'parting gift' from a friend."

"Lots of young girls bask in the attentions of an older man, especially if he comes along with gifts," Maggie said.

"Come to think of it, I didn't see that coat in the bedroom," Polly said, looking over her shoulder. "I wonder where it is."

Since we were speaking so easily about Rowena, I ventured to ask what had been on my mind since I arrived. "Do you know what caused her death? Have you heard anything about the autopsy?"

Polly shook her head. "It's a mystery. There're no heart problems in my family, not that I can remember anyway. I can't speak for my sister-in-law's family."

"Was she anorexic? Could she have starved herself?"

Polly chuckled. It was the first break in her somber mood. "No way. That child could outeat you and me and Maggie together when she wanted to. Not that she wanted to very often, but she was one of

144

the lucky ones. If she splurged, she'd just cut back for a day or two and was down to her fighting weight."

"Have the police said anything to you?" I asked.

"Only that these things take time."

Maggie lowered her voice even though it was just the three of us. "Could she have taken something for her nerves that day? She looked a little anxious to me."

"Well, give her a break. It was her first appearance. But Rowena had nerves of steel. Plus, she hated pills of any kind, so I doubt she would have taken anything."

"Babs mentioned that Rowena had been a little sick to her stomach before the show," I said.

"Maybe she was more nervous than you thought," Maggie said.

"Or maybe she ate something that disagreed with her," Polly said, dusting her hands. "Thanks for getting the lunch, Maggie. How much do I owe you?"

"Not a penny," Maggie replied. "I'll clean up. Then you can tell us what you'd like us to do."

"Yes," I said. "How may I help?"

"I wasn't going to put you to work, Jessica," Polly said, "but if you're volunteering —"

I raised my hand. "Whatever you need."

"Give me five minutes in the bedroom to sort things out and I'll let you know."

I followed Maggie to the kitchen, carrying the plates, but she sent me back to the table. "I don't have room for those yet," she said, turning on the water. "I'll sing out when you can bring them back."

I turned around to see a tall young woman with red hair standing in the open door of the apartment. I recognized her as Isla, one of the models from the show. She was wearing a full-length mink coat over a white angora sweater and black pencil skirt. She eyed me warily. "Who are you?" she said, pulling off her leather gloves. "And what did you do with my mail?"

"I'm Jessica Fletcher, a friend of Polly Roth." I set the plates back on the table. "Everything that was on the table is over there," I said, gesturing to the paper bag and pile of magazines and catalogues. "My friend Maggie and I are here to help Polly pack up Rowena's things."

"Well, you'd better not pack up anything of mine," she said, shrugging out of the coat.

"Is the coat yours?" I asked.

She thrust the coat into my arms as she rushed past me toward the bedroom. "I only borrowed it for my go-see."

Maggie was standing outside the kitchen, the dish towel over her shoulder again, her lips pursed. "In case you were wondering, a go-see is like an open casting call for models."

"I gathered as much."

As I draped the fur coat over the arm of one of the sofas, I glanced at the label. *Chi-Chi Quality Furs.* I don't own a fur coat because I don't believe in killing animals for a woman's vanity, but that's a personal feeling that I don't impose upon others. I had seen newspaper ads for Chi-Chi Furs featuring beautiful women wrapped in expensive mink and sable fur coats. It obviously carried high-end furs for those who could afford them.

"I guess she thought no one would find out if she borrowed her dead roommate's fur coat," I offered.

"Makes me wonder what else she's wearing of Rowena's," Maggie said, turning back to the kitchen.

Made *me* wonder if Detective Aaron Kopecky's "funny feeling" about Rowena's death had merit. For a newcomer to New York, the young woman had managed to alienate an awful lot of people.

Isla emerged from the bedroom wearing a different sweater from the white angora, and a pair of torn blue jeans. She flopped down on one of the sofas. "I have to go back into Manhattan. I only came home to change. If I'd known you were going to be here, I'd have stayed in the city," she said to no one in particular. She stood and stretched. "Is there any food left?"

"There's part of a sandwich here that no one touched," I replied.

Isla walked to the table and used her index finger to flip off the top piece of bread. "What is it?"

"I believe that one's corned beef and Swiss," I replied.

She peeled off the cheese, rolled it up, took a small bite, and returned to the sofa. She picked up the remote and aimed it at the television. The room filled with rock music and an announcer's voice extolling the virtues of a dishwashing soap.

I walked in front of the screen, blocking Isla's view. "Do you mind if I ask you something?"

"Is it about Rowena?"

"Yes."

"I already told the cops I didn't know anything," she said, raising her voice to be heard over the commercial playing behind me.

"Well, maybe you know more than you

think," I said. "I just have a few questions."

"All right. Get out of the way and I'll shut it off." She pushed the rest of the cheese into her mouth, wiped her fingers on her jeans, and switched off the television.

I turned around the desk chair and sat in front of her. "I understand you and Janine were not good friends with Rowena."

She shrugged. "We got along okay." She glanced toward the bedroom and leaned forward. "She was a selfish brat," she whispered. "And she was weird, too."

"How was she weird?"

Isla looked uncomfortable. "I don't know. She was always going down to Chinatown to buy stuff. She made her own lipstick and eye shadow, tried to get me to use it."

"Did you? Use it?"

"No way! Who knows what she put in it? She sent away for stuff on the Internet and videoed herself, like a mad scientist. Although I have to admit, it looked good on her."

"Did you tell her?"

Isla had the grace to look down. "No," she said softly.

"Do you happen to know what she had for breakfast that day?"

"Oatmeal."

"That was a quick answer," I said, smiling.

"She had oatmeal every morning. Disgusting stuff, but she liked it."

"I take it you don't like oatmeal. What do *you* eat for breakfast?"

"Black coffee, and if we have anything left over from dinner the night before, I might finish that. I know. Please don't give me a lecture on good eating habits."

"I wasn't going to."

"Why do you care what Rowena had for breakfast?"

"She was a little sick to her stomach before the show and I just wondered what she might have eaten."

"The policeman told me she probably had a heart attack. Can you believe it?" She gave a shiver. "He said she probably had an inborn weakness."

"It's certainly possible. Did she seem sick here at home before you went into Manhattan for the show?"

"Even if she was, she wouldn't have admitted it. We had to be at the venue by eight. I'm not even human at that hour, so I wouldn't have noticed anything. I don't think Janine would have either. She didn't say anything to me anyway." She was silent a moment. "We were a little freaked out when Rowena dropped dead. It's odd, isn't it?" She gave a big sigh. "And now we have to find another roommate. It's such a hassle."

I had to work not to let my shock show. Wasn't there anyone, other than her aunt, who mourned the loss of this child?

Isla left shortly thereafter wearing a hooded down jacket for the return trip into Manhattan.

When Maggie finished cleaning up the kitchen, she handed me a grocery bag of garbage to leave by the door. "We'll take it downstairs when we go," she said.

As I set the bag by the door, I noticed a crushed cereal box inside and pulled it out. With it came a crumpled receipt from a Chinatown apothecary for fu zi. I looked at both. Rowena had scrawled on the oatmeal box "This belongs to RR. Don't touch!" over the front panel. I opened the box to find a half-used packet of oatmeal. When Maggie wasn't looking, I wrapped the packet in a paper napkin and tucked it and the receipt in my shoulder bag.

CHAPTER TEN

I spent the afternoon after leaving Rowena's apartment shopping for gifts to bring back to friends in Cabot Cove. I seldom returned from a trip without such token gifts and didn't want this one to be an exception. Truth to tell, however, I found meandering through some of the city's wonderful shops and choosing what to buy a welcome respite from thoughts of dying models and what is obviously a competitive, somewhat nasty business — fashion, and the week celebrating it.

I stopped at my hotel to drop off my purchases, which I'd had gift wrapped, and to freshen up. I had some time before I had to leave for dinner at Grady's and Donna's apartment and used it to go back online to find what I could about Sandy Black's time spent in Hollywood, which I'd been in the process of doing when Maggie Black called to ask me to accompany her to Rowena's apartment. Google turned up several Sandy Blacks, including a few in the fashion industry, but none of them were familiar to me. I scrolled through a few more mentions until coming to an abrupt stop at a two-paragraph news item from a Los Angeles weekly newspaper. It was a report of a costume design assistant, Sandy Black, having been convicted for theft of costumes from the studio where he was employed, and who was sentenced to a year's probation in return for a plea of no contest and the return of the stolen items.

"Oh, my," was all I could muster.

If I'd had any doubt about the identity of this Sandy Black, it was dispelled by the grainy photo that accompanied the piece. It was clearly of Sandy, even though the dark circles under his eyes and the unkempt hair were not part of his usually well-groomed appearance. I read the piece again in search of more details, but there weren't any. I continued to Google Sandy's name but came up with nothing else. Now I knew why his mother preferred to forget about his stint in L.A. As I signed off I reminded myself that he hadn't pleaded guilty. A "no contest" plea, also called a nolo contendere, means the defendant does not admit guilt but assumes a conviction will take place, and allows the court to determine punishment.

Had he stolen the costumes? I preferred to believe that he hadn't. But they must have been found in his possession. At least he hadn't received jail time. Why would Sandy want to steal costumes from a film studio? Were they famous outfits from iconic movies for which collectors would pay handsomely? Or did he want them for himself as a souvenir of his profession? I hoped it was all a crazy mix-up, but it certainly explained why Sandy Black had become Xandr Ebon, and had left California for New York.

I typed in Latavia Moore's name and pressed the "Images" link. My screen filled with row upon row of the beautiful celebrity model and — to my surprise — what appeared to be other Latavia Moores, black, white, and Asian, in both formal photographs, candids, and selfies. Focusing on the famous face I recognized, I scrolled down the page. Latavia was featured on myriad magazine covers and in articles, frolicking on the beach, posing on a red carpet with her then husband, pursued by the paparazzi, and — "Wait a minute," I said aloud. I clicked on one of the paparazzi photos of Latavia in huge sunglasses, her left hand holding the scarf that covered her head. Who was that next to her? A man had his arm wrapped around her waist, his head ducked down and shoulders hunched as though trying to hide inside the collar of his windbreaker. But even behind his dark sunglasses, it was impossible to disguise his handsome face. It was Sandy Black.

So Sandy had a relationship — romantic? — with Latavia Moore. It sure looked that way. I searched for a date on the picture. There wasn't one, but Latavia was wearing a wedding ring. Had they been secretly married? It couldn't be. Sandy had barely had a reaction to learning of her death. But clearly they knew each other. What did it mean?

An hour later, I headed for Grady and Donna's apartment. As I got closer to their building, my spirits were boosted. Anticipating seeing Grady, Donna, and their son, Frank, always put an added spring in my step. I walked briskly into the lobby and told the doorman that I was visiting the Fletchers. He went behind the desk to call the apartment, saying as he did, "The other guest has already arrived."

Who could that be?

My question was answered the minute Grady greeted me at the door. I looked past him and saw Detective Aaron Kopecky

155

standing at the window with Frank. Grady read my puzzled expression and said, "The detective working the case, Detective Kopecky, is joining us for dinner. Hope that's okay with you."

"It's — yes, of course, that's fine. Which case?"

Kopecky broke away from Frank the minute he saw me and said, "Hello, Mrs. Fletcher. Uh . . . Jessica. Nice to see you again."

"Yes," I said. "It hasn't been very long."

"Nice apartment, huh?" Kopecky said, indicating the living room with a sweep of his hand.

"Lovely," I replied, giving a quick hug to Grady's son, who had come to greet me. "I'm eager to read your story," I told Frank. I was also eager to find out what had transpired between Kopecky and Grady to lead to his being invited.

"Your nephew and his wife were kind enough to ask me to join you for dinner," Kopecky said.

Grady added, "Detective Kopecky interviewed me this afternoon about the death of the model."

"Which one?"

Grady frowned. "Rowena. Polly Roth's niece. You were there."

"Yes, of course."

I was about to ask what Grady could contribute to the detective's investigation when Aaron added, "We've discussed other cases, too." He gave Grady a wink before turning to me. "I get obsessed when I work a case, Jessica. I never want to think that there's something or someone I've over-looked. I figured that since your nephew here helped set up the fashion show through one of his clients, maybe he could give me a look inside how these things work."

"I'm sure he can."

Grady grinned at me. "The detective —"

"Please, it's Aaron," Kopecky interrupted. "I'm off duty now."

I wondered if he really was.

"Aaron was free tonight," Grady said, "and he said that you and he had had din-ner before, so I figured that since you already know each other, it would be nice to get you two together again. Donna's making her famous angel-hair pasta with lobster meat. Oops! I'd better get in the kitchen and whip up the salad. That's my assignment. A drink, Aunt Jessica, before I disappear?"

"No, nothing, thank you."

"Don't forget that you have to read the short story that Frank wrote. He's dying for your reaction."

"I'm looking forward to it," I said.

I would have been happy to read the story right then and there, but Frank had disappeared, leaving Kopecky and me alone. I noticed that he wore the same gray suit he'd had on when we had dinner at Jeremy's Ale House, but his shirt was blue this time, his tie a bright yellow.

"So," he said, "had a busy day?"

"It turned out that way. You?"

"It's always busy. I like it better that way."

"Anything new on Ms. Moore's death?"

"If you mean do I know what killed her, the answer is no. Not yet, at least."

"The chief of detectives said there was nothing suspicious. True?"

He laughed. "So you caught the press conference. Well, that's what we're hoping. If the ME comes back and says it was a heart attack or stroke, that'll put to rest all this sensational serial killer nonsense that the media is stirring up."

"But you still have doubts?"

He nodded. "Nature of the beast," he said. "We always treat any untimely death as a homicide until proven otherwise. Doesn't necessarily mean anything evil took place. You know, if you run someone over and they die, it's a homicide. That's not the same as murder unless you were aiming the car at 'em."

"Yes, I know."

"I forgot. You're the expert on murder."

"Hardly an expert."

"Yeah, but you know more than the average guy on the street. I should say gal on the street."

Donna emerged from the kitchen wearing an apron. "Aunt Jessica," she said, "sorry to not have welcomed you." She hugged me before disappearing back into the kitchen from which a lovely aroma emanated.

"Nice people," Kopecky commented.

"The best."

"Like I was saying," he said, "I have a problem buying the idea that two young women, both in great shape, drop dead on the same day from causes unknown."

"There is such a thing as a coincidence," I said.

"I don't believe in coincidences. Do you?"

I hesitated. "Occasionally."

"Yeah, well, on this occasion I've got my doubts. My wife, she always said that if somebody said the sun was shining, I'd have doubts even though I could see that the sky was blue."

"I suppose that goes with your job."

"I suppose it does. Tell me about this

designer you knew from Maine, Xandr Ebon." He snickered. "Some name, huh?"

"I knew him as Sandy Black, although not well."

"I did some checking on him."

"So did I," I said.

"You are way ahead of me, Jessica. Must be some of that Scotland Yard fella rubbing off on you." He laughed to soften the comment.

"What did *you* find?" I asked.

"Seems Mr. Ebon, or Black, had sticky fingers when he was working out there in La-La Land."

"He claimed that he hadn't done anything wrong."

"They all do. Not that stealing costumes some actress wore means he had anything to do with his model's death, but it does say something about his character."

"Do you suspect that he might have been responsible for Rowena Roth's death?" I asked, unable to keep the incredulity from my voice.

"Everything's on the table, Jessica. Everything's on the table."

Frank came into the living room carrying a binder and looking uncertain. "Excuse me, Aunt Jessica," he said, "but Dad said that you wanted to read my story."

"I can't wait to see it," I said. "I hear your teachers think it's terrific."

"It's okay, I guess. It's not like I'm a real writer or anything."

"Why don't you let me be the judge?"

"I'll see if I can help in the kitchen," Kopecky said. "My wife always said I was more of a nuisance than a help, but we just did things differently. She never did learn how to load a dishwasher."

Frank and I settled on the couch and I began to read. He interrupted me once to explain what he meant in the story, but I hushed him. "Either I'll understand what you intended by reading the story, Frank, or I won't. If you have to explain it, then the story lacks something."

He sat quietly as I read through the pages. When I was finished I applauded and exclaimed, "An A-plus is too low a grade. It's wonderful!"

He blushed as he thanked me. Grady poked his head out of the kitchen and asked, "Do we have another bestselling author in the family?" he asked.

"I think we do," I said.

Kopecky came from the kitchen. "The kid has talent, huh?" he said. "I heard you clapping."

"It was very good," I said. "Maybe Frank

will let you read it, too."

"Is dinner almost ready?" Frank asked.

"I think so," Kopecky said. "Your mom is a good cook. I got to taste the sauce." He bunched his fingers together and kissed them. "*Delicioso!* That's Polish for yummy."

"No, it isn't," Frank said, laughing.

Kopecky was right. Dinner was delicious, and the mood at the table was upbeat. I tried not to grapple with why he'd ended up at dinner with us, but other topics pushed those thoughts aside. When they were present I couldn't help wondering whether he had accepted Grady and Donna's dinner invitation because he truly enjoyed their company, or because he knew that I would be there. I also couldn't get my hands around Kopecky having interviewed Grady regarding Rowena's death. What could a CPA for production companies know that would be of interest about a model's untimely death?

These and other musings really didn't matter, however. What was important was that I got to spend time with my great-nephew and his lovely parents, even though our usual relaxed atmosphere was stiffened by the presence of another guest.

Donna turned down my offer to help with the cleanup in the kitchen. Grady pitched in, and Frank excused himself after dinner to do his homework. That left Kopecky and me alone again in the living room.

"Terrific dinner, huh?" he said.

"Donna has always been a good cook."

"You're lucky to have such nice family," he said.

"I certainly agree."

"Look, uh, I was wondering what you were doing tomorrow night."

"Tomorrow night? I —"

"The reason I ask is that I have a pretty nice family, too." He launched into a long monologue, and I wondered if Kopecky talked so much and so fast to cover feelings of inadequacy. "My daughter, Christina, is a sweetheart. How she ended up my daughter, I'll never know. My wife, she always said that Christina took after her, not me, and she got no argument. I mean, I'm a cop. I see the world different than most people. Anyway, Christina is my only daughter. I've got a son, too, Paul, but he's out in Oregon working for some real estate company. We don't talk much. But me and Christina are pretty close. She's a college graduate like her mom. So's Paul. Me? I got through a couple of years at John Jay but dropped out to join the military. I was military police. I guess that's what got me into law enforcement when I got out. So what I'm saying, Jessica, is that I'd like you to meet Christina."

"I'm sure I'd love to meet your daughter, but I'm busy tomorrow."

"Like I say, she's a sweetheart, a straight shooter. She works for the city, an administrative job with the Health Department. I was telling her about meeting you and she got all excited because she's read some of your books and is a big fan, a really big fan. I thought that maybe we could have dinner together, some nice place, your choice, of course. Pick your kind of place." He laughed. "Nothing like Jeremy's, huh?"

I thought before saying, "I really appreciate the invitation, but I'm afraid tomorrow doesn't work for me."

Which wasn't true.

What *was* true was that I'd become increasingly uncomfortable with his invitations — we'd already had dinner together three nights in a row — and I wasn't anxious to establish an ongoing relationship with him. There was nothing objectionable about him. He was a decent man, and his frequent references to a deceased wife whom he obviously loved very much were touching. But I wanted to be free of social obligations during the rest of my stay in New York.

"Sure, I understand," he said, forcing a smile. "You're a busy lady and —"

"Now, don't try to make me feel guilty."

Grady and Donna's arrival from the kitchen ended that conversation. I was ready to head back to my hotel, but Grady insisted that everyone taste a new liqueur he'd bought on the advice of a client. We all agreed that it was good, and conversation wound down. I announced that it was past my Cabot Cove bedtime. "I'll get a cab," I said.

"No need," Kopecky said. "My car's right out front."

"Better than a taxi," Donna said.

"Nothing like having a real-live detective drive you home. Right, Aunt Jess?" Grady said.

I could only nod.

We said good-bye to Frank, who thanked me again for reading his story, and Kopecky and I left the building and got into his car. We said nothing as we drove to the hotel. But as we pulled up in front, he turned to me and said, "I forgot to mention this while we were with your niece and nephew, Jessica, but when I dug into Mr. Black's background, I found some other interesting information besides his being accused of theft."

He had my attention.

"But I know you're tired. Sorry we can't get together tomorrow night. Christina will be disappointed. Like I said, she's a really big fan of yours."

"I'd enjoy meeting her one day," I said, dying to probe what other information he'd unearthed on Sandy Black.

"You have a good night," he said, yawning. "It's past this guy's bedtime, too."

CHAPTER ELEVEN

While I'd grown sleepy toward the end of the evening at Grady and Donna's dinner party, I found myself wide-awake once back in my hotel room. As I changed into night-clothes I thought about Detective Kopecky and my interactions with him since arriving in New York. On the surface he seemed like a pleasant, guileless man who'd spent his life in law enforcement, and who was obviously still grappling with the loss of his wife of many years.

But a pattern of sorts had emerged. While he might be all those things, there was also a devious side to him. Every detective develops a sixth sense about what buttons to push to get someone to open up and co-operate. Kopecky had found my buttons. My innate interest in police procedure and the solving of murders had become evident to him, and he dangled the possibility of sharing "inside" information with me as a means to entice me to spend time with him. The question was, what did he hope to accomplish?

It was possible that he'd taken a shine to me, that his invitations to dinner were a legitimate attempt to establish a closer personal relationship. After all, he was now a widower. Seeking female companionship to replace what he'd lost when his wife died was perfectly understandable.

But I also had the nagging suspicion that because of my reputation as a writer of murder mysteries, coupled with my friendship with some of the players at Fashion Week, he might be seeking insights that he felt he lacked.

Both scenarios were pure speculation on my part, of course, and I abandoned that train of thought as I settled in an easy chair and did what I try to do each evening, empty out the bag I'd been carrying and get it ready for the next day.

I unwrapped a napkin to find the folded packet of oatmeal Rowena had eaten for breakfast the day she died. I wasn't certain why I had rescued it from the garbage. I checked online to see if there had been any reports of contaminated cereal or recalls, and there weren't. But I decided to save it just in case something surfaced in the future. The receipt from the Chinatown apothecary was for fu zi, which an online search revealed was aconite root, used for "devastated yang," whatever that was, and to restore circulation. Isla had said Rowena bought things in Chinatown for her home-made makeup, so I assumed the receipt was hers. But what Rowena needed with an herb to restore circulation I could not imagine.

Two other items I extracted from the bag were cards I'd found in my jacket pocket that afternoon. I'd forgotten that I'd tucked them there when I cleaned up the table in the apartment that Rowena had shared with the other models. One was an appointment card for the plastic surgeon Dr. Edmund Sproles, about whom Claude de Molissimo had spoken so disparagingly. The other was the note written to Rowena, presumably about the fur coat one of her roommates had borrowed for her "go-see." The note had been signed "Love, P." Whoever P was had written "R — Sorry for the disappoint-ment. Hope this cheers you up." It was hard to assign any meaning to the note that didn't indicate a romantic relationship between Rowena and the mysterious P.

Who could that be? I wondered.

I passed the time waiting for sleep to prevail by reading and watching TV. My eyes finally became heavy and I climbed into bed. Before dozing off I remembered what Claude de Molissimo had asked when I mentioned Vaughan Buckley, my publisher, to him: "What're you doing at Fashion Week? Researching your next book? If you are, I can tell you where all the bodies are buried."

There was a good chance I *would* use New York's Fashion Week as the backdrop for my next mystery. But even if I eventually decided not to, it was a perfectly good excuse for me to make contact with people who could give me an understanding of this tumultuous world of fashion that I'd found myself in.

I'd start the next day with Dr. Edmund Sproles.

CHAPTER TWELVE

I was going to pretend that my interest in Dr. Sproles was born purely of curiosity about the lives of the beautiful young women who made their living modeling new designs on the catwalks of Manhattan. Of course my innate inquisitiveness — and having spent a number of years turning the knowledge gathered by that trait into murder mystery novels — made Dr. Sproles a natural target for my imagination. According to Claude de Molissimo, Sproles was *the* plastic surgeon to the modeling profession, and that obviously included Rowena Roth. What kind of doctor would operate on teenagers who were beautiful to begin with? Of course I was sure that the exorbitant fees he charged for his questionable services was a strong underlying motive. Did he also manipulate their young minds, promising fame and fortune with a nip here and a tuck there? I doubted whether he would agree to see me if I posed such questions directly. And I certainly wasn't looking for a face-lift or other procedure under which pretext I could ask for an appointment. But powerful men have powerful egos; he might respond to a writer looking to pick his gifted professional brain for the novel I intended to write.

Detective Kopecky hadn't cornered the market on deviousness.

I called the doctor's Park Avenue office first thing in the morning. A pleasant woman with a British accent answered.

"My name is Jessica Fletcher," I said brightly. "I write novels. I was wondering if —"

"Jessica Fletcher, the author?"

"Yes.

"Oh, I've read some of your books. They're quite good."

"Thank you. That's very kind. I live in Maine, but I'm in New York researching Fashion Week for my next book."

"How exciting."

"I'm excited about it, too, but I admit that I'm a bit of a fish out of water. I'm trying to speak with people who can give me insight into the fashion industry, and Dr. Sproles has been mentioned by a number of people. His brilliant reputation precedes him. I was hoping to benefit from his expertise." I hoped I hadn't overstated my case.

"Oh, the doctor is extremely busy," she said. "But you're right. His clients are the biggest names in the fashion industry. I'll tell him about your call and see if he can fit you into his schedule. Do you have a number at which we can reach you?"

I gave her my cell number.

Ten minutes later it rang.

"Jessica Fletcher?" a man asked.

"Yes."

"This is Edmund Sproles."

"Oh, yes, Doctor, how good of you to get back to me so soon."

"So you're in New York researching your next novel set in the fashion industry."

Since using the fashion industry as a milieu for a mystery novel was not out of the question, I said, "Yes." But I couched it with "I'm not totally committed to it yet," salving my conscience for not being completely straightforward. "It will depend on how much information I'm able to collect. I need a real feel for the industry before I can move forward."

"Well," he said, "you've certainly come to the right man. I'd be more than happy to take you into the swinging, swirling world of fashion modeling. I just hope you aren't intending to kill off a plastic surgeon."

I joined in his laughter. "I haven't decided who the victim is yet, Dr. Sproles, but I doubt if it will be a physician. I really appreciate your willingness to spare me some time. When can we get together?"

"How about today at noon? I've had a cancellation just before that, and I usually take a break from noon until one."

"That sounds perfect."

"My receptionist is quite a fan of yours, Mrs. Fletcher. Any chance of getting a book signed to her? Her name is Susanna." He spelled it for me.

"I'd be happy to give her a signed book."

"I'd appreciate one, too," he said. "If it's okay with you I'd like to arrange for my personal photographer to take a shot of us together along with the book. I have a wall of photos of celebrity patients and friends. I'd like to add you to that wall. You'll be in good company, I can assure you."

His personal photographer? His wall of celebrities?

"I look forward to meeting you," I said.

"The pleasure will be all mine."

Before ending the call he gave me the address of his offices, which I already knew.

Since I had a few hours before my meeting with the doctor, I considered who else could possibly give me an understanding of the world of big-time fashion, and settled on Philip Gould, whose firm, New Cosmetics, had sponsored the show during which Rowena Roth had died. He had been very gracious the two times we met, and I hoped I could prevail upon him to answer some questions that had been floating around my brain. His secretary put him on the line.

"Thank you for taking my call, Mr. Gould."

"Philip."

"Philip, of course. I hope I'm not taking you from something, Philip."

"As a matter of fact you are, but I can spare a few minutes."

"I'll make it quick," I said. "First, I want to thank you again for inviting me to the post-show party."

"Happy to do it," he said.

"I'm so sorry that the tragic death of that young model took the edge off the festivities," I said.

He said nothing.

"The other reason I'm calling," I said, "is to ask a favor. I've been toying with the idea of setting my next novel in the fashion world, specifically during Fashion Week, and I'm looking to interview those who know a great deal about it. I think your insights would be helpful."

"I'm in the cosmetics business, Mrs. Fletcher, not the fashion industry."

"It's Jessica, please.

"Jessica, I don't see how I can help, but I'll be happy to recommend others more knowledgeable than I."

"Oh, I was really hoping to speak with you. You deal every day with models and designers, don't you?"

"When I have to."

His blunt comment stopped me for a moment. He filled the sudden silence with "I suppose I can find a few minutes for you. What would you like to know?"

"What I'd like to learn is more than we can cover in a brief phone conversation, and I know I'm taking you away from something important. Could we arrange to meet later today?"

"This is a pretty full day," he said. "I have a series of meetings, and there's the panel I'm moderating."

"What panel is that?" I asked.

"On new advances in makeup."

"I haven't looked at my schedule today," I said as I pulled it from my bag. "Ah, yes, here it is. Four o'clock. I'd like to attend."

"I can't promise that you'll learn anything from it."

"But I'm sure I'll learn *something,*" I said. "Any possibility of getting together following the presentation?"

Another pause. "Yes, I suppose that will be all right, but it will have to be quick. I'll see you there."

While Dr. Sproles had seemed eager to meet with me — adding to his "celebrity wall" undoubtedly helped spur his reaction — I had the distinct feeling that Philip Gould didn't share the plastic surgeon's ready acceptance of me. Not that my call out of the blue should have been welcomed with open arms by anyone. These people led busy lives, and while it's appealing to many to be asked to provide insight for a writer, it doesn't resonate that way with everyone. Maybe it was my sense of guilt for intruding into their lives under false pretenses that caused me to misread Gould's mood. Oh, well. As the saying goes, "nothing ventured, nothing gained." And I was eager to gain information. I thought of my Scotland Yard friend, George Sutherland, and knew that he would approve.

I decided to use the time I had before going to Sproles's office to call on Sandy Black. Since seeing the photograph of him with Latavia Moore, I'd been grappling with myriad thoughts and questions. Clearly, they knew each other in Los Angeles, and judging from their efforts to escape recognition by the paparazzi, it was possible that their friendship might have been more than platonic. I wondered if the picture had been taken before her divorce or after. Not that Sandy's interest in Latavia suggested anything sinister. But it struck me as one of those odd examples of coincidence that I'd told Kopecky I occasionally believe in. Sandy had been involved in one way or another with both of the models who'd suffered untimely deaths. Could his involvement be explained away simply by noting that lots of people in the same industry know one another? Or was there more significance to the connection? I was afraid Kopecky thought there was and might be zeroing in on Sandy as a suspect.

When I called Sandy's Garment District studio to see if he could squeeze in some time for me, his assistant told me that he hadn't arrived yet but was expected within the hour. I passed the time reading that morning's New York Times and catching up on e-mail. When I called an hour later, Sandy had arrived and got on the phone.

"Got a minute?" I asked.

"That's exactly what I have, Jessica, one minute," he said breathlessly as though he'd run up the stairs rather than taken the elevator.

"I know you're busy," I said, "but there are a few things I'd really like to ask you about."

"Such as?"

"I was hoping I could stop by this morning."

"Impossible."

"I understand," I said, "but maybe you'll answer one question for me."

"Go ahead and ask."

"When you were in Los Angeles working as a costumer in motion pictures, you became friends with the model who recently died, Latavia Moore."

He said nothing.

"I saw a photo of you with her taken in Los Angeles and —"

"What is this about, Mrs. Fletcher? What are you insinuating?"

"I'm not insinuating anything, Sandy. I'm just curious how well you knew her and perhaps if —"

"My mother warned me that you were a busybody who pokes her nose into everybody else's business. Well, stop poking your nose into mine, Mrs. Fletcher. Sorry I can't see you. I'm unavailable."

I was stunned at his tone and abrupt

hang-up. I mentally went over our conversation. As far as I was concerned, I hadn't been rude or asked my question in an accusatory manner. But I also understood what he read into my call, that I was in some way trying to implicate him in Latavia Moore's death. In retrospect I decided my first instinct to speak with him personally had been the correct one. I shouldn't have asked the question over the phone, especially after he'd just arrived at his studio and was rushed. A lesson learned.

But despite my finding justification for his reaction to my call, the question still lingered. How well had he known Latavia Moore while in Los Angeles? And had his relationship with her, whatever it was, continued after she'd moved to New York and achieved modeling stardom?

I was also taken aback at his contention that his mother, my friend from Cabot Cove, had said such a nasty thing about me. Maggie Black didn't strike me as the sort of person who would gossip behind my back, and I wondered whether her son had attributed his own view of me to his mother. Rather than stew about it I decided to ask her directly the next time we were together.

In the meantime I'd set into motion a busy schedule that shucked my role as simply a happy, wide-eyed visitor to New York City. Two fashion models had died suddenly under unexplained circumstances, and I'd taken it upon myself to at least find out *why* they'd died. Maybe Sandy Black, aka Xandr Ebon, was right. Maybe I was a busybody who poked her nose into other people's business. But I certainly hadn't asked to be present when Rowena Roth dropped dead, nor was it my initial intention to delve into Sandy Black's past.

But now that I had done that, there was no way that I would back off from seeking the truth.

CHAPTER THIRTEEN

Dr. Edmund Sproles's offices had the look of a Hollywood movie set. I stepped through the door and was in the midst of a reception area the size of my entire first floor in Cabot Cove. My feet disappeared into thick ruby red carpeting. Framed photographs of well-known people posing with a man I assumed was the doctor were arranged in groups on the walls. At least a dozen young women and some older ones sat on the gray leather sofas and chairs that defined the room's perimeter. Tall black marble sculptures depicting Greek and Roman goddesses stood sentry in three corners. The fourth corner of the room contained a brightly lit eight-by-ten-foot glass atrium containing a variety of exotic plants, some with vividly colored leaves or blue or purple flowers. To complete the room was a massive gray marble desk at which an attractive middle-aged woman, dwarfed by the desk's size, sat.

"Hello," I said as I approached her. "I'm Jessica Fletcher. The doctor and I have an appointment."

"Yes, of course, Mrs. Fletcher. How nice to meet you. I'm Susanna."

"I've brought something for you." I retrieved a copy of my latest hardcover book from my bag, one of two copies I'd purchased at a bookstore on my way to the offices. "I've signed it to you," I said. "The doctor told me your name."

"How sweet of him," she said in her British accent, "and of you. Thank you."

"It's my pleasure."

"Please take a seat. I'll see if the doctor is available," she said, and disappeared down a long hallway. I stepped closer to the hall and saw that its walls, too, contained multiple photographs of Dr. Sproles with his better-known patients. I recognized Latavia Moore in one, and was that Babs Sipos in the background?

I didn't have time to scrutinize the photo as Susanna returned and waved me toward the seating area. "The doctor will be with you shortly," she said. "He's had a last-minute emergency. He won't be long. Would you like mineral water or perhaps a glass of white wine while you wait?"

"No, nothing, thank you."

She went back to her desk, and I took an empty seat. While I waited, several women in white uniforms — Nurses? Technicians? — collected some of those waiting and led them through another door marked TREAT-MENT ROOMS.

On a table next to my chair was a plastic holder containing pink brochures. I plucked one out and idly opened it. Inside was a catalogue of the various services Dr. Sproles and his staff offered. In addition to the usual spa services, the list included such treat-ments as Jelly Masks with Sea Kelp, Enzyme and Lactic Exfoliation, Synthetic Snake Venom Facials, and something called Radio Frequency Jawline Treatments. I was read-ing with fascination the descriptions of those treatments, and many others, when Susanna called my name.

"The doctor is ready for you now," she announced.

As we passed the atrium I asked about it.

"The doctor is interested in horticulture," she said, pausing to admire the display. "Aren't they beautiful?"

"Lovely."

"He likes to grow plants that have medic-inal properties to try in his treatments."

"Isn't he a surgeon?"

"Of course, but he says wherever you can spare the knife, you should."

"Interesting philosophy for a plastic surgeon."

"He loves to study Chinese medicine. That yellow flower is called birthwort, and it's supposed to help the pain of childbirth."

"Not something this doctor would need in his practice, would he?"

She shook her head. "He just likes the shape of it."

"What's the purple flower?" I asked.

"I think it's soldier's helmet or hood, something like that."

"Do you take care of these plants for him?"

"Oh, no!" She lowered her voice to a conspiratorial level. "They're very delicate. If you handle them incorrectly, they can die. Or give you a terrible rash. Some can be poisonous, like the purple one. The doctor has a specialist to take care of them."

"So the specialist has a specialist for his plants?" I said, smiling.

She seemed to think I was making fun of the doctor and stiffened. "Dr. Sproles is a dedicated doctor and is always conducting research into areas that can help his patients."

"I meant no offense. I'm sure his patients

are in excellent hands."

Susanna quickly led me past Dr. Sproles's "celebrity wall" in the hallway and we eventually reached his office, a handsome room decorated in muted brown tones; the furniture, including a large desk, appeared to me to be made of some rare — and expensive — wood.

The doctor was seated when I entered. He stood, flashed a gleaming smile with teeth that appeared to have been enhanced by cosmetic dentistry, came around the desk, and extended his hand. I judged him to be in his late forties or early fifties, although it was hard to tell. His pale blue eyes were set in a face that was wrinkle free without a freckle or mark on it, a walking advertisement for his medical specialty. I assumed that his hair was his own, but it also could have been a perfectly executed hairpiece. He wore a pristine white lab coat over a pink button-down shirt and burgundy tie.

"What a pleasure," he said, "to meet such an esteemed author."

I thought that was a bit much but simply thanked him.

"Please, have a seat. My culinary adviser is preparing a light repast for us, a special vegetable platter she whips up. I trust you haven't had lunch."

Culinary adviser?

"Susanna says that you were kind enough to have brought her a signed book," he said, taking his chair behind the desk.

"And I have one for you as well," I said, handing it to him.

"I am extremely grateful." He weighed the hardcover in his hands, turning it over to admire it like a precious gem. "Sy, my photographer, will be here shortly."

"May I ask why you have a photographer?"

His grin was both reassuring and condescending. "I take multiple photographs of my patients before and after. I used to do it myself, but there's nothing like a professional's touch, I always say."

"I see."

"But you're not here to discuss photography. What can I tell you about the fashion world?"

"I suppose we can start with the death of the young model Rowena Roth. I was present when she died on the runway."

His face assumed an expression of profound sorrow. "Oh, yes, poor Rowena. What a tragedy."

"She was a patient of yours?" I asked, wondering how Rowena could afford to see the most popular plastic surgeon in New York.

He eyed me carefully. "This is off the record, I presume."

"Of course," I said.

"I have to be careful, you know, just in case patient confidentiality still applies after the patient has departed this world."

"I understand."

"After she died I pulled her records and photographs from the files. Such a beautiful young woman. I did only minor procedures on her. It mostly involved her lips. I added a slight bit of form and contour to them to better match her other facial features."

"She needed that work?"

He smiled. "My goal with the models I see is to achieve perfection in their looks. That's why they come to me. Some involve more extensive work, but Rowena wasn't among them. Who could ever have guessed that within that exquisite body was a ticking time bomb, a heart that would fail her at such a ridiculously young age?"

"When you saw her did she give any indication that she might have had a medical problem? I assume that you're informed about someone's overall health before you work with them."

"Of course. We have them fill out an

extensive medical history, everything from diaper rash to acne."

My eyebrows flew up.

"Just kidding. No, Rowena seemed in the best of health. She was, however —"

I cocked my head and waited for him to finish his thought.

"She seemed to me to be a difficult young woman, perhaps psychologically unsuited for modeling. She was easily provoked, snapped at my nurse for silly things. Of course she didn't dare do that with me or risk losing my attention. I'm successful enough to pick and choose my patients. And I don't tolerate rudeness. But my staff found her very unpleasant to deal with."

"I've heard that from other people," I said. "Do you mind if I bring up something contentious?"

Before he could answer, his "culinary adviser," an attractive young redheaded woman, entered the office carrying a tray.

"Ah, my savior," Sproles said. "Haley keeps me healthy along with my fitness adviser."

Haley flashed me a smile. "He's such a flatterer." She was accompanied by a young man pushing a cart covered in white linen. He pulled up the sides to create an oval table, and took the tray of food from her, arranged its contents on the table, and drew up two chairs.

Haley adjusted the angle of the linen napkins and nodded at her assistant, who took his leave.

Instant restaurant, I thought, admiring the silver, china, and bud vase with a single pink rose.

"Time to dig in, Mrs. Fletcher," Dr. Sproles said, pulling out a chair for me.

Haley portioned out two plates of steamed vegetables and brown rice, and set them before us. *"Bon appétit,"* she said with a smile, and left the office.

I ate some of what was on my plate to be polite, but made a mental note to stop somewhere for a different lunch after leaving.

Sproles cleaned his plate quickly. "Not hungry?" he asked, patting his mouth with a sigh.

"This is very good, but I had a late breakfast."

"Now," he said, "where were we?"

"You were saying that Rowena had a chip on her shoulder."

"Right. Yes, that was my impression of her. Don't get me wrong. She could be charming when she wanted to be, a cuddly little kitten, but the kitten had sharp claws. Yes,

190

there was an edge to her that was unmistakable."

"Did she mention to you anyone she might be having trouble with?"

"Hmm. Just the usual, you know, roommates. These aspiring models tend to live in crowded quarters. It's all they can afford until they make it big."

"Do many of them 'make it big'?" I asked.

He shook his head. "Afraid not," he said. "I see hundreds of girls — and quite a few young men, too. You'd be surprised. They all have big dreams, but those dreams seldom lead to fame and fortune."

"There are exceptions, of course, like Latavia Moore," I said.

His face turned solemn. "Oh, yes, Latavia, dear, sweet Latavia. Another tragedy."

"I saw her photograph on your wall. Was she also a patient of yours?"

"When she was in New York. Although if I had to depend upon her for a living, I'd be destitute. Her beauty was the most natural of all. There was little I could to improve on it. Strange, isn't it, that two models die of natural causes during Fashion Week?"

"Very. Do you think that they died of natural causes?"

He cocked his head and fixed me in a quizzical stare. "My goodness! Are you suggesting that it wasn't natural causes that took their lives?"

I started to reply, but he began chuckling. "Oh, you had me there. I forgot for a moment that you're researching your next murder mystery. What a character you are. I thought you might be playing a real-life detective."

I laughed, not because what he'd said was funny, but to make the point that what he'd suggested was amusingly untrue.

There was a knock on the door, and a short, bald man poked his head in.

"Sy! Your timing is perfect," the doctor called in greeting. "We've just finished lunch."

"I'll set up while you wash up," Sy said, lugging in a tripod, a sizable camera on a strap over his shoulder.

Sproles opened a door to his private bathroom and I waited while he brushed his teeth and gargled noisily. On the way back, he stopped at his desk for my book and pressed a button on his phone.

Sy positioned me in the middle of the room. "We don't want any shadows on the wall," he said.

The doctor came to my side, holding my book, cover facing the camera, with one hand. He wrapped his other arm around my shoulder and revealed his bright, minty smile to the lens.

"Got it!" said Sy. "I'll have the print to you this afternoon."

"In the silver frame, please," Sproles said, glancing at his watch. "I'm afraid we have to wrap this up," he said to me. "My next patient will have arrived, and I've got a full slate today."

His arm was still around my shoulder as he escorted me toward the door behind the departing photographer.

"I appreciate your time and expertise," I said.

"I'm afraid I had very little to offer," he said. "I'm just a fortunate doctor who gets to make beautiful young women more beautiful."

I remembered Claude de Molissimo's rant about Dr. Sproles and his ilk who, according to the cynical Mr. de Molissimo, preyed on gullible young women.

We shook hands as Susanna arrived to escort me back to the waiting room. "If you ever want some plastic surgery on that lovely face of yours, Mrs. Fletcher, all you have to do is call. I'll fit you in no matter what my schedule," Sproles said.

"That's very kind of you, Doctor."

"You're very attractive for a woman your

age. A little tweak here and there, and you'll look twenty years younger."

"I'll keep that in mind," I said, eager to find a mirror to see whether I'd suddenly aged during the past forty-five minutes.

Susanna accompanied me back to the sumptuous waiting room. I immediately spotted someone I knew sitting on a couch, reading a magazine. It was Linda Gould, whom I'd met at the party her husband had hosted. She was wearing a low-cut cashmere sweater with her ample bosom on display. A fur jacket was folded in her lap.

I thanked Susanna for her courtesy, but instead of leaving I took the empty seat next to Mrs. Gould.

"Hello," I said. "I'm Jessica Fletcher. We met at the party your husband's company hosted the other night."

She looked at me with an expression that said both that she was trying to remember who I was and that she was uncomfortable being recognized in the swank offices of a leading plastic surgeon.

"Oh, yes," she said.

"It was good of Philip to hold that party after what happened to the young model on the catwalk, don't you think?"

I couldn't tell whether she agreed with me, or found the subject distasteful, because she eyed me carefully. "And just how do you know my husband?" she asked.

"We met at a fashion show New Cosmetics was sponsoring. The mother of one of the designers is an old friend of mine. Philip generously gave me a ticket to come to your party."

"Yes. Philip can be very generous. Is that all he gave you?"

I ignored her question and posed one of my own. "You're here to see Dr. Sproles?" I asked, knowing the answer.

"Yes. Are you a patient of his?"

"Not yet," I replied. "I was just interviewing him."

"Oh, are you a reporter?" She shifted in her seat, which caused her fur jacket to open, enough for me to see the satin label for Chi-Chi Quality Furs. She closed the coat and hugged it, as though it were a cuddly dog, and I had the feeling that she wanted to move farther away from me.

"No. We just had a little chat and had our picture taken together."

"How nice."

It was obvious that she didn't wish to engage in further conversation. But while we were talking, I'd looked closely at her face. Previous plastic surgeries — and I had no idea how many procedures had been performed on her — had given her a "false" look, her skin stretched tautly across prominent cheekbones and a shiny, smooth forehead. Her lips were puffy, her neck firm, and her eyebrows arched high over green eyes that lacked any acceptable bags natural aging would have created. But the back of her hands, with ropy veins and spotted skin, revealed the age she fought so valiantly to hide in her face.

"It was good seeing you again," I said, and left.

As I rode the elevator down to the lobby, I was suddenly and inexplicably troubled by my brief encounter with Linda Gould. What drove her to keep looking for a more youthful appearance? Was it vanity, or a self-image so fragile that she was willing to go under the knife to stave off the natural progression of nature?

Or was it to remain attractive to her husband, whose work brought him into constant and close contact with youthful beauties?

Whatever the answer was, it only saddened me further, and I stepped out onto the street feeling very sorry for her.

CHAPTER FOURTEEN

I made straight for a nearby luncheonette and ordered a bacon, lettuce, and tomato sandwich and a Diet Coke. As I enjoyed my meal I reflected on my time spent with Dr. Edmund Sproles, plastic surgeon to the stars of the modeling world.

When Sproles had asked that I bring a book for him and his receptionist, my first thought was that it would have been nice if he'd purchased two books for me to sign, rather than expecting freebies. But on reflection, I thought it was a small price to pay to take up the doctor's valuable time in my attempt to better understand the fashion industry. As it turned out, I didn't learn much of anything except that he was a man with an outsize ego who had "advisers" for every aspect of his life, and who basked in having his picture taken with famous people. I suppose I should have felt flattered to have my photograph added to his "celebrity wall." I was sure he expected that I would. But I wasn't flattered at all. Here was a man who collected images of himself with public figures like the way Grady used to collect baseball cards when he was a boy. I was convinced the celebrity wall was a rotating gallery depending on whether the person standing next to the doctor was in or out of favor at the moment.

My thoughts drifted to the atrium in the doctor's reception area for which he had a plant adviser, a "specialist," according to his receptionist. She'd indicated that some of the plants were poisonous. Why would anyone raise poisonous plants? Did he really cultivate them so he could experiment on his patients with a plant's unique "medicinal properties" as Susanna had said? Or was it simply to be different from other gardeners who contented themselves with more run-of-the-mill flora? Dr. Sproles struck me as the sort of man who needed to be associated with unusual possessions in order to set himself apart from the rest of us.

Of course he had confirmed everything I'd heard about Rowena Roth. His comments mirrored aspersions of her that I'd heard from others. Her aunt Polly attributed Rowena's unpleasant edge to insecurity, but I had my doubts. Like the doctor, Rowena had her own collection of people. In her case, it was those she'd managed to alienate, and they constituted a sizable number.

Now that she was dead, was it unfair of me to be critical of her? As Seth Hazlitt often says, "When you're dead, all bets are off." But if there were any questions about whether her sudden collapse was caused by something other than natural causes, those with whom she was on bad terms during her young life would become "people of interest" to anyone investigating her demise.

Speaking of casting aspersions on people, I couldn't shake my disappointment at what Sandy Black quoted his mother, Maggie, supposedly saying about me. Could it be true that she'd made that comment? You like to think your friends are honest with you. If they become annoyed at some aspect of your personality, isn't it better to say so directly to your face rather than pass along nasty comments about you to others? It isn't as if I don't recognize my weaknesses. I know I'm inquisitive, certainly persistent, and perhaps occasionally nosy, but I hope I'm not a busybody. I like to pursue facts, but only as a path to the truth about a situation. I don't dig up dirt on people to spread gossip or damage their reputations.

Rather than stew about Sandy's comments, I decided to spend the time I had before attending Philip Gould's panel to see if I could track down Maggie and ask.

She was staying at the same hotel I was — she'd said Sandy didn't have room for her at his apartment — so I headed to the Refinery on the off chance I might catch her, but when I called her room from the lobby, she didn't pick up.

A cup of coffee appealed and I went up to the rooftop bar, where I took a chair in the corner next to a long window overlooking the city and near a fireplace filled with candles. It was a perfect atmosphere in which to contemplate life. The building had been a factory at one time, and even though the room had brick walls and a stone floor, it was warmed considerably by an exposed-wood ceiling and the perfect placement of an antique rug, cozy chairs, and sofas. I sipped a latte as I gazed out the window at a slice of Manhattan's tall buildings silhouetted against a gray sky. I was thinking that while I loved New York, I missed being in Cabot Cove, where the chilly winter wind held a tang of salt from the sea. And just then, Maggie appeared at my table.

"This is a pleasant surprise," I said. "I've been looking for you."

"You have? Then you won't mind if I join

you?" she asked.

"Not at all. Please do."

I waited until Maggie had settled herself on the chair next to mine. I set down my coffee and looked across the table at an unhappy woman.

"Something wrong?" I asked.

She started to say something, but emotion overwhelmed her. I could see her struggling against tears. She took out a tissue and held it balled in her fist.

I reached over and placed my hand on hers. "What's the matter?" I asked.

"It's Sandy."

"Is he all right?"

It was more of a guffaw than a laugh. "Oh, sure, he's fine," she said, "as obnoxious as ever."

It wasn't a characterization I'd have expected from his mother, from any mother for that matter. But from my personal experience that morning, I couldn't disagree. I waited for her to elaborate.

"He's become impossible," she finally said. "I don't know what's happened to him. He's always been high-strung, but I chalked it up to his artistic nature and his frustration at not getting recognition for his talent. But ever since —" Her eyes welled up. She pressed her lips together and took a deep

201

breath. "I will not become 'a whiny, weepy old lady.' I'm sorry, Jessica. I shouldn't burden you with this."

"Did Sandy call you a whiny, weepy old lady?"

"He did."

I laughed. "Well, he called me a busybody who pokes her nose into everybody else's business."

A look of horror passed over her face. "No!"

"Yes! And he said you were the one who told him that."

"Oh, Jessica, I hope you don't believe for one second that I would ever say something like that about you."

"It didn't sound like you. It was meant to hurt, and it certainly found its mark."

"I've always prided myself on being straightforward," Maggie said. "If I have a beef, I'll confront you. I wouldn't go around telling tales behind your back."

"That's nice to hear. I feel the same way."

She lowered her chin and shook her head. "This day is getting worse and worse. I'm so sorry, Jessica. Sorry my son was so rude to you, and sorry he had to blame me for his bad behavior."

"*I'm* sorry to see you in such distress," I said. "Why don't you have a cup of coffee or tea with me? My treat."

"Tea would be wonderful," she said, sinking back into the pillow on the chair.

At least the shock of hearing Sandy's remark had dried up her tears. And her response had gone a long way to pacifying my disgruntled feelings.

With our cups between us, I asked, "Do you think the situation that Sandy found himself in while working in Los Angeles contributed to his behavior?"

Her eyebrows went up into question marks. "You know about that?"

I nodded. "I happened to find it when I Googled him."

"Why did you do that?" Her tone was annoyed.

"Grady wanted to know if Sandy worked on any exciting movies when he was in Hollywood. I told him I'd look it up for him."

"Oh. I guess you found more than you bargained for."

"I did. You never mentioned the court case. I was surprised that Sandy would steal anything, but perhaps it was a misunderstanding." I was hoping she would say that it was.

She drew a deep sigh and sat back. "Nothing is private anymore, is it, with the Internet and social media?"

"I'm afraid not," I said. "If you'd rather not talk about this, I understand."

"Why *not* talk about it? It's obviously already common knowledge."

"Well, if not common knowledge, at least easily accessed. I also found a photo of him with Latavia Moore, the other model who died. Did you know that he knew her, too?"

"What do you mean by 'too'?"

"Only that he knew Rowena and also Latavia, both models who died under mysterious circumstances."

"I don't like what you're suggesting, Jessica."

"I'm not suggesting anything, Maggie, but you should know that the detective investigating both deaths, Detective Kopecky, is aware of Sandy's legal problem while in Los Angeles."

She gasped. "He doesn't think that — ?"

"Oh, no, no, Maggie, I'm sure not. But he has a job to do and is trying to put all the pieces together in the unlikely event that some sort of foul play was involved."

"Is that what he thinks, that someone actually *killed* Rowena Roth and Latavia Moore?"

I shook my head. "I'm sure he hasn't come to any such conclusion. As I said, he's responsible for finding out everything he can. He has an equally important responsibility to rule *out* foul play, if there was none."

I filled the next void in our conversation by asking, "Maggie, how well did Sandy know Latavia Moore?"

I wasn't sure whether her sour expression resulted from my probing, or because the answer was distasteful.

"They dated for a brief period of time," she said, "while Sandy was working for the studio. She was in Hollywood trying to become an actress."

"She certainly was beautiful enough."

"Hollywood is loaded with beautiful young women, Jessica. Whether she could act is another story. She dated anyone she thought could help her get a movie role."

"But Sandy wasn't in a position to do that, was he? From what I understand, he worked in the costume department on some — well, some smaller films."

"But his work on them was noticed. And he had high aspirations, Jessica. I really believe it was just a matter of time before bigger things came his way."

"I'm sure you're right, Maggie. Sandy is very talented. But since we're on this subject, what actually transpired in Hollywood when he was accused of stealing costumes?"

Again, her expression changed. It was angry now. "He was set up."

"Who set him up?"

"Her husband."

"Whose husband?"

"Latavia Moore's."

It was my turn to sit back and exhale. "She was still married when she was dating Sandy?" I said.

"If you can call it that. Her husband was a Hollywood hustler, a so-called talent agent. When he learned that Sandy and his wife were seeing each other, he got even by accusing Sandy of stealing the costumes. When the police searched Sandy's apartment, they found them."

"Oh, dear."

"Sandy swore to me up and down that he had never seen them before. But her husband had clout with the studio. They believed his accusations, and when the police said they had the evidence, Sandy was in a bind. He had no choice but to accept the plea, but of course that was the end of his costume designing days."

I hesitated before asking, "And you're convinced that Sandy had nothing to do with those thefts?"

"That's right, Jessica." She came forward, elbows on the table, her face closer to mine. "Look," she said, "I don't make excuses for Sandy dating a married woman. He was brought up better than that and should have known better. Latavia was a user, Jessica. She'd do anything to further her career."

"But she didn't succeed in Hollywood," I said. "I'm not aware that she ever appeared in a film."

"She never did. She divorced her husband and returned to modeling."

"And became very successful."

"With the help of that two-faced Jordon Verne."

"Why do I know that name?"

"He's Sandy's business adviser and financial backer."

"Yes, I remember him now. He was at Sandy's studio when I visited there."

"He's bad news, Jessica. I've pleaded with Sandy to get rid of him, but he's convinced that Verne knows how to elevate his career in the fashion world, and help him return to Hollywood. Look what he did for Latavia. She was an unknown and he made her into a supermodel. He has connections. Sandy's determined to get back in the studio's good graces, or if not them, another studio. Costume design was always his first love."

"But isn't fashion design satisfying as well?"

"Believe it or not, fashion is more cut-throat than movies. You have all these editors and reporters and bloggers you have to make up to. Not to mention the wealthy women who want to look twenty when they're sixty, and talk trash about you to their friends if they don't like your attitude, much less your designs. One false step and they can ruin your career."

"And Verne can protect him from that?"

"So Sandy thinks."

"I have to admit I was shocked to hear you say that Latavia Moore was married when she took up with Sandy. Would it be out of place for me to ask whether Sandy has been personally involved with other models?" When she didn't answer I added, "Rowena Roth?"

Her response was a staunch "Sandy had nothing to do with her death."

"I'm not sure anyone had anything to do with her death, Maggie, but —"

My cell phone rang. "Please excuse me," I said, and answered it.

"Jessica, it's Aaron."

"Aaron?"

"Detective Kopecky."

"Yes, Detective. Sorry. I'm in the midst of a conversation and —"

"Sorry to interrupt, Jessica, but I thought you'd want to know that the medical examiner's preliminary report has come back on the Rowena Roth case."

"Oh?" I glanced at Maggie, who held her teacup in both hands and stared into it.

"Can we get together?" Kopecky asked.

"What did the report say?"

"I'd rather not get into it over the phone," he said. "How about I buy you a drink, or maybe dinner?"

"Listen, I'm being rude to a friend. May I call you later?"

Maggie looked up and waved. "It's okay."

Kopecky continued pressing. "I know you're busy. I just figured that since you seem to be involved in what's going on, you'd be interested in what the ME has come up with."

"I'm attending a panel at four, but I'll be free after that."

"Good. I'll meet you in the rooftop bar at your hotel, say five?"

"Six. I'm interviewing someone after the panel."

"Six it is."

"Not even a hint what the medical examiner had to say?"

He laughed. "Nope, not even a hint. Let me just say that —"

Maggie stood to leave and I asked Kopecky to hold.

"Sorry," I said to her. "I'm getting off now."

"That's all right, Jessica. I see that you're busy. And I have things to do, too. What's this about the medical examiner?"

"Oh, nothing. I'll fill you in next time we're together."

"Thank you for the tea."

I watched her walk away and was disappointed at not having been able to extend our conversation.

"Sorry," I said to Kopecky. "My friend was just leaving. You were saying?"

"I think you wanted me to give you a hint about what the ME's report said."

"And you said that you wouldn't."

"I'll save it for when I see you this evening. Let me just say that I knew it right away."

"What was that?"

"That we might have a murder on our hands."

CHAPTER FIFTEEN

If Detective Aaron Kopecky's intention was to grab my attention and give me a reason to meet with him again, he certainly had succeeded. I signed the tab to my room but remained in my chair reflecting on his final words.

He'd sounded upbeat on the phone, and I could only surmise that he was pleased that his suspicions had been confirmed — that it was too much of a coincidence that two models had died suddenly on the same day during Fashion Week. He'd suspected foul play — if not from the outset, as he claimed, soon after — and must have felt vindicated that his instincts had been validated by the medical examiner. I could understand that. A policeman's job is to prevent or solve crimes, and without crime a policeman's reason for being ceases to exist. I remember once speaking with a career army officer in Cabot Cove who was unhappy that we were between wars at the time. I expressed my dismay at his attitude, but he explained that he was a soldier, and without a war to fight his purpose was stifled and his chances of advancement in rank were limited. I still disagree with his view, but I understood where he was coming from.

I realized that if I lingered any longer I was going to be late for the panel on which Philip Gould was appearing. The venue was a short walk from the hotel and I arrived just as the discussion was starting. I'd had minimum interaction with Gould at the fashion show and party that he'd hosted, but I remembered that he carried himself with the self-assurance of a company CEO, a man of short stature who bounced on his toes and spoke in a louder voice than necessary.

I thought back to having bumped into his wife, Linda, at Dr. Sproles's office and wondered about the tenor of their marriage. As a man who spent his days with beautiful young women, he had an obligation not to allow that to intrude on his marriage and his wife's happiness. It seemed to me that Linda Gould spent a lot of time and money pursuing a more youthful appearance through plastic surgery. Did Gould demand that of his wife? Or did she believe that going under Dr. Sproles's knife and whatever other procedures the doctor suggested would ensure her husband's love and devotion? I hoped that neither was the case. If anything, I hoped the sacrifices Linda Gould made were for her own satisfaction and not someone else's.

I glanced down at the program I'd been handed when I arrived and noted that New Cosmetics was offering several more upcoming lectures in conjunction with Fashion Week, plus a demonstration of how new products were developed at the company's headquarters. That one was taking place the next day. The event promised a sample of custom-made cosmetics for the first fifty attendees. I took out a pen and circled the address.

Philip Gould stood at the podium as the moderator of the panel, which included Ann Milburn, the makeup artist I'd seen backstage at the fashion show, and two other cosmetic company executives, both of whom were involved in research and development of new product lines. The topic was advances in cosmetics and what breakthroughs the cosmetic industry would enjoy in coming years. Although it wasn't a subject in which I had any particular interest, I found myself fascinated at everything that went into creating new kinds of makeup, using sophisticated scientific methods to create "organic" compounds to achieve a "natural" look, and the marketing of, not just the goods, but the elaborate philosophy behind them, aiming to slide smoothly into the life-style of busy women, *busy wealthy women,* I amended in my mind when the discussion turned to pricing. Gould was especially interesting as he took the attendees into the world of big-time cosmetics. He was a dynamic speaker, and the applause at the end of the presentation was well deserved.

I waited in a line of people eager to speak personally with the New Cosmetics CEO. When I reached him I said, "Jessica Fletcher, Mr. Gould. It was a wonderful discussion."

"Thanks," he said.

"You said that you'd grant me some time following the panel."

"I did? Right. Only a few minutes, though." He threw out an arm and looked at his watch.

"Whatever time you can give me will be appreciated."

He ushered me to a corner of the room and we sat at a small table.

"What is it you want to know?" he asked stiffly.

"I've been toying with the idea of setting my next murder mystery novel in the fashion world, during Fashion Week to be more precise. It's a fascinating world that I know nothing about, and thought you might be able to give me insight into the role the cosmetics industry plays in it."

He dusted an imaginary speck of lint from the vest of his three-piece blue suit, and chewed his cheek while deciding what to say. Finally, he said, "Look, Mrs. Fletcher, the cosmetics business is a competitive one — ruthless, you might even say. There are people who will do everything but kill a competitor in order to grab market share." His smile was small. "Maybe that's what you should write about in your novel, how a cosmetic manufacturer kills a competitor."

I jotted a note in the pad I'd taken from my bag to indicate I was taking what he said seriously. But my interest was in models and how they factor into a cosmetics company's business.

"A good idea," I said to Gould, who seemed anxious to leave. "What about models?" I asked quickly. "Are models cut-throat, too?"

His eyebrows went up. "Do you mean will they kill each other to get ahead?" He chuckled. "Close enough. Yeah, I'd say that you could make that your story."

"I ask because of what happened recently to Rowena Roth and Latavia Moore."

He immediately sobered. "You're asking the wrong person," he said, making a show of glancing at his watch. "I know, they were too young to die, but such things happen. I read an obit the other day of a guy, aged twenty-six, who dropped dead while jogging. Heart attack. Some of these models starve themselves, go on crazy diets to stay thin. You can imagine what that does to their hearts and other organs. They're young and reckless, stay out late drinking too much, skipping sleep, and expect my staff to fix the damages before they walk the runway or pose before the camera. At least with photography, you can fix their faces in the computer. In real life, it's not as easy."

"I imagine not," I said. He held up his index finger to Ann Milburn, the makeup artist who'd been on the panel with him. She'd been leaning against a wall during my conversation with Gould, and judging from her body language she was impatient.

"Time's up," he announced to me.

"And I appreciate the time you've given me," I said, returning the pad and pen to my bag. "What you've said about models and their lifestyles is very interesting."

He stood and tugged at his vest to straighten it. "Some of them are like that. Not all, of course."

"Of course. Not Rowena Roth, for instance," I said as he prepared to walk to where Ms. Milburn waited. "I'm pretty sure that Rowena Roth didn't die as a result of constant dieting."

He stopped and turned. "And why are you so sure of that?"

"I just learned this afternoon that she might have been murdered."

He returned to where I sat.

"Who told you that?" he asked, a frown creasing his brow.

"A source with the police."

"Why would the police confide something like that in *you*?"

"I suppose because I've shown interest in why Rowena died, and the coincidence — sometimes there are coincidences — of Latavia Moore's sudden death."

"That's nonsense," he said loudly. "Why would anyone kill either one of them?"

"That's what the police intend to find out, and I share their interest. Thank you again for your time today. I really appreciate it."

He walked to where Ann Milburn waited for him and said something in her ear. She glared at me as they left the room together, and I had the feeling that Philip Gould had not been happy with my news.

CHAPTER SIXTEEN

By the time I arrived at the hotel, the rooftop bar was filling up fast. Kopecky had already secured a small table for us by the window, the same table that Maggie Black and I had occupied earlier. He stood when he saw me enter the room and displayed a wide grin, his hand outstretched. "Here you are," he said, "looking as beautiful as ever."

I thanked him for the compliment and took the chair he held out for me.

"So," he said, "what have you been up to today?"

"It's been busy," I said, "but judging from what you said on the phone, you've had a busy day, too."

"Not so much busy as interesting. What are you drinking?"

"A white wine would be nice."

He motioned for the waitress and gave her my order. His glass of beer sat on the table.

"You were saying that your day was interesting," I said.

"Right." He raised his glass. "Here's to seeing you again."

I mirrored the gesture and we touched rims.

"You know, Jessica, there's something I have to say to you, get off my chest."

"I'm listening."

"Ever since Mary died — that's my wife, God bless her — I've met lots of women, you know, nice single women who maybe I could get interested in. But then I met you."

Oh, no, I thought. *Where is this going?*

"What I mean is, you have this way about you that makes a guy, makes me feel really important. You ask a lot of questions instead of mouthing off with your own opinions and ideas. That makes me feel — well, it makes me feel comfortable, right at home, if you get my drift."

"I, uh — yes, I think I do, and I'm pleased that you feel that way. You said on the phone that you thought that Rowena Roth's death might have been murder. Or were you referring to Latavia Moore? Or maybe both?"

"I'll get around to that in a minute. You know what I did?"

"I haven't the slightest idea."

"I bought a couple of your books and started reading them."

"That was very good of you."

"Not at all," he said, waving away my appreciation. "I know that they're novels, fiction and all, but they really give me a look inside you, what makes you tick, the things that are important to you. You're a really nice person, a real lady."

His barrage of compliments was sweet, but put me on alert. While I thanked him for each nice thing he said about me, what I wanted to get to was the reason I was there with him. It certainly wasn't to bask in his ego-boosting comments. But as he continued, my eagerness to hear about the possible murder of Rowena Roth would have to be put on hold, at least until he was finished speaking of other things.

"I was talking to Christina — she's my daughter; you haven't met her yet — and I showed her your books, which of course she'd already read. I told you she was a big fan. So I began telling her all about you and you know what she said?"

"No."

"She said, 'Daddy, I think you've got a crush on this lady Jessica Fletcher.' "

He sat back and smiled, held out his hands in a gesture that said, "What can I say?" and added, "That's what she said, and she knows me pretty good."

The trend of his monologue had to stop, I told myself. I struggled with what to say. I didn't want to insult him. He was a nice man, and it was evident that he missed his wife terribly and needed another woman in his life. But I wasn't that woman.

"Detective," I said, deliberately not calling him Aaron, "we don't know each other very well, and I've already indicated to you that there's another man in my life."

"Yeah, but when do you ever get to see him? He lives far away."

"That's true. Nevertheless, he's very important to me. You have been very attentive and certainly flattering, but I'm feeling uncomfortable being on the receiving end of all these compliments. I really would appreciate hearing about what you alluded to on the phone earlier today, that we might have a murder on our hands. Did you mean in the case of Rowena Roth, or was it Latavia Moore?"

His response was to ask whether I wanted a second glass of wine, which I declined, and to order another beer from our waitress. I glanced around to make sure that we weren't being overheard by those at neighboring tables. "Why do you suspect a murder took place?" I asked.

"Okay," he said, "down to business. You

know, I looked you up on the Internet, Jessica."

I waited to hear more.

"I saw that not only do you write about murder, but you've been involved in solving a few of them in real life."

"I've been fortunate to be in the right place to help out at times, and I've made a number of lucky guesses."

"I think it's a lot more than that. So I'm seeing you as a partner of sorts."

"A partner in solving a murder?"

"Yeah. Right. If you insist."

"That's the only way I'll partner with you."

He looked at me for a long moment. "Okay. I get the message."

"I appreciate that."

"Look, let's start over. You've been doing your own investigation into Ms. Roth's death. Am I right?"

I stifled a sigh of relief. "I wouldn't call it an investigation, but I am naturally curious why she died."

His pause was pregnant, as though making a dramatic statement. Then he said, "Ms. Roth, the model, might have been poisoned!"

" 'Might have been'?"

He leaned closer. "This is between us, right?"

I looked around. "Who else would I tell?"

"Not the pretty-face design guy. Not his mother. Not the model's aunt. No one. I *have* to insist."

"You have my word."

"Good. I figure your word is gold. Here's the skinny, Jessica. The medical examiner's office has a couple of young hotshots working in it whose only goal is to cut down on the backlog of cases they have. One of them did the original autopsy on Ms. Roth and came to the conclusion — a premature conclusion, I might add — that she died of a heart attack. Convenient, huh?"

"And not entirely far-fetched."

"Even though she wasn't even twenty years old and had been in good health?"

"She was seventeen actually," I said.

"Just proves my point."

"I admit that young people dying of a heart ailment is unusual, but it does happen from time to time." I thought of Philip Gould's comment. "Wasn't there a jogger who died at twenty-six?"

"Yeah. I saw that, too. They said it was natural causes. But maybe not *this* time," he said smugly. "Like I told you before, I've had this funny feeling about it from the get-go, so I put the arm on my boss at headquarters to request a second autopsy, this time by Doc Barden."

"Barden? He's a famous medical examiner. I have two of his books."

"He sure is, and for good reason. He was the best. He retired a year ago, but they bring him in on tough cases, the ones that the young turks in the office of the chief medical examiner can't get a handle on. Anyway, Doc Barden agrees to perform a second autopsy on her — and he did."

"I take it that he came up with a different conclusion from the others."

"He sure did. Want to know what he says?"

I would have preferred that he simply say what the result of the second autopsy was and not prolong the story, but he had the floor. I nodded.

"Doc Barden says that her heart was damaged by a foreign substance that he's betting will show up in her liver and kidneys."

He watched as what he'd said sank in to me.

"Poison? What sort of poison?" I asked.

Kopecky shrugged. "The doc is working on that as we speak. Whatever it was, it did something funny to her lips. The regular toxicology report takes forever, but Barden's putting a rush on it. 'Stat,' they call it in the medical business. He named a couple of possibilities, names I'd never heard of. But that's why he's the best."

"Well," I said, "I certainly appreciate your sharing this with me. When does Dr. Barden expect to have a definitive answer?"

"I don't know, but based upon his track record, it won't take long."

"What about Latavia Moore's death?" I asked. "You were suspicious of that one, too. Is there anything new on that case?"

He shook his head. "I still think I'm right about that one. We'll see."

The rooftop bar was now filled to capacity and the noise was giving me a headache. I desperately needed some quiet space, fresh air, or a nap.

"So," Kopecky said, "I've told you everything that's new, Jessica. You have anything to add?"

He'd shared a great deal with me, and I decided I had to return the favor. "Rowena was a patient of a prominent Park Avenue plastic surgeon, Edmund Sproles."

"How do you know that?"

I explained that I'd come across the doctor's card in Rowena Roth's apartment while there with her aunt and Maggie Black. "I spent some time with Dr. Sproles today," I added. "He did some work on her, including reshaping her lips."

He grimaced.

"I know," I said, "it hardly seemed that she needed any sort of restructuring. Oh, I should also add that Dr. Sproles grows exotic plants in his waiting room as a hobby, including some poisonous ones."

"Really? Now, that's interesting," he said, and asked me for the doctor's name again, which he noted in a pad.

"Rowena also received an expensive fur coat from an admirer, perhaps someone with whom she'd had an affair."

"Past tense?"

"It seems that way. Polly Roth said her niece was attracted to older men, but at Rowena's age almost all men were older men." I picked up my bag and rummaged inside. "Oh, and this is for you."

"What is it?"

"It's half a packet of oatmeal that Rowena had for breakfast the morning she died. I took it in case there had been any incidence of contaminated cereal, but I couldn't find anything to support that. I kept it anyway. It's probably not relevant, but perhaps you should have it tested."

Kopecky leaned back and grinned at me. "You're in the wrong profession, lady. This is all incredible stuff. You make a great partner. We should have another drink to celebrate."

"Detective Kopecky, I'm not feeling well. I'm sorry to bail out on you, but I'd like to go to my room and lie down."

"You all right?"

"Just very tired."

"Sure, sure, I understand."

While he waited for the waitress to bring the bill, he walked me to the elevators.

"Thanks for sharing information with me," I said.

"Same here. I'll look into this Park Avenue doctor, and I'll have this tested." He waved the oatmeal packet at me.

"Thank you for the wine."

"Hey, my pleasure. We'll do it again soon. Christina is dying to meet you and —"

The elevator arrived. I got in and pushed the button for my floor. My last image of NYPD Detective Aaron Kopecky was of him smiling and waving good-bye as the door closed.

CHAPTER SEVENTEEN

I'd told Kopecky that I didn't feel well and needed to lie down. It was close to being accurate. I *was* tired, tired of fending off his advances. And truth to tell, I simply had to get away from him and the noisy bar crowd and enjoy some moments of solitude.

The detective's interest in me had spilled over into the personal, which made our exchanges awkward. And while I thought I'd made it abundantly clear that I was not interested in a personal relationship, perhaps in my efforts not to offend him I hadn't been firm enough. In any case, he was intent upon wearing me down. And I was weary of his efforts and in danger of losing my patience. The best action under those circumstances was to climb out of the frying pan and try to avoid a fire.

I knew that Kopecky must be lonely. The years following my husband Frank's death were not so far in the past — and probably never would be — that I couldn't instantly recall the feelings of misery and longing for what had been lost. The death of Mary Kopecky had created a gaping hole in Aaron's life. That he was looking to fill it was understandable, and I was sure that one day he would find another woman — not to take Mary's place, but to recapture the warmth and comfort of companionship and sense of belonging that being part of a couple can provide. What he didn't yet realize was that there are benefits to being on one's own as well: the freedom to make choices without consulting anyone else; the pride in being self-reliant; and the satisfaction of deciding what your soul requires at the moment, whether it's to spend an evening with friends or enjoy some time alone.

Once I was ensconced in my room at the Refinery Hotel and had traded my shoes for a pair of slippers, I turned my attention to what he had told me regarding the deaths of Rowena Roth and Latavia Moore. Without the ambient roar of the crowd and the distraction of deflecting Kopecky's amorous interest, I was able to quietly review what I knew and what I needed to know.

What was blazingly clear was that the brass at headquarters must have a lot of confidence in Detective Kopecky's ability to ferret out foul play to go so far as to bring in the esteemed Dr. Michael Barden to perform a second autopsy on Rowena Roth. It was going to be quite a feather in Aaron's cap, since his hunch proved correct that Rowena was murdered, as Barden's preliminary conclusions seemed to indicate that she might well have been.

I had been reluctant to believe that Rowena died from anything other than natural causes. But I wondered how much of my resistance was bound up in trying not to agree with everything Aaron said. I'd raised so many objections I began to sound like a resident of Missouri, the "show me" state, instead of my beloved Maine. And yet, even while I was demanding proof, my subconscious had me busy gathering evidence and tracking down leads in the event I was mistaken. And it looked as though I was.

Barden was a legendary figure in the medical examiner's office, a man who stubbornly refused to accept nebulous results, and who kept digging for the truth. I'd once attended a lecture given by him and was impressed with his depth and breadth of knowledge of forensic medicine. He'd been consulted on many high-profile cases across the country, and even abroad, and had received every accolade and award available to men and women in his specialty. His books were considered the go-to source for insight into postmortems and their role in solving crimes.

Kopecky said that Barden had seen something during his autopsy that made him suspect Rowena's heart had been damaged, and most likely her liver and kidneys as well. While those findings represented a preliminary report — the official toxicology results were still days away despite his having put a rush on them — his initial evaluation was provocative. Would the eventual toxicology findings support it?

As to Latavia Moore, apart from the fact that Sandy had had an affair with the beautiful model when they lived in California, there was little I knew about her or her death. Kopecky had seen the body and challenged the young medical examiner about some physical findings he'd seen. But unless the ME's office called in Dr. Barden a second time, which was highly unlikely, Latavia's passing might remain unexplained. I knew from previous consultations with police authorities that there are tens of thousands of such cases across the country each year. In many cases the cause of death is an undetected infection. There are hundreds, perhaps thousands, of bacteria and viruses medical science hasn't encountered yet. With all our medical advances — and they have been impressive — there is a world of unknown pathogens waiting to be discovered. Where had Latavia been in the days leading up to her demise? What had she eaten? Who had she seen? I didn't know and suspected I never would. But I had been there when Rowena succumbed, had seen her in the hour before she perished, had visited her apartment, met one of her roommates, talked with her doctor, and I hoped I could contribute in some modest way to solving her death.

I picked up the phone and dialed Dr. Seth Hazlitt in Cabot Cove. I fully intended to honor my pledge to Kopecky not to share what he'd told me with any of the people I'd met or knew in New York. But I felt that bouncing my thoughts off Seth was an acceptable exception. Seth had nothing to do with the case, and was many miles away. He would never meet Kopecky or anyone who knew Rowena. And, anyway, he was always a model of discretion.

When he picked up the phone, I heard an electric noise in the background.

"Catch you at a bad time?" I asked.

"As a matter of fact, you have, Jessica. I'm

performing surgery."

"Really?"

"No. I'm trying out my new electric knife."

"Am I interrupting dinner?"

"Not yet. This roast I'm preparing for my guests requires delicate apportioning. Of course Tobé Wilson refuses to eat meat, so she will enjoy a vegetable lasagna instead."

"You've been cooking up a storm, I see. Who else is going to be there?"

"The Wilsons, Jack and Tobé, Tim Purdy, Eve Simpson, and yours truly."

"Please say hello for me."

"I will be happy to do so. Enjoying Fashion Week in the Big Apple? Eve expects you to come home dressed in the season's best and most expensive finery."

"She knows me better than that, Seth."

"I expect so, but hope springs eternal. She's eager to debrief you the moment you get home."

"She'll be better off talking to Maggie Black. Maggie knows all about the fashion industry."

"I'm sure Maggie is on her interrogation list as well. Speaking of interrogation, I see that your holiday in Manhattan has a bit of intrigue. I read about that model dying. Moore, was it?"

"Latavia Moore."

"Looked pretty as a picture in the article. Tragic. Only twenty-five, it said. Did Sandy Black know her?"

"I believe he did."

"By the way, how is Cabot Cove's gift to the fashion world?"

"He's known as Xandr Ebon now. He's fine. But there was another death on the same day that Latavia Moore's body was discovered. One of Sandy's models dropped dead on the runway."

"My goodness. All these young women dying. How old was this one?"

"Seventeen."

"Too young to be traipsing around on a runway, and certainly too young to die. You were there?"

"Along with a hundred other onlookers."

"Sounds fishy to me."

"The detective assigned to the case feels the same way. Dr. Michael Barden was brought in to perform a second autopsy. He evidently has suspicions, too, about how she died."

"Can't get better than that man, Jessica. Excuse me. Something on the stove is about to boil over."

I waited until he'd attended to his kitchen obligations and came back on the line.

"You were saying?" he asked.

"I was talking about the second model who died."

"And I suppose you've found yourself smack-dab in the middle of things."

"I have been doing a little probing of my own, nothing heavy-duty."

"I'll take your word for it," he said, his skeptical tone all too familiar to me.

"Seth, you've taken a number of forensics courses over the years."

"Ayuh."

"Do you know of any poison that would cause a young person's heart to give out, and that might also affect the liver and kidneys?"

"Off the top of my head, just like that?"

"I just thought that —"

"Can't say that I do, but I'll do some checking for you."

I heard his doorbell in the background.

"My guests are here," he said. "Have to run, Jessica. Good of you to call. You're still at that hotel called the Refinery?"

"Yes."

"I'll give you a call tomorrow if I come up with that poison you're looking for. But I warn you, there's probably a slew of them."

"I appreciate it, Seth."

"Have a good night, Jessica. I'll give your best to my guests."

I felt a little homesick after the call. Jack Wilson is Cabot Cove's top veterinarian, and his wife, Tobé, works with him. Tim Purdy is the town's historian, and Eve Simpson is our most successful real estate agent. All old friends of mine. I would have enjoyed spending the evening with them.

I didn't have any plans for my evening in Manhattan, which suited me fine. But that changed when my phone rang. It was Maggie Black calling from her room in the hotel.

"I'm calling for two reasons," she said. "First, I need to apologize for the way I acted in the bar, crying, then getting up and leaving while you were on the phone."

"No need to apologize," I said.

"I feel better doing it," she said.

"Apology accepted."

"The second reason for the call is to invite you to a party tonight."

I couldn't help laughing. "Another party? It seems there are more parties than fashion shows during Fashion Week."

She joined in my laughter. "There's lots to celebrate," she said. "Sandy has some big news."

"Oh? That's wonderful. What is it?"

"The actress Jeanne Rogét has approached Sandy through her agent to see whether he'd be interested in lending her a gown for the Academy Awards."

"That *is* big news," I said. "Jeanne Rogét is hot these days."

"She sure is. Anyway, that troll Jordan Verne, Sandy's financial backer, is hosting a party tonight to celebrate. I want you to come as my guest."

"I'm not sure that —"

"You have to come, Jessica. I laced into Sandy about what he claimed I'd said about you. He wants to apologize in person."

"That's not necessary, Maggie, but I'm relieved to know he feels that way."

"Please come with me. After everything negative that's happened, we need something positive to celebrate."

"That's true. Who else will be there?" I asked.

"The usual group of suspects, models, other designers, and media. The press is so important. Jeanne Rogét's interest in Sandy's designs could make all the gossip columns, and I wouldn't be surprised if some publications will want to interview him."

"I'm delighted for him, and for you."

"Meet you in the lobby at eight?" she said.

"That sounds fine."

I had to smile. There was a moment when I almost declined Maggie's invitation to accompany her to the party. I'm someone who covets downtime on a regular basis to recharge my batteries and clear my head before another round of party chitchat. But the realization that I'd committed myself to finding out what I could about the mysterious death of Rowena Roth changed that. Here was another opportunity to immerse myself in the fashion industry's intrigues and cast of players. It was too tempting to pass up. I'd have plenty of time to recoup once I was home in Maine.

As I dressed for the party, I thought back to my conversation with Seth Hazlitt. He's become quite the cook in recent years. I pictured him sitting down to dinner with my friends and exchanging news about the goings-on in Cabot Cove.

I missed being there.

CHAPTER EIGHTEEN

Xandr Ebon's party was held in a basement bar at the Dream Downtown Hotel on West Sixteenth Street, in the Chelsea section of the city. Maggie told me during the short cab ride that the bar, the Electric Room, was one of the city's trendiest venues. "It doesn't even open until eleven in the evening, but they make it available earlier for events. Sandy said Jordan was lucky to be able to book it on such short notice," she said. "They've been having parties there all week, but it was free tonight because someone had a last-second cancellation."

"I'm getting a real education about Manhattan's *in* places," I said.

"A far cry from Cabot Cove," she said.

"Yes," I said, "but both places have their special appeal."

The hotel had a lovely lobby, and we received a friendly greeting at the door. Maggie asked how to get to the Electric

Room and we were directed past a wall of Andy Warhol portraits to a spiral staircase leading downstairs, although the sounds of loud recorded music emanating from the basement space made the need for directions moot. We descended the stairs and were greeted inside by Jordan Verne, Sandy's business adviser and his mother's least favorite person.

"Ah, Mrs. Black," he said, flashing Maggie a smile. "Or under the circumstances should I call you Mrs. Ebon?"

"Black will do," Maggie replied, forcing a return smile.

"Here to celebrate your son's looming success?"

"Of course. I'm excited for him," Maggie said. "Do you know Jessica Fletcher?"

"The bestselling writer," he said. "Setting one of your mystery novels during Fashion Week?" He didn't wait for me to answer, and added, "There are plenty of people around here who deserve a knife in the side." He made a stabbing motion with his hand.

When neither Maggie nor I responded, he added with a smirk, "Just joking. Come, have a drink, some food."

With that he looked past us to the next arrival.

"I detest that man," Maggie grumbled to me as we entered the small dark room with high ceilings.

"Why do you dislike him so?" I asked. "Sandy seems to have confidence in him."

"It's not a matter of confidence. These money people exact their pound of flesh for every favor they provide. In exchange for funding Sandy's collection, and making selected introductions, Jordan not only dictates Sandy's every move, but he has demanded a huge cut of his profits regardless of how Sandy earns a living. Even if my son decided to leave fashion design and pursue, say, acting — which, given his looks, is not inconceivable — his contract with that man requires him to pay a fee to Jordan Verne for the rest of his life, even if the initial investment is recouped ten times over."

"Good heavens! No wonder you're upset. Didn't Sandy consult an attorney before he signed such an agreement?" I asked, shocked that Sandy would bind himself to such restrictions.

"Oh, Jessica. The ego of an ambitious man knows no boundaries. He was desperate to keep designing and was convinced that he knew best. I told him about people who had raised money on the Internet. He pooh-

poohed it. I begged him to call my cousin who's a lawyer in Chicago, just to get some advice, but of course he wouldn't. And there's more."

"What's that?"

"The worst of it is that the man who introduced him to Jordan Verne was Latavia Moore's husband."

I turned my head to look back at Sandy's "financial adviser" and wondered if Latavia's husband, who'd accused Sandy of theft, was still orchestrating that young man's punishment from behind the scenes.

Maggie spotted Sandy at the bar and we made our way toward him. From what I could make out in the room's dim lighting, the far wall was studded with metallic bricks. Wood paneling separated niches in the wall, featuring avant-garde art on mirrors hung over leather benches — most of them occupied. In the center of the room, Chesterfield sofas were arranged facing one another to form conversation areas. One sofa was piled high with winter coats, and I was surprised to see several furs among them. Whoever left a mink nestled along with the other outerwear was a very trusting person.

Small tables were arrayed in what leftover space was available. Maggie and I skirted them and the groups of animated people sitting and standing with drinks as we headed toward the bar. I was surprised at how many people I recognized, including the *Post* reporter Steven Crowell who was talking to Dolores Marshall, whom Babs Sipos had pointed out as her roommate.

"Mom, Jessica," Sandy said, hugging Maggie and kissing my cheek. "I owe you a big apology, Jessica." He cocked his head and gave me his best little-boy look. "I shouldn't have said what I did at the studio, and even worse, I laid it off on my mom. I hope you'll forgive me."

"It's completely forgotten, Sandy." I was pleased that he'd seen fit to apologize, but I wondered how often he got away with saying terrible things thanks to his good looks and charm.

"This whole week is just a blur," he said.

"You've been under a lot of pressure," his mother said.

"I heard about Jeanne Rogét's interest in your designs," I said. "Congratulations."

"That's why Jordan decided to throw this party," Sandy said. "Man, if she follows through and wears one of my gowns on the red carpet, I'll be over-the-moon. But if she gets me in to design costumes for her next flick, that's the best. I'll have it made." His look of satisfaction faded to a scowl. "The kicker is that the dress she wants is the gold one, and I never got it back from the police. It's going to cost me a small fortune to duplicate it. What am I saying? It's going to cost me a large fortune. Thank goodness Jordan has deep pockets."

Sandy waved at a woman who had arrived at the party, and left us to greet her. The newcomer was about my age, whip-thin, with a complexion that suggested she spent a great deal of time under a sunlamp. He wrapped his arms around her, kissed both of her cheeks, and smiled as if she were the love of his life.

"That's Pamela McQuaid," a voice whispered in my ear.

I turned to see Sandy's model Babs. "I was just thinking about you," I said. "And who is Pamela McQuaid?"

"Her husband is a biggie on Wall Street. She spends a fortune on clothing. All the designers court her like she's the Queen of England." Babs waved at Maggie, who was standing next to me. "Hi, Xandr's mother. Boy, you must be proud of your son."

"I certainly am," Maggie agreed. "Jessica, will you excuse me? I see the editor of *Catwalk* magazine and I need to make nice."

"Of course."

"So, how are you, Mrs. Fletcher? See? I remembered your name," Babs said. "I never remember anyone's names."

"Yet you remembered mine."

"That's because you're famous. Did you hear about the actress Jeanne Rogét? She wants Xandr to lend her a frou for the red carpet."

"What's a frou?"

"That's designer talk for a party dress. And I hear Rogét is quite the party girl. Who knows what that dress will look like by the time he gets it back? She'll probably drip champagne on it. That's if she gives it back at all."

"Would she keep it without paying for it?"

"Depends on what you think is payment. If she likes what her stylist picks out for her, she promised that Xandr could be in the running to design the costumes for her next movie. He's stoked. He's been telling everyone."

"In the running, you say? But nothing definite."

"Yeah. Nothing is ever guaranteed in this business or, I guess, any business. Promises are broken every day."

"That's quite a cynical point of view for one so young," I said.

"I know. I'm not very trusting. You learn

246

fast or get pushed to the side."

"Do you think that's why Rowena didn't make any friends? She didn't trust anyone?"

Babs shrugged. "I was nice to her — most of the time — but she didn't like me anyway. I think she was annoyed that I refused to try her homemade concoctions."

"You mean her makeup?"

"Yeah. I have very sensitive skin. I'm not putting her goop on my face."

"That's understandable."

"To you, maybe, but not to her. She was very independent. I think she saw herself as a future entrepreneur in the business. She just wasn't sure which part of the industry she wanted to bestow her many talents on."

"Now, Babs," I started to say.

"Hey, Babs, you didn't tell me you knew Jessica Fletcher." Peter Sanderson, the male model I'd seen at the show, slid an arm around Babs's waist and pulled her back against him. He glanced at the phone in his other hand before flashing a smile. "Isn't this little one a beauty?" he said to me.

"Hardly little," Babs said, pushing away from him. "I'm five-ten."

"You're still a little girl to me," he said. "So cute."

I remembered that at the show Ann Milburn had warned him away from Rowena, calling the first-time model "jailbait." Apparently Sanderson liked to tease the younger women.

"Nice to see you again, Jessica. I was disappointed that you didn't call me. Still have my card?"

"I do," I said.

"I've got some great ideas for film projects we could work on together."

"I'm really busy with book projects right now," I said, "but thanks for thinking of me."

His phone must have vibrated, because he frowned down into the screen and turned his back to Babs and me for the moment. She looked around to ascertain that we weren't being overheard before asking, "Is there anything new about how Rowena died?"

"Nothing as far as I know," I said, remembering my promise to Kopecky not to share what he'd told me with others. "But I was hoping to have a few minutes to talk with you about her."

"Sure. Anytime." Babs looked around the room. "I heard that she might have been murdered," she said, leaning toward me to be heard over the recorded music emanating from the DJ's booth.

Maggie had returned to my side in time

to hear Babs's announcement. "That's ridiculous," she said.

Babs shrugged. "I'm just repeating what other people are saying."

"Well, don't go around spreading those kinds of rumors. Poor Polly Roth. She would die if she heard you talking that way."

"I don't think Rowena's aunt is here," Babs said, pouting.

"It's an open investigation," I said, hoping to shift the conversational emphasis.

Sanderson turned around and wrapped his arm around the young woman's shoulders. "Hey, Babs!" he said. "I want you to meet someone." He winked at me. "See you later, Jessica Fletcher. Don't forget me, now."

Babs excused herself and the pair went off.

Maggie gave me a knowing look. "What about this rumor that Rowena was murdered?" she asked.

I gave her my best confused expression.

"That call you got when we were together in the rooftop bar. I couldn't help overhearing that it was the detective who is investigating Rowena Roth's death, and you mentioned the medical examiner during your conversation with him. You obviously know more than you let on, Jessica."

"I've heard a few things," I said, wishing that someone would approach and get me off the hook.

Now it was Maggie's turn to glance left and right before speaking. "Level with me, Jessica. If the police suspect that Rowena was murdered — and I stress *if* — do they consider Sandy a suspect?"

"Not that I'm aware of," I answered honestly, not adding that if Rowena had been murdered, no one was excluded as a suspect until proven innocent, and that would include Sandy Black, aka Xandr Ebon, the man she worked for at the time of her death, and possibly his mother. Even me, for that matter. I'd been there when she died.

"I just don't trust the police," Maggie said. "They're lazy. They focus in on the easiest mark. That's what they did in L.A. I don't have any reason to think it would be different in New York."

The arrival of the writer Claude de Molissimo captured our attention as he descended the spiral staircase, stopped, and took in the gathering. Immediately behind him was the redheaded model who'd lived with Rowena, the one who'd "borrowed" Rowena's fur coat. Her name, I remembered, was Isla.

"That's one of Rowena's roommates," Maggie said.

"Yes. I met her at Rowena's apartment when I was there with you."

"Do you know the man who's with her?"

"I do," I said.

"You're amazing, Jessica. How did you meet so many people so quickly?" she asked.

"It's just a knack I have."

De Molissimo took Isla's arm and escorted her to where Sandy stood with Jordan Verne and a knot of partygoers, which included the makeup artist Ann Milburn.

"Is he in the fashion business?" Maggie asked, referring to de Molissimo.

"He's a writer. He wrote a controversial book about the design business."

"So he's the one? Sandy mentioned that book. He said it was an unfair criticism of the fashion industry and the people in it."

"I haven't read it yet," I said, "but I did get to meet him."

"Can't believe you're in New York less than a week and you already know more people in the fashion business than I do."

"I sincerely doubt that." I didn't know from the way she'd said it whether she was impressed or being snide. I didn't get to find out, because she broke away when she saw another editor she needed to buttonhole.

Babs, who'd been gyrating to the music in a corner of the room with Sanderson and several others, left her dance partners and rejoined me.

"You wanted to talk to me, Mrs. Fletcher?" she asked. "Is now a good time? I figured you didn't want to chat in front of Xandr's mother."

"That's true. Thanks. But the music here is a bit loud for conversation," I said.

She laughed. "Listen, I hope I didn't say anything out of line before when I mentioned the rumor that Rowena —"

"Not at all, Babs. But let me ask you a question."

She nodded.

"You were with Rowena right before she died, right next to her on the catwalk."

"I don't think I'll ever forget it," she said.

"You said she had to run to the bathroom. Had she complained of not feeling well?"

Babs screwed up her face in thought. "Not really. I mean, I told her it was okay to be nervous and she said she wasn't. But she was sweating a lot. And — oh, yeah, she was afraid that it was going to ruin her makeup. That's right. She said she felt all sweaty."

"Not good for a model about to go on the runway," I said.

"It's weird how you remember things later. She also complained about her lips. Her tongue, too."

"Really? What did she say was wrong with them?"

"Nothing that I can recall. She'd had her lips done over."

"I know," I said, "by Dr. Sproles."

"Oh? You know him?"

"We've met. You can't remember precisely what she complained about?"

She shook her head. "Maybe something about her lips and tongue tingling. But, you know, people who have work done sometimes have side effects like that. Does that make sense?"

"I suppose it does," I said.

"Who do you think did it?"

"Did what?"

"Killed her."

"I'm not sure that anyone 'killed her,' Babs. Let's not jump to conclusions."

She seemed disappointed. "Anything else, then?"

"Well, yes. Did you know any of the men Rowena might have dated?"

She laughed. "No one really dates anymore, Mrs. Fletcher. Rowena might have hooked up with a guy every now and then, but I don't think she was attached to anyone, if that's what you mean."

"Was Peter Sanderson one of the men?"

She shrugged. "Maybe. He flits from one girl to another all the time."

"Could he have pursued her, sent her gifts?"

She laughed again. "Peter expects to *get* gifts, not the other way around — or at least he expects the older women who chase after him to keep him well supplied."

I wasn't sure I wanted to know what "supplies" Sanderson received from his admirers, but at least I thought I could discount him as the lover who had sent Rowena a fur coat.

Babs moved on to other people, and I gravitated toward Claude de Molissimo, who was engaged in what appeared to be a spirited conversation with Sandy Black, Jordan Verne, and Ann Milburn while the model Isla stood by. Sandy saw me approaching and broke off what he was saying to the others to welcome me into the conversation.

"Have you met Claude de Molissimo?" Sandy asked.

"Yes, I've had the pleasure," I said.

"The pleasure was mine," de Molissimo said in a loud voice. He seemed even bigger than the first time we'd met, a whale of a man dressed this day like a big game hunter in Africa. All he lacked was a pith helmet.

"You were saying, Ann?" Sandy said to the makeup artist.

"I was saying that today's crop of models leaves a lot to be desired."

I glanced at Isla to see whether she was offended, although it was hard to tell. She was scanning the crowd, striking poses as if cameras were focused on her, and for all I knew some might have been. Almost every young person in the room was checking a cell phone, taking selfies or using a stick to extend the phone's reach to capture a group of people on their cell phone cameras.

"What was better about previous models?" de Molissimo asked.

"To begin with," Ann replied, "their beauty was more natural, required less makeup."

"But that's your business," Verne said. "You mustn't be very good if you complain about having to use more makeup."

"I'm one of the best makeup artists in the industry," she said angrily. "I can make anyone look good, even the half-sober, sleep-deprived whiners who call themselves models these days."

"You've been doing it long enough, considering how old you are," Isla said through what passed as a thin smile.

For a moment I thought that Ann was going to strike her. Her fists curled into balls at her sides, and her dark brown eyes shot daggers at the model.

"Let's act like ladies," de Molissimo said.

"She's no lady," Isla said as she pirouetted and sauntered away.

Ann heard her and I thought she might go in pursuit, but Verne stopped her with a hand on her arm.

I looked at de Molissimo, who had a bemused smile on his broad face. To my surprise he then placed his hand on my back and steered me away from the group to an area of the bar that had just opened up.

"The claws are out tonight," he said through a hearty laugh. "Two proseccos," he called to the bartender.

"It certainly was an unpleasant exchange," I said.

"Ann Milburn is a tough cookie," he said.

"Is she well-known as a makeup artist?"

"Oh, yes, and she's equally well-known for having a heck of a temper. She's been charged with assault at least twice."

"Assault? My goodness. Who did she assault?"

"A former husband, for one," he said. "And I remember a time she smacked a model who gave her a hard time."

"I see what you mean about being tough. Yet she's also a very attractive woman."

"Sexy, you mean. She has that sort of sexual allure that certain special actresses have, you know, not especially beautiful women, but ones who exude sensuality. Colleen Dewhurst and Lauren Bacall come to mind." He took two glasses from the bartender and handed me one.

"You say that she attacked a former husband. How many times has she been married?"

"Twice, at least officially. There's a rumor that there was a third husband back when she was the same age as the models she works on."

"She's currently unattached?"

He tipped his glass to clink with mine, took a big gulp of the sparkling wine, and set the glass down on the bar with a tap. "Maybe. Maybe not. Current gossip — and this business thrives on gossip — has it that she's the sometime paramour of several titans of industry, including the CEO of New Cosmetics."

"Philip Gould?"

"The very same. Of course that's just a rumor. Just talk to someone and you end up the object of speculation on Page Six.

By tomorrow they'll have you and me in bed together." He waggled his eyebrows up and down, and it took everything I had to keep from rolling my eyes. I would have taken a step back away from him, but the crowd around the bar prevented it.

"Her relationship with Gould is a professional one," I said. "She can't help being in his company when she works for him." I don't know why I was defending Ann Milburn. It's just that rumor mills have always been distasteful to me. So many people are hurt through insinuation and innuendo, including in my beloved Cabot Cove, Maine, where a casually dropped comment soon makes its rounds via the town's usual gathering spots and pretty soon a rumor is no longer considered a rumor. It becomes a "fact" thanks to the reasoning that if enough people say it, it must be true. Having been a victim of that kind of scandal-mongering in the past, I'm highly suspect of hearsay. At the same time, being human, I'm as susceptible as the next person to interesting "news," and there have been times when a rumor actually did turn out to be factual.

Ann Milburn and Philip Gould? Well, I would withhold judgment for now.

Gould was a married man, albeit to a wife who didn't seem to be enjoying marital bliss. I thought back to when I briefly interviewed Gould and noticed that Ann Milburn waited impatiently for him to join her. Was this volatile, attractive makeup artist Gould's mistress? One of many? It was none of my business unless . . . unless it had something to do with the death of Rowena Roth. But if it did, how?

"I saw you come in with Isla tonight. How did you happen to bring her?" I asked de Molissimo.

"Didn't bring her at all. Bumped into her outside the hotel," he said. "She's not my type. These skinny babies turn me off."

I started to respond, but he added, "Somebody like you is more my style. You have a brain, writing all your books, and you're not bad-looking."

My guffaw came out involuntarily. "Thank you, I think," I said, at a rare loss for words.

"Speaking of that," he said, "how about you and I get together tomorrow night for dinner at my place? I make a mean tuna casserole."

"You're having a party?" I asked, having regained my composure.

"Yes. You and me. I bet we both have great stories to swap."

I noticed Maggie at the far end of the room talking with the *Post* reporter.

"Thanks, but I'm busy tomorrow night," I said to de Molissimo.

"Another time, then. Promise me one thing."

"What's that?"

"That if you end up finding out who killed Rowena Roth, I'll be the first to know. The rumor that somebody did her in is all over town."

I didn't promise anything as I disengaged from him and returned to where Sandy stood just as Maggie rejoined her son.

Should I be flattered that both Detective Aaron Kopecky and now fashion industry gadfly Claude de Molissimo had indicated an interest in me as a woman, even if de Molissimo's compliment was certainly a backhanded one?

The answer I gave to myself was that I fervently wished that George Sutherland was there.

I announced to Maggie and Sandy that I was leaving and thanked them for inviting me to the party. It was wearing having to talk over the incessantly loud music, and I was feeling hunger pangs. While there was finger food at the party, it was scarce; it seemed that whatever was offered disappeared into the hands and mouths of those closest to the kitchen the moment a waitress appeared with it.

"Mind if I stay?" Maggie asked.

"Not at all," I said. "I'm so happy for you, Sandy — or should I say Xandr?"

"I'll answer to anything, Jessica," he said, kissing me on the cheek. "Thanks for helping me celebrate."

I sought out others to say good night to on my way out, including Babs Sipos and Jordan Verne, who'd hosted the party for Sandy. I avoided Claude de Molissimo and was making my way toward the exit when Ann Milburn stopped me with a hand on the shoulder.

"Leaving so soon?" she said. "The party's just getting started."

"I'm sure it is for these young people. But it's getting late for this lady," I said.

"I'll go up with you," she said. "I could use some fresh air."

We ascended the stairs and walked through the hotel lobby, out into the chilly night.

"People say you're researching a murder mystery here during Fashion Week."

I was tempted to dissuade her of that notion but held my tongue. I'd been saying it to a number of people to justify asking questions and thought I might as well continue with that story.

"Has that detective been part of your research?" she asked.

"Detective Kopecky? He interviewed me after Rowena died," I said, trying to be noncommittal. "I imagine he interviewed you, too."

As I spoke with her I kept thinking about what Claude de Molissimo had said, that she'd demonstrated a violent streak in the past, and had been a mistress of sorts to some powerful people in the fashion industry, including possibly Philip Gould of New Cosmetics. Her personal life certainly wasn't any of my business, of course, and I'm not someone who makes moral judgments about people when their actions don't directly impact me. Besides, de Molissimo appeared to delight in being a rumormonger of the first order. His gossip about people in the fashion industry served him well; he'd even landed a publishing contract with a leading publishing house, the same one that published my books. But I knew whatever he said had to be taken with the proverbial grain of salt until proven true.

"Mind a word of advice?" Ann said as we stood together on Sixteenth Street.

"Not at all."

"The fashion world is a small, tight-knit

community, Mrs. Fletcher, sort of like Las Vegas being a small, close-knit city. You know the saying about Las Vegas: 'What happens in Las Vegas stays in Las Vegas.'"

"Yes, of course."

"It applies to the fashion industry, too. We hate to give up our secrets, especially to strangers. Don't believe everything you hear. It will get you into trouble. And I'm sure you're not looking for trouble, are you?"

She said it slowly and emphatically, as though to make sure that every word had meaning, and that I understood the thought behind the words. As she said it, her attractive, expertly made-up face was set in a stony glare.

"I'll remember that," I said.

"Make sure you do. Have a good night, Mrs. Fletcher, and enjoy the rest of your stay in New York."

CHAPTER NINETEEN

I decided to walk back to the Refinery Hotel rather than take a taxi. My mind was swirling with thoughts and I needed the brisk air to help sort them out.

What was intended to be a pleasant trip to New York City to enjoy Fashion Week and to spend time with close friends and family had ended up a tension-filled, provocative stay in which murder had once again injected itself.

The police were looking at Rowena Roth's case as a homicide. While nothing tangible had been established yet in that regard, it was possible that someone had deliberately taken her young life, and I was determined to get to the bottom of it.

I know, I told the voice of Seth Hazlitt in my mind, *it's not my business to solve crimes. I'm a widow who writes mystery novels and helps host civic events in Cabot Cove, Maine. You're right — except that one of my genes dictates something different. Sorry, but it's who I am.*

As I neared the hotel it occurred to me that I'd spent too little time with Grady, Donna, and Frank, and made a silent pledge to rectify that. I was thinking about Frank's excellent short story while crossing a street, not realizing that I wasn't paying attention to traffic. A car whizzed by close to me, causing me to jump back. I tripped on the curb behind me and landed on my bottom.

"Are you all right, lady?" a man said, helping me to my feet.

"I . . . I think so."

"Okay, then." He smiled and continued on his way.

I dusted off the back of my coat and took a mental inventory of my body. No bones broken, although I expected to be good and sore the next day. Rattled, yes, but it was my own fault. I'd been so immersed in my musings that I neglected to watch where I was going, like all those people who walk the streets peering into their cell phones, oblivious of everything and everyone around them. *That's how people get killed on the streets of New York, Jessica.*

Several people gave me strange looks as I stood rooted to the pavement before I felt confident enough to cross the intersection.

No one could have done that on purpose, I assured myself. I looked around. A couple with their arms around each other seemed to be engrossed in a store window. A man across the street stopped to light a cigarette. *You are not being followed!* But there was still a niggling suspicion that perhaps someone wasn't happy with my inquiries. I remembered all of Seth Hazlitt's cautions to me over the years and my dismissals of his concern.

As I reached the street on which the hotel was located, my cell phone sounded.

"Hello?"

"Jessica?"

"I was just thinking of you, Seth."

"What's all that noise I hear?"

"Traffic. I'm on the street."

"What are you doing on the street at this hour?"

"I can't hear you, Seth. I'll be at my hotel in a few minutes. I'll call you back."

"I'll stay on the line."

I walked faster, reached the hotel, and went to a quiet corner in the lobby.

"Seth?"

"Ayuh, I'm still here."

"Why are you calling?"

"I'm calling because you asked me to check into poisons."

"Yes, right. I'm sorry. I forgot."

"Are you still interested, Jessica?"

"Of course I am, and I appreciate your taking time to do this for me."

"Always happy to oblige my good friend Jessica Fletcher. I did some research as promised."

"What did you find?" I asked, hurriedly removing a pad and pen from my purse.

"Well, there are many naturally grown substances that can be used to poison someone, things like water hemlock. That's what the old Hemlock Society was named after. They call it Compassion and Choices these days."

"I know," I said. "I donate to it every year."

"Could be rosary pea, or even lily of the valley."

I scribbled down what he was saying. "That's such a pretty flower."

"Mebbe so, but you don't want to eat it. Then there's kudu, also known as desert rose. Good old castor oil can be lethal, too, if taken in large quantities. The list goes on and on."

"But have you narrowed *down* the list?" I asked.

"Ayuh, I have. I can't be certain, of course, and only testing can nail it down, but a good bet might be aconite. Care to hear more?"

"Fu zi," I whispered, remembering the Chinatown apothecary purchase.

"What was that?"

"I'm listening," I said, my pen poised over the pad.

"Aconite's from the buttercup family of plants," he said. "You'd think those pretty flowers would be safe, but one of them is monkshood. It's been used in Chinese medicine for years — in small doses, of course."

"I remember reading about monkshood. It's also known as wolfsbane and was considered the queen of poisons in ancient Greece."

"It's plenty toxic, that's for sure. Somebody who ingests aconite, either in liquid or food, or absorbed through the skin, can die pretty quickly. The first symptoms can show in just a few minutes, things like numbness, nausea, staggering, a tingling sensation, difficulty breathing, cold and clammy skin, sweating. The heart takes a hit; so do the kidneys and liver."

"I assume a blood test offers a definitive finding," I said.

"Ayuh, but it's more likely to show up first in the urine. By the way, Jessica, the Lepchas — that's a tribe of sorts in Nepal and environs — poisoned the water supply of British troops with it back in the late eighteen hundreds when the Brits were out to conquer the world."

"That's interesting," I said, having stopped writing.

"Just thought I'd throw in a bit of history," my doctor friend and inveterate history buff said. "Beats me how it's still a basic part of Chinese pharmacology, and apparently it's widely available in homeopathic remedies. You wouldn't find me taking it, although there's some who say it staves off aging. Lot of nonsense. But I guess it's true: if you die, you won't grow older."

"And so you say that if — and I stress *if* — one of these models was poisoned, it was possibly aconite."

"I didn't say 'possibly,' Jessica, but it's my best guess, only because it's so easily available." He rattled off a list of ailments it could be used for. "If anyone can come up with the definitive answer, it's someone like Michael Barden. He's the best."

We chatted about other things including his recent dinner party that I wished I'd been able to attend.

"Everyone missed you," he said. "I gave them your best."

"I'll be home the next time you cook a

roast," I said, smiling at the contemplation.

"We'll all look forward to that," he said. "And, Jessica."

"Yes?"

"If that model was murdered by somebody, it's not your business."

"Yes, sir," I said. "And thanks for the information about aconite."

"You're welcome, Jessica. Stay safe. You're not as young as you used to be."

Those final words rang in my ear as I clicked off my cell phone. It seemed as though I'd aged considerably in the few days I was in New York for Fashion Week, at least in the eyes of people like Claude de Molissimo, Dr. Edmund Sproles, and everyone else involved in what is decidedly a young person's game. Promptly, I decided not to look in the mirror until I got back home to Cabot Cove, whose mirrors are more flattering to those of us on the wrong side of forty.

I was pondering my accelerated aging when I looked in the direction of the lobby bar and saw Detective Aaron Kopecky emerge from it. He spotted me and came to where I sat.

"My lucky night," he said.

"You just happened to be having a drink in this hotel?" I said.

"I cannot tell a lie," he said, placing a hand over his heart. "Mind if I join you?"

He sat next to me before I could answer.

"I called your room a couple of times, but you weren't there. I was sure you would be because you told me you needed to rest."

"I did rest," I said, a little irritated at having to account for my time. "But Maggie Black called and insisted I come to a celebratory party."

"Another Fashion Week bash?"

I nodded.

"Anyway," he said, "when I couldn't reach you in your room, I figured I'd stop in here for a drink and hope you'd arrive. You did. How was the party?"

"It was fine. Why have you been trying to reach me?"

"Oh, I figured you'd want to hear the latest on the model murder."

He had my attention. I sat forward and said, "It was murder? Rowena was murdered?"

It was his turn to nod. "Join me for a drink and I'll fill you in."

"I don't need a drink, Detective. I don't *want* a drink."

"Had dinner?"

"No, I — I'm not hungry," I said, hoping

my rumbling stomach wouldn't give me away.

"Keeping your figure?"

I'd had enough of the banter. I said firmly, "Detective Kopecky, I —"

"Hey, come on. It's Aaron, remember? We're old friends."

"Why not just tell me without a drink or dinner why you've decided that Rowena Roth was murdered?"

"Okay," he said, "provided that after I do you at least join me in the bar for a night-cap."

"Maybe," I said.

"You drive a hard bargain, Jessica."

I fixed him in my best hard-nosed stare.

"It's like this," he said. "My boss called me this afternoon and told me to be at headquarters for a meeting with Dr. Barden."

"About Rowena Roth's death?"

"You've got it. Barden is quite a guy, a straight talker, no beating around the bush. I felt like I was back in grade school being lectured by a teacher."

"He has a wonderful reputation," I said.

"That he does. Anyway, Barden had come to headquarters to give his latest findings on the autopsy he did on Ms. Roth."

"And?"

"Looks like she didn't die of natural causes. Somebody *wanted* her dead."

When I didn't say anything he added, "She was poisoned."

"Could it have been aconite?" I asked.

It was as though I'd punched him in the stomach. He stared at me, looked down, looked up again, blinked a few times, started to say something, stopped, held up his hands in a surrender gesture, and finally said, "I really need a drink now."

CHAPTER TWENTY

I felt obligated to accompany him back into the bar after having obviously unsettled him. I certainly hadn't intended to. My conversation with Seth Hazlitt about poisons was fresh in my mind and I'd just blurted out "aconite." I suppose that Kopecky expected to surprise me with what he'd learned that day and I'd taken the wind out of his sails.

We found a table. He ordered a bourbon, neat; I asked for a club soda with a wedge of lime. He stared at me and we said nothing until the drinks had been served. He looked down at his glass with its shimmering amber liquid, shook his head, smiled, sipped from the drink, and said, "Aconite."

"Is that what Dr. Barden found during his follow-up autopsy on Rowena Roth?" I asked, nibbling at the bowl of pretzels on the table.

He started to say something in response,

shook his head again, took another sip, and finally asked, "How did you know it was this poison called aconite?"

"I didn't know. I was guessing."

He guffawed. "*Guessing?* You just *guessed* that it was this aconite stuff?"

"I'm misleading you," I said, "and I'm sorry. I didn't mean to. My friend back in Cabot Cove, Seth Hazlitt, is a respected physician who is constantly keeping up on advances in medicine, including forensics. I was chatting with him on the phone and asked if he would look up poisons that could affect the heart. He named a few and felt that aconite was the most logical choice. But he was guessing, too."

I asked again whether Dr. Barden had found aconite during his autopsy of Rowena.

"That's right," he said, "but he *wasn't* guessing. He said aconite was found in her urine and liver. No doubt about it."

I pondered what he'd said before saying, "So the obvious question is, how did Rowena Roth ingest it, and under what circumstances?"

"Why do I have the feeling that you already have the answer to that question?"

It was my turn to shake my head. "No," I said, "I haven't a clue why aconite would be found in her body."

Kopecky pulled a slip of paper from his pocket and read from notes he'd jotted on it. "Doc Barden said that he discovered the poison using what he called a liquid chromatography tandem mass spectrometer, whatever that is."

"It's a —" I stifled the urge to explain how that piece of laboratory equipment works. He didn't need for me to one-up him again. "My friend Seth said that aconite is sometimes used as a medicine for all sorts of ailments in Asia, things like gout, facial paralysis, pleurisy, and many other maladies."

"Your doctor friend sounds like a pretty smart guy."

"He certainly is, as well as a close friend. Detective Kopecky, I —"

"What happened to calling me by my first name? Because you've trumped not only me but Dr. Barden, too, it's all formality now? No more Jessica and Aaron?"

I didn't debate what we called each other and took a sip of my drink.

Kopecky broke the silence. "You think it's possible that Ms. Roth used it herself for some medical problem she was having?" he asked. "Like one of those problems your doctor friend mentioned?"

"I can't imagine that," I replied, "although

since I've been here at Fashion Week talking to people, it seems that there's nothing these young models won't do to enhance their natural beauty. Did she use it as some sort of cosmetic concoction? It's possible, I suppose. She liked to experiment, creating her own makeup and buying potions from Chinatown."

"Yeah? Who told you that?"

"Her roommate. And I found a receipt in her garbage for fu zi, which turns out to be aconite root. Of course, nothing on the receipt indicated who bought it, and I didn't realize at the time that it could be poison. It was supposed to be good for circulation."

Kopecky downed what was in his glass and motioned for another. My fatigue of earlier in the evening had returned, and I was beginning to feel the effects of my fall on the street. I was eager to call it a night. I told the detective that I would be leaving.

"Sure, sure, I understand," he said. "But before you go, let me ask you a question. Did this doctor in Maine tell you how aconite can be used to murder someone?"

"He said that it can be mixed in liquid or food and ingested, or can be absorbed through the skin."

"Since you seem way ahead of me, what's your best guess how it ended up in Ms.

Roth's body?"

"I haven't the slightest idea," I said, pleased that I could say it with conviction and not further attack his already fragile ego.

He suddenly perked up from his sour mood and asked, "Feel like dinner?"

"Afraid not," I said, "but thanks anyway."

"Suit yourself," he said, his words exhibiting disappointment.

I stood and offered my hand. "It was good seeing you," I said, feeling a modicum of guilt at leaving him alone.

"Yeah, I'm sure. See you around."

I went to my room, happy to be by myself. I ordered a sandwich from room service and was about to run a hot shower for my aching body when the phone rang. It was Maureen Metzger, Sheriff Metzger's wife, from Cabot Cove.

"I hope I'm not calling too late," she said.

"Not at all, Maureen. It's nice hearing from you."

"The reason I called is to remind you that the library fund-raiser is coming up in a week. You'll be back for it, won't you?"

"I certainly intend to," I said. "How is Mort?"

"He's fine," she said. "Are you okay?"

"Me? Yes, of course. Why do you ask?"

"Well, Mort was talking to Doc Hazlitt and he told Mort that you were involved with that famous model who died, Latavia Moore."

I laughed. "It always amazes me how things become skewed in the retelling," I said. "No, I have nothing to do with her unfortunate death, but I have been talking with the detective who's investigating that case as well as that of another model, Rowena Roth."

"Another one? Is there a serial killer loose in New York?"

"No, of course not. I don't think they're connected. She was modeling one of Sandy Black's creations when she died. Remember him? From Cabot Cove?"

"Can't say that I do. So, you're working with the detective on those two cases."

I had to laugh. "No, Maureen, I'm not *working* with anyone. The detective and I have become friendly, that's all."

"Were those models murdered, Jessica?"

"That hasn't been determined yet," I said, eager to change the subject. "It was good hearing from you, Maureen. Give my best to Mort."

"Oh, wait," she said. "He wants to talk to you."

"How's my favorite sheriff?" I asked when

he came on the line. "Keeping crime down in Cabot Cove?"

"Everything's under control, Mrs. F. I couldn't help overhearing your conversation with Maureen. What's this about a serial killer and a detective you're working with?"

I sighed. "I'm not working with anyone, Mort. I explained it to Maureen."

"Seems like every time you travel you get yourself mixed up in somebody's murder."

"I'm not mixed up in —"

"You know, Mrs. F., not all cops are like me. Some professional law enforcement officers don't like having amateurs butting in. Not that you butt in exactly. But take it from one who knows. I was on the force in New York City for years. The detectives I worked with would get their backs up if you made suggestions about one of their cases."

I started to respond, but he pressed on.

"I know, I know," he said, "you're familiar with how law enforcement and criminal investigations work because you write murder mysteries and all, and I'll be the first to admit that you've been a help to this law enforcement officer a few times." He paused before adding, "Maybe even more than a few times. But a good cop takes pride in what he knows and does, and having an outsider offer advice can be — well, it can be downright annoying."

I'd heard this speech from Mort before and knew there was nothing to be accomplished aside from telling him that I understood and that I agreed with him, which I did.

"Just some friendly advice, Mrs. F."

"And I appreciate it, Mort."

He put Maureen back on the phone.

"Hope you don't mind Mort saying what's on his mind," she said.

"I never have," I said.

There was a knock on the door.

"Time to run. My dinner has arrived."

"And, Jessica, you take care of yourself. If there *is* a serial killer in New York killing fashion models, he's liable to mistake you for one. You're pretty enough."

Bless Maureen Metzger.

After room service delivered my very late dinner, I turned on the TV just in time to catch a local newscast. The anchor came out of a commercial break with an update on the deaths of the two models, Latavia Moore and Rowena Roth. She read from the teleprompter, "An unidentified source in law enforcement has told this station that the sudden death of the model Rowena Roth, who collapsed on the catwalk while modeling a dress designed by Xandr Ebon, is now being considered a possible homicide." The anchor went on to mention Latavia Moore's unexplained death, her words accompanied by a stunning photo of Ms. Moore wearing a luxurious mink coat in a magazine advertisement.

I sat back in my chair and remembered having seen the labels for Chi-Chi Quality Furs in the fur coat worn by Philip Gould's wife, Linda, and the one that had belonged to Rowena Roth, a gift from someone with whom she presumably had a romantic relationship.

"Chi-Chi Furs," I said to myself. I consulted my schedule for the next day. I'd circled a demonstration of makeup manufacturing that Philip Gould was giving at New Cosmetics. *Maybe I'll stop by Chi-Chi Furs before the program and see what I've been missing all these years.*

Chapter Twenty-One

A good night's sleep and a hot shower had done wonders for this lady's sore body, and I faced the morning with renewed energy. Before heading off for Chi-Chi Furs, I used my smartphone to check out the city's Fur District. Fur manufacturers tended to group together in parts of the city the way other industries did. According to what I read, the area in which more than eight hundred fur manufacturers were once cloistered is now home to fewer than a hundred, gentrification at work, replacing buildings that were once warehouses with pricy condominiums. Bawdy Times Square is no longer bawdy, and Brooklyn, once looked down upon by Manhattan dwellers, has become such a fashionable borough in which to live and work that its housing is as expensive as its sister borough across the East River.

The Fur District is on the West Side of Manhattan, its vague boundaries defined by the upper Twenties and lower Thirties. I was surprised that the Chi-Chi Furs retail outlet, on West Twenty-ninth Street, wasn't located in a more upscale neighborhood considering how much fur coats cost, but maybe its owners felt that there was a certain cachet being in the midst of where many of their furs were manufactured.

On my way to Chi-Chi Furs, I passed a building from another era and was attracted to a pair of garish gargoyles on its façade, each depicting a furrier working at his trade. One featured what appeared to be a squirrel biting the furrier's finger; the other could be interpreted as a furrier skinning a mink. Or maybe he was giving the animal a spanking. No matter. I just hoped that some developer wouldn't tear down the building and destroy the gargoyles in order to erect a high-rise apartment building with rents that only wealthy foreigners could afford.

Outside the glass door of Chi-Chi Furs, I pressed a buzzer and looked up to see a closed-circuit television camera watching me. My buzz was answered with a corresponding beep, releasing the lock, and I pushed the door open and entered. I looked around and was surprised at the Spartan surroundings. Instead of a posh retail store, the space had the look of a small warehouse.

The floor was concrete painted red, and the ceiling was a maze of gray metal ducts and pipes. The furs hung haphazardly from shiny movable racks that took up the majority of the shop.

A young man emerged from the rear and greeted me.

"May I help you, madam?" he asked. He was a short, slender gentleman wearing a double-breasted midnight blue blazer, pale yellow shirt, and purple bow tie.

"Perhaps in a moment. Right now I'm just browsing," I replied, but added as an afterthought, "Philip Gould recommended you highly. I thought I'd see what might be available."

He smiled. "You're a friend of Philip's?"

To claim that I was would have stretched the truth, so I replied airily, "We certainly know each other."

"Philip Gould is one of our very best customers," the young man said, drawing out his words for emphasis. "As you can see, we have a large selection of only the finest furs."

"So I understand. His wife has a darling jacket that I admired. And I met someone else who had a fur from Chi-Chi Furs," I said. "Unfortunately, she died recently."

He adopted a sorrowful expression.

"She was a model, Rowena Roth. Do you know the name?"

"Yes, of course. I heard about her death. So tragic when someone so young passes."

"It was a shock for everyone," I said, "including, of course, Philip."

His nod was solemn. "I understand he was very close to her."

I hadn't expected such a quick confirmation of what I'd conjured as a possible scenario that the fur coat owned by Rowena Roth might have come from Philip Gould. The note that I'd taken with me from Rowena's apartment had been signed "P," and the fact that Gould's wife wore a fur from Chi-Chi Furs, which was also the label in Rowena's coat, meant that both had come from the same source. Whether that added anything to the resolution of Rowena's poisoning was pure conjecture, but I was pleased that my impromptu visit to the fur shop had reaped minor support of my speculation.

The salesman shifted gears and insisted on showing me some coats that he "just knew" had been created with me in mind. There was a full-length mink that would set me back $29,999; a snappy little sable jacket that cost *only* sixteen thousand; and if I preferred something less pricey, I could walk away with a coat made from the fur of raccoons that would cost a mere four thousand.

I, of course, did not mention my aversion to fur coats. Instead I said, "I'm afraid I'm just not in a buying mood today, but I appreciate your courtesy."

"Of course," he said, walking me to the door and joining me on the sidewalk. "Please give my best to Mr. Gould."

"I'll be happy to," I assured him. "I'm on my way to see him now."

His face assumed a knowing grin. "Mr. Gould certainly has an eye for pretty things."

"Pretty things? Pretty girls, you mean?"

"Well, I didn't say that, now, did I? But it would be more accurate to say pretty women in general."

Pretty young fashion models? Pretty women like Ann Milburn?

The salesman lowered his voice. "You tell him that whenever he says the word, we'll wrap you up in any glorious fur that takes your eye, like that elegant sable jacket you admired. You obviously have very good taste."

I didn't hint that he might have been misinterpreting my response. Instead I thanked him again and strolled away.

Because Sandy Black's studio was only six blocks away, I decided to stop in before going to the makeup demonstration at New Cosmetics. I'd navigated two of those blocks when my cell phone rang.

"Aunt Jessica, it's Grady."

"Hello, Grady," I said, suffering instant guilt at not having spent much time with him and his family. One of my primary reasons for coming to New York City was to see my nephew, his wife, and their wonderful son. "I apologize for being out of touch," I said, "but —"

"We understand," he said. "You've been busy. Have you heard about Sandy Black?"

"As a matter of fact, I'm on my way right now to his studio."

"Well, you won't find him there."

"Oh?"

"He's been arrested."

"Arrested? For what?"

"It was on the news this morning. Remember that famous model Latavia Moore who died? We talked about her at lunch."

"Yes, of course."

"Sandy Black has been taken in for questioning about her death."

"Being taken in for questioning and having been arrested are two different things, Grady."

"Maybe arrested isn't the right word. Anyway, the police are questioning him about her murder."

" 'About her *murder*'? I thought it had been determined that she died of natural causes."

"Well, they must have changed their mind. It was on WCBS this morning. They didn't have many details, but the announcer did say that an eyewitness saw him at her apartment building the night she died."

"Oh, dear, his mother, Maggie, must be frantic. I'd better call her right away. Thanks for letting me know."

"Aunt Jessica, that really wasn't why I was calling. I know that you're busy, but you'll be going back home soon and Donna and I — and Frank, too, of course — want to see you again before you leave. Are you free for dinner tonight?"

"As a matter of fact, I am," I said, "and I'd love to spend the evening with you. What time?"

"Six?"

"I'll be there."

My mood at the anticipation of spending the evening with Grady and his family was upbeat but tempered by the news that Grady had just delivered about Sandy Black. Until that moment my thinking about a model dying had been focused on Rowena Roth. I knew that Detective Kopecky was working both cases but had limited my questioning of him to Rowena.

But things had obviously changed.

The emphasis was now on the much more famous and successful model, Latavia Moore. There was no doubt that Sandy knew her. The photo of them together taken in Los Angeles proved that, as did his mother's acknowledgment of their relationship. Had he maintained contact after they moved to New York and she became a top model? If the unnamed eyewitness was correct — although eyewitnesses were notorious for being mistaken when identifying someone — Sandy could still have been seeing her.

I considered abandoning my plans to visit Sandy's studio but changed my mind. I wanted to know more about his having been taken in for questioning, and what better place to gather information than his workspace?

As might be expected, the scene at the Thirty-fifth Street studio was subdued. Sandy's investor and business manager, Jordan Verne, was on the phone in Sandy's office. Sandy's assistant and a few others on his staff worked quietly at the long table against the wall. To my relief I saw Maggie Black sitting in a yellow director's chair by the smeared windows that overlooked a blackened brick wall.

I went to her. She looked up and I could see that she'd been crying.

"Oh, Jessica. Can you believe it?" she said in a cracked voice. "They've arrested Sandy."

Correcting her semantics as I had done with Grady would accomplish nothing, so I said, "I'm sure that the police will soon realize that Sandy had nothing to do with Latavia Moore's death."

She grabbed my hand. "Jessica," she said, "you know the detective who is handling the case. Would you call him and see how Sandy is doing? I asked to visit him, but they wouldn't let me."

"Does Sandy have an attorney?" I asked.

"Only for his business, but he's not a criminal lawyer. Jordan is trying to find one now."

"I'm not sure that Detective Kopecky will talk to me about Sandy being held for questioning."

"But would you try? Please. I'll never ask you for anything again."

I didn't have any choice but to agree.

Maggie left me as I dug out my cell phone

from my purse and dialed Kopecky's number.

"Kopecky here," he answered sharply.

"It's Jessica Fletcher."

"What can I do for you?" he said coldly.

"I'm here at Sandy Black's studio with his mother. She asked that I try to check on him."

"He's fine," he said. "We stopped using rubber hoses years ago."

I looked at the phone in surprise. Had I dialed the wrong number? "May I ask what evidence you have against him?"

"He's seen on surveillance tape entering Latavia Moore's apartment building the night she died."

"But the police said her death was not suspicious."

"We don't always make our suspicions public. The fact is the autopsy showed she had been strangled."

"You certainly led me to believe that her death was from natural causes."

"I never lied to you. I told you about the petechial hemorrhages I saw."

He pronounced the word "petechial" perfectly now, and I began to wonder whether I'd completely misjudged Aaron Kopecky. Were his amorous advances all an act to solicit information from me, knowing that I would be interested in the mystery surrounding the deaths of the two models?

"Will his lawyer be given a copy of the surveillance tape to review?" I asked.

"If we decide to give him one," he said curtly. "We're only required to turn over all the evidence we have against him if he's charged with a crime. So far, we haven't charged him with anything. He's just here as a guest of the NYPD so we can hear his side of the story — and to explain what he was doing there when she was killed."

"Of course," I said, still grappling with the change in his tone toward me.

"Anything else, Mrs. Fletcher?"

"Did he say why he was at Ms. Moore's apartment building?" I asked, not expecting an answer.

I was right. Kopecky replied, "What a suspect tells us during an interrogation isn't for public consumption, Mrs. Fletcher, even for someone like you who makes a living snooping into police matters for the sake of writing a book."

Oh, my, I thought. I'd received a lecture from Mort Metzger, our sheriff back home in Cabot Cove, and now I was on the receiving end of another one from a New York City detective. I was poised to ask what had led to his stern admonition when he said,

"Anything else, Mrs. Fletcher? We're busy here."

"I'm sorry to have disturbed you, Detective Kopecky," I said, fully aware that we were on strictly formal footing. "But one more question."

"Go ahead."

"Since Mr. Black hasn't been charged with a crime, I assume that he'll be released sometime later today."

"If he is, you can ask *him* your questions. Nice talking to you."

The sound of him clicking off our connection was loud in my ear.

Maggie had been watching me from the far corner of the room. When it was obvious that our conversation was completed, she returned to where I sat.

"What did he say?" she asked.

"He said — well, he didn't say much, Maggie. Sandy hasn't been arrested or charged with anything. The police evidently have a videotape from a security camera that shows him at Latavia Moore's apartment building the night she was killed."

"She was killed? Someone murdered her?"

I nodded.

"Oh, no," she said, slowly shaking her head, her eyes pressed tightly closed.

I patted her arm and said, "It'll work out

fine," not at all certain that it would.

"Why did he go there?" Maggie moaned. "He told me he was through with her."

"I'm sure you'll have a chance to ask him that yourself," I said, "once he's released. And maybe he wasn't there," I added. "The images captured by security cameras aren't always clear."

But as I said it I had the sinking feeling that this camera hadn't lied, and that Sandy had, for whatever reasons, elected to visit Latavia Moore the night she was killed.

Since there wasn't anything I could do to help Maggie until Sandy was released, I assured her that I'd stay in touch. I didn't want to be late to the makeup manufacturing demonstration being hosted by New Cosmetics' Philip Gould. I had more questions for him.

On my way out, Jordan Verne emerged from Sandy's office.

"Did you find a criminal defense attorney for Sandy?" I asked.

He looked at me strangely, as though I'd asked an inane question.

"His mother said that's what you were doing."

"He's a fool," Verne snarled.

"Pardon?"

"I told him to stay away from Latavia, but

he wouldn't listen. She was nothing but trouble for everybody who got close to her, including Xandr, and now he's in the biggest trouble of all."

"Are you saying that he had something to do with her death?" I asked, surprised at his premature assumption that Sandy had been involved in some way with Latavia Moore's murder.

"Sure looks that way, doesn't it?" he said, and walked away.

CHAPTER TWENTY-TWO

The New Cosmetics Company Store was on the ground floor of a six-story building a block away from Capriccio's, where its CEO had hosted the party for Sandy and the other designers after their fashion show. Inside the door a young woman dressed in black wearing bright green eye shadow and yellow lipstick accosted me. "Are you here for the demonstration?"

When I indicated I was, she directed me to an elevator in the building lobby next door. I had only a moment to admire the decor of the store, with its sleek gray cabinets and counters accented with Corinthian columns topped with what I assumed were imitation marble busts of Greek goddesses. Glass and mirrors sparkled everywhere, and even though I don't wear a lot of makeup, I was intrigued to see what was on display. But I'd have to wait.

The elevator took me and a dozen other

ladies to the manufacturing floor, where Linda Gould, Philip's wife, elegantly dressed in a light blue cashmere sweater with an angora collar and matching pastel skirt, took our cards and welcomed us. She gave no indication that she'd met me before, although she brightened considerably when a woman I recognized from one of Sandy's parties as a magazine editor entered.

A young man in a white lab coat, safety goggles, and yellow steel toe guards over his sneakers ushered us down a hall and into a room with long counters with stainless steel tops. On one side folding chairs were set up in rows in front of a screen. Most of the seats were taken, but I managed to find a chair in the next-to-last row before the lights were dimmed.

The opening image on the screen showed row upon row of young models. I searched for a familiar face, but the pictures went by too quickly before ending with the question WHO WILL BE THE NEW FACE OF NEW COSMETICS?

The film, accompanied by swelling music, was a pastiche of images of merchandise the company offered, including — in addition to every kind of makeup imaginable and the tools with which to apply it — skin creams, fragrances, hair products, and elegant pouches in which to carry all your beauty supplies when you leave home. At the closing credits, there was a round of enthusiastic applause as Philip Gould came forward to explain what would happen next.

We were divided into smaller groups, each led by one of a dozen lab-coated staff members, one of whom was Ann Milburn. I maneuvered myself to follow the group Philip Gould was accompanying, even though I had been directed to join that of a young woman with blue stripes in her hair. Philip led us down the rows of stainless countertops and stopped where another woman in white was filling lipstick molds with a magenta liquid concoction, stopping every so often to hold up a color chart to ensure that her blend was a proper match.

"This is what we call the 'dirty room,' " he said. "It's where we work with color." He launched into a complicated explanation of the elements that go into a new lipstick, including aromatic oils and the minerals that give lipstick its color.

At the next table, arrayed in front of a woman mixing up the lipstick formula, were pots of colored minerals in every shade imaginable, and rows of bottles and vials. She used a metal tool to scoop up a small amount of a mixture in a bowl and deposited it on a piece of glass, using a gloved finger to spread it.

"What she's doing now is checking for grittiness," Gould explained. "We mill our own minerals until they are as smooth as talc. Any grittiness and the mixture is discarded and we start again."

Satisfied with the texture of her mixture, the woman poured her concoction into a lipstick mold and put it on a freeze table to solidify.

"The Food and Drug Administration governs everything that goes into our cosmetics," Gould said. "Of course, they're a little lax when it comes to ingredients from the Far East, which is why it's so critical for you ladies to buy American-made cosmetics. We only use the purest and safest materials in nature: beeswax, shea butter, jojoba, to name a few."

I thought of the Chinatown receipt I'd found in the garbage at Rowena's apartment. Fu zi was not a safe ingredient, yet someone there had bought it. Had one of Rowena's roommates made that purchase? Had Isla? And had she pointed a finger at Rowena to deflect suspicion from herself?

Gould wrapped up his speech with "New Cosmetics makes roughly ten thousand lipsticks a day between our New York and our Cleveland plants. That's more than three-and-a-half million lipsticks a year. Who buys them, you want to know? You do."

An assistant carrying a box of lipsticks came up beside him. Gould plucked one out and held it up. "Back in the eighties, the average woman used to own seven lipsticks. Today, she's more likely to have twenty-five or more. Surveys of our customers show the numbers run much higher." He handed each of us one of his lipsticks. "Lipsticks from New Cosmetics have greater staying power, more vivid color, and are completely natural, so if you chew it off, there will be no adverse effects. Thank you for coming today."

As we filed out of the "dirty room," each of the attendees received a coupon to use at the New Cosmetics store downstairs. I looked for Ann Milburn but didn't see her. I wanted to follow up with her about something Philip Gould had said. I lingered near the elevator, waiting until the others had left before asking one of the white-coated employees if she'd seen Miss Milburn.

"She went downstairs with the first elevator group."

I thanked her and asked where Mr. Gould's office might be. She pointed me to an open door. "But he isn't there right now," she said, smiling.

"Do you mind if I wait for him?"

"I don't mind," she said, "but I have no idea when he'll be back. He might have gone out."

"I'll take my chances," I said.

I entered Philip Gould's office and looked around. The walls were painted a pastel blue, similar to the color his wife wore that day. Someone once told me that sky blue is a color that inspires creativity. I wondered if Gould had considered that when selecting the paint for his office. Large photographs of models' faces marched across one wall, and a huge framed advertisement asked WHO WILL BE THE NEW FACE OF NEW COSMETICS?

Who indeed? I wondered. Rowena considered herself in contention for the role, and Polly Roth had said she was lobbying for Rowena to get it. How had she been lobbying? Had she been using her friendship with Gould to advocate for her niece? Was Polly just a friend or another of Gould's paramours? Claude de Molissimo had suggested that Ann Milburn was his mistress. Could the New Cosmetics' CEO have more than one? Were any of these rumors true?

"What are you doing in here?"

Philip Gould stood in the doorway to his

office, his face set in a cold expression.

"Waiting for you," I said, taking a seat in one of the chairs in front of his desk.

"And if I don't have time to talk with you? I've already given you more of my time than I have any other stranger. What makes you think you can just waltz in here and demand my attention? I'm not interested in the needs of your books, Mrs. Fletcher."

"Actually, I'm not here to ask you about Fashion Week," I said.

"Then what is it you want? Tell me and get out!"

"I wanted to ask you about this," I said, handing him the card signed "Love, P" that I'd taken from Rowena's apartment.

The bluster seemed to seep out of him.

Linda Gould stepped through the door. "Are you all right? I could hear you yelling down the hall. We still have some VIPs here."

"I'm fine," Gould said. "Close the door and I'll be with you soon."

Linda gave me a worried look but did as he'd said.

When we were alone, he sank into the chair behind his desk. "Where did you get this?"

"At Rowena's apartment. That was quite an extravagant gift you gave her."

"What do you mean?"

303

"The mink coat from Chi-Chi Furs. She referred to it as a 'parting gift.' "

"What do you want? Are you blackmailing me, too?"

"Nothing of the kind," I said. "I'm only after information."

"What kind of information?"

"Rowena Roth was poisoned."

"Oh my God, it's really true?"

"Did you have anything to do with her death?"

He shook his head slowly and when he looked up I could see that his eyes were damp. "If I tell you everything, will you swear not to tell my wife?"

"Absolutely, but I cannot promise not to tell the police if what you say sheds light on her murder."

"What do you want to know?"

"Why did you give Rowena a fur coat? Were you having an affair with her?"

"I'm bad, but I'm not a cradle robber. Even though she was accustomed to wrapping men around her finger in Ohio, New York is another story. There are a million Rowenas in this city. I think that came as something of a shock to her."

"What came as a shock?"

"That she wasn't the most beautiful, just one of many beautiful models trying to make it in New York. Without the power she was accustomed to, she looked for other means to get her way."

"I'm not sure I understand what you're saying."

"Rowena and her aunt Polly had been pressing me to pick her as the new face of our company. I'd already selected another model, but I didn't say anything at first. Then Rowena caught me with, well, let me just say with a friend, and she threatened to go to my wife, Linda, if I didn't name her as the new face."

"So she tried to blackmail you?"

He nodded.

"But you didn't give in."

"This is business. It's bad enough to be manipulated in your private life. I wasn't about to let her direct my business decisions. She kept pressuring me until I finally told her I'd already chosen Isla Banning as the new face, and it was too late to change my mind. Millions have been invested. All our marketing materials are set to launch as soon as the announcement is made."

"So you gave her the coat as a consolation prize?"

"You could say that." He tossed the card on his desk. "I didn't tell Polly. She was having a hard enough time trying to contain

Rowena. And then the kid drops dead. I swear to you I had nothing to do with her death, but if I'm being honest with myself, I have to admit that I felt a sense of relief."

"And you didn't attempt to get the coat back?"

He waved a hand as if dismissing the idea. "What am I going to do with it? I don't care what happens to the coat. If Polly ends up with it, good for her."

"Does Isla know she's going to be named the new face of New Cosmetics?"

"Sure. She's in all the new marketing materials. We've been shooting ads for a month. But we swore her to secrecy. She had to sign a nondisclosure agreement that threatens financial penalties and to cancel her contract if she breaks her promise."

I wondered if Isla had truly been able to hold back such a delicious secret, especially in the face of an antagonistic roommate with her eye on the same prize. "Just out of curiosity, why didn't you pick Rowena for the role?"

He heaved a sigh, and held up his index finger. "First, she was too headstrong. We need someone on the team who wants it so much she'll accommodate our calendar and all our needs. Rowena was more accustomed to making demands on everyone around her. Second, she was too young and we'd have to go through hoops to complete all the paperwork that hiring an underage model requires. Isla has a little mileage on her. She doesn't know we know that, but it suits our purposes. The women who use New Cosmetics are all ages, not just teenagers. And third, Rowena wanted to be in competition with us. She was always bragging that her eye shadow, her lipsticks were every bit as good as ours. She even posted a video to that effect on YouTube. Why would I want a young woman to represent my company who thinks she can make the same products in her kitchen? And then she tried to blackmail me. After that, her fate was sealed. She screwed herself out of the job in every way possible."

"You'll tell the police all this if they question you again?"

"If I have to. Has any of this been helpful to you?"

"Very much so. But before I leave, I was hoping to speak with Ann Milburn."

Gould held up a hand. "What do you need with Ann?" he asked.

I smiled. "My questions for her have nothing to do with you."

"You're sure?"

I held up my hand. "Scout's honor!" I said.

Gould paged Ann Milburn and two minutes later there was a knock on the door.

"Mrs. Fletcher has a few questions for you, Ann." He looked at me. "Do you mind if I sit in?"

"Not at all," I said.

Ann Milburn gingerly lowered herself into the chair next to mine. "What's this about?"

"It's about Rowena Roth," I answered.

"Don't look at me. I didn't have anything to do with her dying."

"I don't think you meant to," I said, "but you may have inadvertently contributed to her death."

She glanced nervously at Gould. "How did I do that?"

"Prior to the fashion show, Rowena presented you with a lipstick she had made for her roommate Isla, but Isla rejected it. Do you remember?"

"Yes. I was surprised. It was the first nice gesture I'd seen Rowena offer either of her roommates. Usually, she talked disparagingly about them. But she told me she'd made it especially for Isla, and would I surprise her with it? I guess you were there when Isla rejected the gift."

Gould sat up straight in his chair and

glared at her. "And you would have used one of that kid's homemade concoctions on one of our models before a show featuring New Cosmetics? What were you thinking?"

"Philip, it was the same color as the lipstick Xandr Ebon had selected for his models, and I was trying to make nice to her. You know how she was. She was ready to make trouble any time she didn't get her way. I figured no one would know, and maybe she'd leave you alone."

Gould sat back with a heavy sigh. "I wish you hadn't done that."

"Well, it's done and what's the harm anyway?"

"The harm is —"

"Excuse me," I said, trying to interrupt their argument. "Miss Milburn, do you still have the lipsticks that you used on Xandr Ebon's models in the show?"

She turned back to me. "I . . . I don't know. I guess so. I had them in the pocket of my pink smock."

"And where is that pink smock now?"

She looked around in confusion. "I'm not sure. I haven't worn it since then. We wear white lab coats in the manufacturing rooms here. I think it should be hanging in my office on the back of the door."

"Would it be possible to see it?" I asked.

"I think so," Gould said. He picked up the phone and dialed a number. "Caroline, would you please bring me the pink smock that's hanging on the back of the door in Ann Milburn's office?"

We sat quietly until there was a knock on the door, and a young woman entered carrying a hanger holding the pink smock Ann Milburn had worn the morning of the fashion show.

The makeup artist took the hanger and patted the pockets of her smock. She pulled out two tubes of lipstick and held them up. "See, they're basically the same color. This one has an *NC* on it for New Cosmetics, and Rowena copied our style by putting *RR* on hers."

"May I see?" Gould asked.

"Don't touch them," I said.

Milburn's faced paled. "I'm touching them."

"They already have your fingerprints on them," I said. I dug a plastic bag from my purse and held it open in front of her. "Please drop them in here."

"What is this about, Mrs. Fletcher? You're very dramatic, but you're scaring me."

"There's nothing to be scared of," I told her, "unless you applied the lipstick to yourself."

Gould pounded his desk with his fist. "Will you tell me what's going on? Unlike you, I'm not a fan of mysteries."

I looked at Gould. "I believe Rowena was attempting to poison her roommate Isla to eliminate her as a competitor for the position as your company's new face. She even said to you at the fashion show that there was still time for you to choose her. Do you recall her saying that?"

"I do, and I thought that a mink coat was all she was going to squeeze out of me, no matter what she did."

Ann Milburn groaned. "Oh, Philip, did you really try to buy her off?"

"Never mind. It's water under the bridge."

"Miss Milburn, which of these lipsticks did you use on Rowena?" I held up the bag for her to see.

"I'm not sure. I just pulled out whatever was in my pocket and put it on her."

"We need to call the detective who's in charge of Rowena's case. If I'm not mistaken, you used Rowena's own lipstick on her. It was the one she'd made for Isla, and if she'd included a Chinese ingredient, it made the lipstick highly poisonous."

"Do you mean I killed her?"

"Clearly not intentionally," I said. "You had no idea what ingredients Rowena used

311

in her experiments making lipsticks. But she ended up dying from aconite poisoning, and I found a receipt for aconite in the girls' apartment that had been purchased at an apothecary in Chinatown."

Chapter Twenty-Three

Aaron Kopecky was not happy to see me when he and a colleague arrived at New Cosmetics, but he listened carefully to my theory and pocketed the two lipsticks from Ann Milburn's smock.

The makeup artist, rattled that she might have unknowingly applied poisonous lipstick to a child, eagerly gave Kopecky a blow-by-blow description of all the makeup plans she had designed for the show and recalled for him each conversation she'd had with the models.

I was sure it was Rowena who had purchased the aconite, but I couldn't prove it, and until that loose end was confirmed we didn't have a solution to the seventeen-year-old's untimely death. Rowena had been an annoyance to her roommates, but was that enough of a reason for murder? I didn't think so. Isla had coveted Rowena's fur coat. Would she have killed for it? I doubted it.

Not with a pending boon to her income as the new face of New Cosmetics. Instead I was betting that Rowena thought she could eliminate her chief competition for that prize. For me that was enough of a motive in the mind of a spoiled young woman accustomed to getting her way.

When Kopecky had finished interviewing Ann Milburn, I gave him the receipt I still held from the Chinese apothecary.

"You found this in the garbage?"

"Yes, when I pulled out the oatmeal bag."

"You already told me about this."

"Yes, but I never went to the store to ask about who bought it," I said, also offering him Rowena's model card that Maggie had given me at the fashion show.

"The oatmeal bag was a dead end," he said, looking at the photographs of the beautiful young model and shaking his head.

"I can't promise you this won't be as well," I said, "but I'm hoping that someone at the herbal remedies shop will recognize the young woman who'd purchased the fu zi, which is another name for aconite root."

"And if they don't?"

I shrugged. "It's my best guess at the moment."

"I have to say I'm not sure I trust your best guesses."

"I'm sorry you feel that way."

"I'll have it checked out this afternoon." He tucked Rowena's card and the receipt in a plastic evidence bag and handed them off to his colleague. "By the way, we let your buddy go — for the moment. He's swearing up and down that he didn't kill his old girlfriend, but I don't believe him. We had to release him because of lack of evidence aside from the surveillance tape showing him at her apartment building around the time she died. But he's still number one on my list."

Kopecky walked me to the elevator.

"Where are you headed, Mrs. Fletcher?" he asked, making certain I knew that we were still on formal, perhaps even adversarial ground.

"Why are you interested?" I asked.

"Just curious."

"If you must know," I said, "I'd like to see Sandy Black now that he's been released."

"What do you think you can accomplish by seeing him? He'll just tell you the same lies he told us."

"He may very well tell me the same story he's told you, Detective Kopecky, but I'd prefer to be the judge of his honesty."

"Suit yourself."

He turned to walk away but stopped and

retraced his steps to me. "You know, Mrs. Fletcher, I'm not some bumbling cop you like to write about in your books."

"Detective Kopecky," I said, struggling not to allow my ire to surface, "did you ever see the movie *Cool Hand Luke*?"

"Yeah, maybe years ago."

"There's a famous line from that film, 'What we've got here is a failure to communicate.' Unfortunately, that seems to be true of you and me. One, I've never considered you a 'bumbling cop.' Two, I don't portray police officers in my books as 'bumbling cops.' And three, it has never been my intention to involve myself in the cases you're handling. May I remind you that you *offered* to tell me about those cases and *invited* my input? All I've wanted to do is to be helpful to you. Now please excuse me. I'm going to see your number-one suspect to provide whatever assistance I can."

I left him standing in the New Cosmetics office, reached the street, walked half a block, and stopped to take a deep breath. As much as I dislike confrontations of any sort, I was glad that we'd had ours. The last thing I wanted was to alienate a New York City detective, especially one whom I'd gotten to know on a relatively personal basis —

which was part of the problem, I suppose. When I made it clear that I wasn't interested in him as a potential suitor, his ego was wounded, which probably accounted for his sudden frostiness. But that was his problem; he would just have to thaw out.

In the meantime I wanted to hear Sandy Black's side of the story, assuming he was willing to entrust me with the information. Based on previous encounters with the temperamental designer, it could go either way. I hailed a taxi and after long traffic delays arrived at his building. I rode the creaky elevator to his floor and entered his studio, where, to my delight, his mother came directly to me, beaming.

"You've heard," she said, giving me a hug. "Sandy's been released by the police."

"Yes, I heard."

"Your detective friend told you?"

"As a matter of fact, he did. I've just left him at —"

Sandy bounded from his office and opened his arms to me. "Jessica," he said. "I'm so grateful that you're here."

I accepted his embrace and said, "And I'm glad to see you, Sandy. Detective Kopecky told me that you'd been released."

He shook his head sadly. "They treated me as though they've already decided that I

317

killed Latavia. Next they'll say I killed Rowena Roth, too."

"What an awful thing to go through," his mother said, rubbing her son's back.

"Cut it out, Mom," he said, shrugging off her hand. He turned to me. "You always help people wrongly accused, Jessica. Will you help me? I don't want to see the inside of that police station again." He shuddered dramatically. "It's a lot worse than what you see on TV."

I thought of Kopecky's sarcastic comment that the police long ago stopped using rubber hoses in their interrogations. Sandy had a tendency to dramatize things most people would allow to slide off their shoulders — not that I thought being interviewed by the police was a pleasant experience. But I withheld my opinion that his recent confrontation with the detectives was unlikely to be his last. They were probably busy investigating every detail they could unearth about his life here in New York and in California.

"If I'm to help you in any way, I'll need to hear from you about your questioning, Sandy," I said. "That is, if you don't mind reliving it."

"I guess I don't mind," he said, "but let's go in my office. I don't want the world to know my business."

I resisted mentioning the fact that his visit to police headquarters had already been on the news. Instead I followed Sandy into his cramped office, where he picked up bolts of material that had been left on both guest chairs along with a large pair of shears used for cutting the fabric.

"Watch out for that glass bowl," his mother said as he set down the fabric. "Your grandmother brought that from Italy."

"Please, Mom. I know what I'm doing."

"I understand that you were seen on the building's surveillance camera about the time Latavia Moore was killed," I said to steer the conversation away from an impending confrontation between mother and son.

He nodded.

"You were there?" his mother said.

Another nod accompanied by "She asked me to come. I wouldn't have gone there otherwise."

"She called you?" I asked.

"No. She sent me a text message."

"When?"

"The same day as my show. That afternoon."

"And she was killed that afternoon," I said. "Did the police indicate a time of death for her?"

He shook his head. "No, they said it was around the time that I received the text message."

"How could she send you a message after she was dead?" his mother asked.

Sandy replied, "The police say that she sent it *before* she died, and that I responded to it and killed her."

I thought before asking, "Do you have a copy of her text message?"

"No," he said. "The police confiscated my cell phone. I showed them the message and they took it from me."

"They have to get a warrant if they're going to use it as evidence," I said.

"Well, they kept my phone anyway. They gave it to some tech guy when I arrived, and they questioned me about the message while I was in their interrogation room."

"What did she say that caused you to go there?" I asked. "Was she in some sort of trouble?"

"I guess. She wasn't specific," Sandy said. "It was a short message, just that it was important — no, she said it was *crucial* that she see me right away. That was the word that she used. *Crucial!*" He paused, his face scrunched up in thought. "I can almost remember it verbatim," he said. " 'I'm in a real mess and need to see you right away.

It's crucial that you come to my apartment. Please, Xandr, come now!' "

I chewed on what he'd said before continuing. "Had you been in touch with her lately?" I asked.

"No. That was the funny part. I hadn't seen her since she came to New York and became a big-time model, even though she was divorced by then. I figured she didn't want to relive bad memories."

"You never even tried to see her?"

He glanced quickly at his mother.

"Sandy, I need to know everything," I said.

"I, um, I did try to see her at first. I went to her building a couple of times, but she wouldn't let me in."

"Oh, Sandy," I heard Maggie whisper.

"Yeah, yeah. I know, Mom. But I didn't see her. It was over. She made her point. That's why I was so surprised to get a text from her."

"Did you ever use the name Xandr Ebon when you were in California?" I asked.

"No. I wanted a fresh start in New York, new name, new direction. But — wait a minute," he said, coming forward in his chair. "I see what you're getting at, Jessica. She called me Xandr in her text message. Why would she call me that?"

Maggie looked at me quizzically. "Why

wouldn't she call him Xandr?"

"She hated the name," Sandy said. "Told me it was stupid, that I should've stuck with my real name."

"She must have thought you'd pay more attention if she called you by your new professional name," Maggie said.

"Or maybe she didn't send that text message, at all," I said. "Maybe someone else used her cell phone to lure you to her building to frame you."

It was his mother's turn to sit forward and become animated. "Like the killer," she offered. "You mean that whoever killed her sent Sandy that message to entice him to go there so he would become the suspect?"

"It's certainly a possibility," I said. "It had to be someone who was pretty sure you would respond to a message from Latavia. What happened when you arrived at her building, Sandy?"

"Nothing. The doorman rang her apartment but didn't get an answer. He let me go up and knock on her door, but she didn't respond to that either. There was nothing more I could do, so I left."

"And left your image on the building's surveillance tape," I said.

"And fingerprints on her doorbell," Sandy added with a sigh. "I'm being set up —

again. It's the story of my life when it comes to Latavia Moore."

"It looks that way," I said.

"Who would do such a thing?" Maggie asked.

"That's for the police to find out," I said. "Did Detective Kopecky show you the entire surveillance tape from that afternoon?"

"No. He just showed me the section with me on it. It was a really clear tape. No doubt it was me. And anyway, I admitted that I was there, but I never saw her. I swear it, Jessica."

"I believe you," I said. "Did he happen to say that he'd reviewed earlier portions of the tape?"

"No," Sandy said wearily. "All he said when I was leaving was that he knew that I'd killed her and that he'd prove it if it was the last thing he did." He looked at his mother. "Was Jordan able to find me a lawyer?"

"Excuse me," I said.

I went into the studio portion of the space, pulled out my cell phone, and dialed Kopecky's cell number.

"Kopecky here," he answered.

"It's Jessica Fletcher," I said. "I'm with

Sandy Black and his mother at Sandy's studio."

"If he tells you we roughed him up, he's lying."

"He hasn't said anything of the kind. I would like to bring Sandy back to headquarters and view the surveillance tape for the hours prior to his arriving at the building."

"Why?"

I'd prepared my answer to that potential question. "It's possible," I said, "that either he or I would recognize someone who'd arrived ahead of him."

"So he's still sticking to his story that he never saw her that day."

"That's correct. And you can't have found his fingerprints anywhere inside her apartment, because he wasn't there."

"So he says."

"He can get a lawyer and subpoena the tape, but you could save us all a lot of money and bother if you'd let us view the tape with you. After all, Sandy knows a lot of people involved in the fashion world, people Latavia Moore would have known, and I've gotten to meet many of them, too. I'm not asking to review it in its entirety, just for, let's say, three hours prior to when Sandy is captured on the tape."

His silence said to me that he was about

to turn down my request. But, to my surprise, he said, "All right, Mrs. Fletcher. You and your fashion designer buddy come here and I'll arrange for the tape to be shown. That satisfy you?"

"Yes, it does, Detective. Thank you very much."

"Be here in a half hour." He gave me the address.

I announced to Sandy and his mother the gist of my conversation with Kopecky. At first Sandy balked. "I'm not going back there," he said. "They might change their mind and lock me up."

"Sandy, they let you go because the evidence they have is circumstantial. I know that this is a long shot, but there may be someone earlier on the tape that you recognize. Isn't it at least worth trying?"

"Jessica is right," Maggie said.

"You'll come with me?" Sandy asked her.

I shook my head. "I don't want to test Detective Kopecky's patience," I said. "Right now he's doing me a favor — and I know it. Why don't you wait here, Maggie? We'll only be a few hours at headquarters, and we'll call you as soon as we leave."

"If you think it best," she said.

"Come on, Sandy," I said. "Let's give it a try. Let's see if we can catch a killer."

Chapter Twenty-Four

Kopecky was waiting for us when we arrived.

"I don't know why I agreed to this," the detective said, glaring at Sandy.

"I'm just pleased and grateful that you did," I said.

He led us to an interrogation room equipped with a video recorder and playback machine. Sandy and I sat at the end of the table; Kopecky took a chair as far removed from us as possible.

"How far back you want to go?" he asked.

I glanced at Sandy before replying. "Can we start at noon?" I suggested. "Sandy has an alibi for that time. He was still at the catering house where the fashion show took place. In fact, he was there for at least an hour or more afterward. You can confirm that yourself, Detective Kopecky. You were there as well. But let's look at the tape starting at noon."

"Suit yourself. I've got other things to do." Kopecky conferred with the officer who would work the equipment and left. "Ready?" the officer asked.

"Yes," I said.

He dimmed the lights and reversed the tape. The numbers rapidly streaming backward on the bottom indicated the time that the tape had been made. There were many figures going in and out of the building, but no one was recognizable at that speed. The officer stopped rewinding when the numbers neared noon, and then began the tape again, going forward at a faster speed than real time, but not so fast that we couldn't get a clear picture of the doorman opening the building's glass front door for visitors, and for people who entered or exited when the doorman was on a break or helping someone out of a taxi. The camera had been situated above the small waiting area in front of the elevators in the lobby, and angled back toward the entrance. Sandy and I sat transfixed by the fleeting images that came and went. At times there was a sizable lull. Then myriad people could be seen waiting for the elevator, tenants, deliverymen, contractors, and members of the building staff. It became boring; we had to fight to maintain vigilance as the tape ran, the fleeting numbers indicating the passage of time.

"What time were you seen on the tape?" I asked Sandy sotto voce.

"About an hour and a half from now," he said, his eyes glued to the screen.

I was beginning to lose faith in the exercise. There hadn't been a single face that he or I recognized; everyone on the tape was a stranger to us.

Until . . .

I turned to the officer. "Would you please stop the tape and rewind it back a few minutes?"

He did as I'd asked.

"It's him!" Sandy blurted, almost elevating from his seat.

"Yes, it is," I said.

The man in the lobby was certainly well-known to Sandy, and was recognizable to me despite my having met him only a few times.

The policeman paused the tape so we could confirm his identity. There was no doubt. The man waiting for the elevator in Latavia Moore's building was Jordan Verne.

CHAPTER TWENTY-FIVE

"I'm sure that Detective Kopecky will want to see this," I told the officer who had frozen the video on the section in which Jordan Verne's face was clearly identifiable. Kopecky came into the room a few minutes later.

"Who's he?" he asked, looking at the screen.

"His name's Jordan Verne," Sandy said. "He's my financial backer and business manager."

Kopecky noted the time at the bottom of the video. "That's close to an hour before you show up," he said. "Did you watch it long enough to see when he left?"

"Yes," I answered. "We watched all the way until Sandy arrives, in case there was anyone else we might recognize. The tape shows Verne exiting the building less than thirty minutes before Sandy comes in."

Kopecky nodded slowly. "It could fit into

the approximate time of death," he murmured to himself.

"Had rigor mortis set in by the time her body was discovered later on?" I asked, knowing that coroners use that sign to estimate a time of death.

"Let's leave the forensics to the medical examiner, shall we?" Kopecky shot back. He turned to Sandy. "So this Verne character knew the deceased?"

"That's right," Sandy said. "From Los Angeles. He also knew her ex-husband, a sleazeball who called himself a talent agent."

"Let's stick to the facts without any characterization," Kopecky said.

Sandy sighed. "Yes, Jordan knows, um, knew, Latavia very well."

"Your mother told me that Jordan Verne was responsible for her success as a model in New York," I said. "Do you agree?"

"Yeah, he was. Of course she worked it good. Never saw a camera she didn't like or an editor she wouldn't kiss up to — and more. Jordan pulled a lot of strings to get her cover work, hired press agents to place stories about her. She was unbelievably ambitious, but he had the connections to make her into a supermodel. That's why I signed with him for my work, signed away my future earnings, signed away my soul. I figured if he could make her into a star in such a short time, he'd do wonders for me."

"And has he?" I asked.

"Not yet, but he says I haven't given him a year yet." Sandy snorted. "It was a bargain with the devil. I can see that now. And look at this — now the guy sets me up to take the rap for his crime. If I give him a year, he'll probably have me behind bars for life."

"Let's not get carried away here," Kopecky said.

Kopecky looked at me. "You know this guy Verne, Mrs. Fletcher?"

"I've met him a few times."

"He's here in New York?"

"He was as of this morning," Sandy said. "He lives in L.A."

Sandy gave the detective the name of the hotel at which Verne was staying.

"I'll have Mr. Verne picked up for questioning," Kopecky said to Sandy, "but that doesn't get you off the hook. I'm keeping my options open. You were at the scene where a model — a former married girlfriend of yours, I come to find out — was murdered."

I knew Kopecky and his team would have been looking into Sandy's background. His "no contest" plea in the theft of the costumes in Hollywood would have raised a lot of red flags for the police. But at least Kopecky was willing to open his mind and consider another suspect.

"Thanks for the tip." He directed the comment at me.

I held my tongue. He should have had someone intimately familiar with individuals involved in the fashion industry screen the video in search of recognizable faces. And for all I knew, maybe he had. And maybe other viewers were not familiar with Latavia Moore's manager from California. But the important thing was that Sandy and I had been given the opportunity to see the video and could identify Jordan Verne. That didn't mean, of course, that Verne had anything to do with his client's murder, but his presence in her apartment building was enough, at least, to expand the field of persons of interest.

As we were about to leave, Sandy said to Kopecky, "I asked you a question when you were interrogating me earlier today, but you wouldn't answer."

"Yeah? What was that?"

"I asked if you'd found my fingerprints in Latavia's apartment."

Kopecky looked at me.

"Sounds like a fair question," I said as sweetly as possible.

"No, your prints weren't inside her apartment, Black. That's why we let you go. We did find them on her door, however."

"I told you they would be there," Sandy said, smiling, trying out his charm on Kopecky. But the detective wasn't letting himself be won over.

"Prints or no prints don't exonerate you, Black. Killers sometimes wear gloves or wipe their prints off anything they touched."

"But you did find some other prints there, I assume," I said, "someone other than Latavia's herself."

"That's right, Mrs. Fletcher, unidentified prints."

"When you catch up with Mr. Verne, I assume you'll check his prints against those that you found in the apartment."

The moment I said it I knew that I'd overstepped my bounds, and expected an angry response from the detective. But I needn't have worried. He smiled for the first time since we'd arrived and said in a high voice, "Gee, I hadn't thought of that — Jessica — but I'll make a note to myself to see that it's done." He was being facetious, of course, but at least he hadn't snapped at me, which I would have deserved.

Sandy and I left headquarters and took a taxi back to his studio.

"He called you Jessica," he said as we neared our destination, "not Mrs. Fletcher."

"Detective Aaron Kopecky is a good and decent man, Sandy," I said, "but I'm afraid that I rubbed him the wrong way somewhere along the line. Our relationship was pleasant until that happened, and I'm hoping to get it back on a friendlier basis."

As we rode the creaky elevator to Sandy's floor, he said, "I can't tell you how much better I'm feeling, Jessica. You just lifted an enormous weight from my shoulders."

"That's good to hear, Sandy, but it's not over yet. I still think you should consult with a criminal attorney for your own peace of mind. But otherwise, let's let the police do the job they're trained for. I trust them not to railroad an innocent man."

"How about you, me, and my mom have dinner together tonight?"

"I'd love to, but I promised to have dinner with my nephew and his wife and son. It's the last chance I'll have to see them before heading home to Maine."

The door to the studio was closed when we arrived. Sandy tried it and it opened.

"We usually leave the door open if we're working," he commented as we entered the empty studio. "Leaving it unlocked if no one is here is a bad idea. I wonder where

334

my mother went."

His question was answered the next moment. Maggie was nowhere to be seen — but when we looked in Sandy's office, we found Jordan Verne with his feet up on the desk.

"Hey, Jordan," Sandy said, "didn't expect you to be here. Where's my mom and my staff?"

"I told your staff to take the rest of the day off. I sent your mother out to get us some coffee."

"Why would you send the staff home?" Sandy asked.

"Hey, I'm not footing the bill for salaries if you're going off to the clink."

"Just a minute," I said. "Aren't you presuming a great deal?"

"Oh, right, you're Jessica Fletcher. You and Xandr been out on the town?"

"As a matter of fact, we've been at police headquarters."

"Yeah, I knew that they brought you in for questioning, Xandr," he said, "something about Latavia Moore's death."

"Her *murder*, you mean," Sandy said.

"Was it murder?" Verne's laugh was forced. "I'm not surprised," he said. "Lots of people hated her, and after what she did to you in California, I'm sure you were first in line among those who wanted to see her dead."

"Mr. Verne," I said, "I think you ought to know that the police would like to interview you about Ms. Moore's — death."

"Me? Why would they want to interview me?"

I waited for Sandy to explain, but he was staring at Verne with a frown. When he didn't say anything, I said, "We've just come from viewing a surveillance tape recorded at Ms. Moore's apartment building the day she died."

"Yeah? Why would that interest me?"

"You were on that tape."

"Was I?"

"Yes, we saw you."

"Must be a mistake. Those video cameras are lousy. You can never recognize who's in them."

"I'm not sure I agree," I said, "but you can make that point with Detective Kopecky when he invites you downtown. He said he and his people were going to your hotel, but since you're here, I'll call and have him swing by the studio." I pulled my cell phone from my bag and punched in Kopecky's number. Verne wrenched the phone from my hand and threw it in the corner.

"What are you up to?" Sandy asked. He

lunged for Verne, who grabbed the heavy glass bowl from the desk and swung it viciously, catching Sandy in the side of the head. He let out a pained groan as he slumped to the floor, blood from the gash running down his cheek.

I bent down. "Sandy, are you okay?" I looked up at Verne. "I don't know what you think you can accomplish by attacking him. The police are already looking for you. If they don't find you at the hotel, they'll check the airports, and it wouldn't surprise me if they showed up here as well."

"Shut up!" Verne snapped. He lifted the glass bowl to strike again, but I kicked his shin. He dropped the bowl and it shattered when it hit the floor. He stumbled backward and grabbed the pair of giant shears Sandy used to cut his fabrics. "Get back," he yelled.

Sandy continued to moan, his hand pressed against his wound, but Verne warned me away. "Leave him," he said, raising the shears and waving it in front of my face.

I drew deep breaths to calm myself, my eyes fixed on Verne and the shears he wielded. "You know what you're doing now is convincing me that you did, indeed, murder Latavia Moore," I said, backing through the office door, trying to put some distance between Verne and me and to get him away from Sandy. "An innocent man wouldn't threaten someone with a weapon."

"And a smart woman wouldn't make the kinds of remarks that encourage violence," he said, following me into the studio, keeping the shears pointed at my chest.

"What do you plan to do?" I moved toward the windows and stepped behind the large worktable, using a chair to keep him a safe distance from me. "A smart man like you must have made plans to get away."

"I'm getting out of here all right," he said, grabbing the chair away and tossing it across the room. He continued to make slashing movements over the table while I pulled one chair after another in front of me to keep my distance from him.

He was wound spring-tight; his eyes darted around the room in search of a way to magically escape. But there was no magic exit, not with Sandy in the office and me there, and that meant — and the thought made me shudder — that he would have to dispose of us if he had any chance of bolting from the studio and enjoying freedom.

I had started to ask him how he thought he could possibly evade the police when out of the corner of my eye I saw Sandy slumped against the wall. I kept my gaze on Verne and continued to pepper him with questions, hoping to rivet his attention on me so as not to notice the injured man sliding along the wall in the direction of the door. Sandy had closed it behind us, but it hadn't latched. It was open a few inches.

Verne stabbed at me, but I leaped out of his way. "Enough games, Jessica Fletcher. Play your cards right and I'll make your death swift and painless. Wouldn't you prefer that?"

I danced back and forth behind the table. "You have to answer my questions first."

"I don't have to do anything," he said, holding the shears above his head like a knife.

"Why did you kill Latavia Moore?" I shouted. "You must have had a good reason."

"She asked for it," he replied, "her and that swindling husband of hers."

"What does *he* have to do with her? I thought they were divorced."

"He still pulls the strings."

"Were you and her husband in business together?" I asked, noting that Sandy had almost reached the door.

"He cut me out, the dirtbag," Verne said. He'd calmed considerably, his body language no longer taut, his eyes now fixed solely on me. "I made Latavia into a big success and then her husband convinces her to drop me. Oh, no! You're not firing me, buddy." He smacked the side of the shears against his palm. "He's the one who should have died. I'll get him when I get back to L.A., after I take care of you, that is." He was composed now, his voice cold.

"You must have felt very upset when Latavia fired you," I said, anxious to establish rapport with him.

"Upset? Yeah, that's putting it mildly. Mad as hell, too."

"Didn't you know Latavia's husband was not to be trusted?" I said. "He set up Sandy Black on the charge that he'd stolen costumes from the studio where he worked."

"Where do you think I got the idea? That's right — poor, dumb Sandy Black, the patsy. I saved him, persuaded him to leave L.A. and become a designer in New York. Even gave him his new name. Without me, Xandr Ebon would be nowhere."

And not bound to an ironclad contract for the rest of his life.

Sandy had reached the door. While I was attempting to distract Verne, Sandy silently opened the door wide enough to slip through it and disappeared into the hallway.

But the moment he was gone, Verne turned and saw the trail of blood on the floor that led to the door. He cursed as he turned from me and ran to the door, out into the corridor. As he did I acted on pure instinct. I raced to the door, put my shoulder against it, and tried to shut it behind him. But an opposite force slammed the door against the wall and I tumbled backward, falling to the floor, scrambling out of the way, trying desperately to escape the deadly shears that were certain to be biting into my body any second. I put my arm up in defense. Someone grabbed my wrist and hauled me to my feet.

"Jessica! Are you okay? Lady, you scared the life out of me."

Detective Kopecky shook me by the shoulders.

"Did you see him? Jordan Verne, the man we saw in the surveillance tape. He just ran out of here. He injured Sandy and threatened to kill us both. He murdered Latavia Moore. He admitted to it."

"Yeah, yeah, yeah. Calm down. We got him. Ran right into our arms."

"But Sandy. He's terribly injured."

"No worries. The EMTs are on the way for your designer buddy. He's got a hard head. He's going to be fine. His mother is comforting him as we speak."

I took a deep breath and ran my shaking fingers through my hair. My heart was racing.

Kopecky grabbed one of the chairs Verne had thrown out of the way and insisted I sit down.

I sank into it gratefully, not sure my knees would stop knocking any time soon. "How did you know to come? Did Sandy call you?"

"No, you did. But then when you didn't come on the line and I heard a big crash, I figured something was wrong and hotfooted it over here, just in time to catch a wild-eyed guy running at me holding the biggest pair of scissors I ever saw. How does anyone use those things anyway?"

I started to giggle. Maggie and Sandy who stood in the doorway started laughing, too.

"What? What?" Kopecky scratched his head. "What did I say that's so funny?"

When I was able to get my adrenaline-fired giggles under control, I wiped away tears of relief and smiled at Sandy. "Are you really all right?"

"My head hurts," he replied, "but I think I'll live, thanks to you. If you hadn't lured him away from me, I think he'd have tried to finish me off with that bowl."

"Was that the bowl your grandmother bought in Italy?" Maggie asked.

Sandy nodded until he realized the movement made his head ache. "Sorry, Mom. We'll have to take a trip there to replace it."

"Oh, no. I never liked that bowl anyway."

The EMTs had arrived and Kopecky righted two more chairs so Sandy and Maggie could sit while they examined Sandy's head wound.

"His financial manager was a whack job in all senses of the word," Kopecky told me with a wry smile. "What was he, some sort of psychopath?"

"I'm not a psychiatrist —" I started to say.

"No? I thought you were an expert on everything."

I playfully slapped at him. "And you're not a psychiatrist, but that's probably an apt description of him."

"Ah, but the real question is, are you hungry? After we book this bozo, we should go out and celebrate. I know this great place —"

"I know you're not going to believe this."

"But you're already busy for dinner."

"Grady and Donna invited me to their home. It's my last night in New York."

"And family comes first."

"Yes, it does."

CHAPTER TWENTY-SIX

My week in Manhattan had come to an end — thank goodness.

Being able to spend time with Grady and his family had been my treat to myself, as limited as it was, and I wish I'd found more opportunities to enjoy it. The problem was that murder had intruded itself into what was to have been a leisurely visit to the Big Apple, soaking up the glamour of New York City's fabled Fashion Week.

My involvement with Detective Aaron Kopecky had introduced a complication I hadn't anticipated. Not that I deliberately set out to befriend him, nor had it been my intention, at least initially, to involve myself in his investigations into the deaths of the teenage model Rowena Roth and super-model Latavia Moore. But I would be less than honest not to admit that once my inquisitive genes were awakened, I was an active participant in trying to unravel what had happened to these two beautiful young women. I suppose you could say that our relationship, as brief as it was, defined a perfect negotiation — I got from him the opportunity to contribute to two NYPD homicide cases, and he got from me certain help in fulfilling his responsibilities. Both sides came out ahead, although his apparent personal interest in me had added an unwelcome dimension that I'm afraid I hadn't handled with much aplomb.

The detective had hoped to establish a romantic bond with me. When I made it clear that I wasn't interested (but flattered perhaps), he'd reacted the way many people do. He was hurt, and put up a defensive shield to avoid further injury to his psyche. But once the pressure of solving the deaths of the two models had abated, he seemed to readily accept that I would not be the woman to replace his beloved wife, Mary, and we could enjoy each other's company without that element muddling our relationship.

My dinner with Grady, Donna, and their son, Frank, was on my final night in Manhattan. Donna greeted me when I arrived and excused herself to finish up preparations in the kitchen.

Grady handed me a glass of wine and

settled me in a lounge chair on their small terrace. "Donna needs my help in the kitchen, Aunt Jess. I'll be back in a few minutes. Can I get you anything?"

"Do you happen to have today's paper? I never got a chance to buy one."

"Only the *New York Post.* I left the *Times* in the office," he said, popping inside and returning with a copy of the tabloid.

I took the paper and thanked him. A headline on the front page immediately caught my eye: "Scalpel to the Stars Cut Down to Size." The article, by Steven Crowell, revealed that celebrity cosmetic surgeon Dr. Edmund Sproles was under investigation by medical authorities for doing unnecessary procedures on underage models, and selling them experimental substances as legitimate medicines. The piece went on to say that Dr. Sproles was the target of myriad malpractice suits from young women who broke out in rashes from his custom creams, prompting officials to launch an examination into his overall practices and procedures.

"Isn't that story something?" Donna said, sliding into a chair next to mine. "That guy was mixing poisonous plants into concoctions he used on his patients." She gave a shiver.

"You can find charlatans everywhere," Grady said, joining us on the terrace.

"I met Dr. Sproles this week," I said, closing the newspaper and setting it aside.

"You did? Where?" Grady asked. "Was he at the fashion party we attended?"

"No. I went to his office to talk with him, and not about any procedures, I hasten to add."

"You certainly don't need anything to make you prettier," Donna said.

"That's very sweet," I replied. "I just had some questions for the doctor about one of his patients, Rowena Roth."

"The model who died," Grady said.

"Yes. He had quite an operation going with a full waiting room."

"Did you see anything nefarious going on?" he asked.

I laughed. "Not exactly, but he did have a large collection of exotic plants on display."

"You've had some exciting week in New York," Donna said.

"Certainly more excitement than I planned for."

"But you seem to thrive on excitement," Grady suggested.

"Do I? Oh, dear, what a dreadful reputation to have. My preference is for my peaceful life in Cabot Cove, where the biggest excitement is when someone has a little too much wine and has to be fished out of the harbor."

"But that's not true, Aunt Jess," Grady said. "People have been murdered in Cabot Cove. Not only that, but you've been involved in helping solve some of those murders."

"True, Grady, but it's never been my intention to get involved." I laughed. "Ask Sheriff Metzger about that. Sometimes I think he'd prefer to solve his cases all on his own."

"He ought to be thankful that you've been there to help," said Donna.

"Oh, I think he is, but his male pride occasionally gets in the way of acknowledging it. Dinner was delicious, Donna, as usual, and the conversation even better. But I'd best be getting back to my hotel. My flight tomorrow morning to Boston is an early one."

"Is Jed Richardson picking you up in Boston and flying you to Cabot Cove?" Grady asked.

"That's the plan," I said. Jed runs our small airport and is my flying instructor.

"Good old Jed," Grady said.

"How are you getting to the airport in the morning?" Donna asked.

Before I could answer, Frank came bouncing to the terrace carrying something that he handed me. It was a copy of his short story bound in a blue plastic binder with the title written on it.

"For you, Aunt Jessica," he said proudly.

"Open it," Grady said.

Frank had inserted an extra page at the beginning of the manuscript: "For my aunt Jessica. The best aunt anyone could have and the world's greatest murder mystery writer."

"How sweet," I said, hugging him to my side, "but I'm afraid it's a gross overstatement."

"I mean it," Frank said.

I kissed his cheek. "I will treasure this," I said.

I was at the door and poised to leave when Donna again asked how I was getting to JFK Airport in the morning.

"Detective Kopecky is driving me," I said.

"Really?" Grady said, stringing out the word.

"He insisted," I said. "I told him I'd be happy to take a taxi, but he wouldn't hear of it. His daughter, Christina, will be with him."

"Interesting," Grady said, glancing at his wife.

"Interesting," Donna echoed.

I ignored the implied editorial comments and said, "Let's not let too much time pass before the next time we get together." I hugged everyone good-bye and added, "I'll expect to see you in Cabot Cove this summer if not before."

I'd initially declined Kopecky's invitation to drive me to the airport for my flight to Boston, but he was insistent. "Christina will be with me," he said. "She's staying overnight. She'll never forgive me if I don't let her at least meet you."

And so I agreed.

Christina vacated the front passenger seat of his battered Subaru as I exited the Refinery Hotel. Kopecky also got out of the vehicle and gave me a wave. He'd parked away from the curb, making it difficult for other vehicles to pass.

"Perfect weather to fly, huh?" he said as we shook hands. "This is the famous Christina I'm always talking about."

"What a pleasure to meet you," I said.

She grasped my outstretched hand and pumped it energetically. She was a pretty brunette, solidly built and with a wide, winning smile. "I am so thrilled to finally get to see you," she said. "I'm a big fan and your books are my absolute favorites. I brought a couple with me for you to sign, if that's okay."

"Of course it's okay," I said. "I'm very flattered."

Her father, dressed nicely in suit and tie, seemed unsure of what to say next. Finally he said, "Hey, we'd better get going. You never can tell about New York traffic."

A driver behind Kopecky leaned on his horn, causing the detective to glare at him. As I'd come to learn, Kopecky's shield on the visor of his car gave him carte blanche when it came to parking, something he freely took advantage of.

Christina climbed in the back, leaving me the front passenger seat. Kopecky put my suitcase in the trunk, slammed it shut, got behind the wheel, gunned the engine, and roared away from the curb, cutting off another car. "New York drivers are the dumbest," he mumbled.

I'd heard the same said about New England drivers but didn't mention it.

Christina chatted away and handed three of my books to me over the seat back. Signing was made difficult because of her father's fast, aggressive driving, but I managed the task and gave them back to her.

As we headed for the airport, Christina

said less and her father became more talkative.

"I'll tell you, Jessica," he said, "I've been a cop in New York for a lot of years, but this case with the models takes the cake. I mean, here's this kid, this beautiful young model who decides to murder another model who's competing with her to become — what do you call it, the 'face' of this guy's cosmetic company? We tracked down her credit card and, sure enough, she bought the aconite that showed up in her homemade lipstick. And then she goes and ends up poisoning herself by mistake. Go figure."

"As they say, truth is often stranger than fiction," I replied.

"That's for sure. I bet you'll write one heck of a book about it."

"To be honest," I said, "I'm not sure I want to write about the fashion industry."

He guffawed. "I get your drift, Jessica."

"You must be pleased that Latavia Moore's murder has been solved," I said as we left the city and entered the borough of Queens. "You suspected from the outset that her death wasn't from natural causes."

"I got lucky with that one, but you played a big role, Jessica, learning from Mr. Sandy Black, or whatever name he uses, that the text message he got couldn't have come from Ms. Moore. Couple that with the other guy on the security camera tape and we nailed Black's so-called manager and financial backer. He cracked like an egg under pressure. Seems Latavia's former husband was trying to pull a fast one by getting his ex to fire Verne so they could pocket the savings. Backfired on both of them. LAPD picked up the ex. They've been keeping an eye on him for years. He copped to the fact that he set up Black in the costume theft. He should've realized he was going to land up in jail one way or another."

"I'm just glad that it's over," I said. "And it's a relief that the two deaths were not related."

He pulled up in front of the terminal, leaped out, and opened the doors for me and Christina.

"Here you are, Jessica," he said. "We made good time."

"I really appreciate the ride," I said to him. I turned to his daughter. "It was a pleasure meeting you, Christina," I said.

"Me, too," she said.

"You have a wonderful father."

"I know it," she said, sliding her arm around his waist.

Kopecky smiled, disengaged from Christina, and gave me a hug. "I am wonderful."

I laughed.

"Gotta admit, I was a little miffed that you weren't as impressed with me as I was with you."

"I'm sorry, Aaron. I hope you're not offended. It's just that —"

"Yeah, yeah. You don't have to explain. The detective in England and all. You're a classy lady, Jessica Fletcher," he said, and planted a kiss on both my cheeks.

"Ooh, very continental, Daddy," his daughter said.

Kopecky blushed and without another word he and Christina climbed back into his Subaru and drove away.

As Jed Richardson circled Cabot Cove prior to landing his single-engine plane at our small airport, I immediately felt at ease and thought of these lines from T. S. Eliot:

We shall not cease from exploration
And the end of all our exploring
Will be to arrive where we started
And know the place for the first time.

It was wonderful to be back.

The ensuing months passed quickly for me once I was again settled and had fallen into the welcome small-town routine Cabot

Cove offered, but events conspired to remind me of my exposure to Fashion Week in New York.

A postcard had arrived from male model Peter Sanderson announcing his role in a new situation comedy on television. A handwritten note on the bottom read "Don't forget me when you're making your next movie." It was signed "Love, P," an echo of another note written to a seventeen-year-old model with aspirations that, sadly, she would never achieve.

A day later, my friend and our local real estate expert, Eve Simpson, had dropped off one of her fashion magazines for me. She had marked a page that contained photographs from the red carpet at several of the Hollywood award shows, among them a picture of the actress Jeanne Rogét in a form-hugging gold gown by Xandr Ebon. I thumbed through the rest of the magazine and was delighted to discover Isla Banning's lovely face in a print ad for New Cosmetics.

Maggie Black called me one day soon after to inform me that Xandr Ebon was going back to being Sandy Black. Her son had decided to abandon his high-fashion aspirations in New York and to return to Hollywood, where he hoped to reestablish himself as a costume designer. "I tried to talk him out of it," Maggie said, "but there was no dissuading Sandy once my cousin, the lawyer, was able to get him out of that awful contract he signed with Jordan Verne. I just hope it works out better for him this time."

"I'm sure it will," I said. "I'll look for his credits whenever I see a new movie. By the way, I saw that the actress Jeanne Rogét kept her promise to wear one of his designs on the red carpet."

"Yes, she did, and he's hoping that the good word she puts in for him, along with the discrediting of Latavia Moore's husband's accusations against him, will help him get back into the good graces of the studios."

"I'll keep my fingers crossed," I said.

I'd not heard from Detective Aaron Kopecky or his daughter since they dropped me off at JFK. But a week after Maggie called, I received a note from Christina.

Dear Mrs. Fletcher,
I hope all is well with you and that you're writing another wonderful book. I thought you'd want to know that my dad is getting married again. She's someone he's known since high school

who is a widow, a really nice lady. And I just got engaged, too. Looks like the Kopecky family might have a double wedding.

I smiled, dropped her note on my desk, raised my half-filled teacup, and said aloud, "Congratulations, Aaron Kopecky. May you and your bride have many happy years together."

I finished what was in the cup, turned to my blank computer screen, and started writing my next novel, which, by the way, has nothing to do with fashion.